The Apostate

Henry H. G. Mungle

BookLocker

Saint Petersburg, Florida

Published by BookLocker.com, Inc., St. Petersburg, Florida.

Printed on acid-free paper.

This book is a work of pure fiction. Names, characters, places, and incidents are a product of the author's imagination, constructed, and used fictitiously. Any resemblance to actual events, locales, organizations, or persons, living or dead, is entirely coincidental.

BookLocker.com, Inc.
2021

First Edition

The views expressed in this publication are those of the author and do not necessarily reflect the official policy or position of the Department of Defense or the U.S. government. The public release clearance of this publication by the Department of Defense does not imply Department of Defense endorsement or factual accuracy of the material.

Dedication

This book is dedicated to the men and women of the polygraph and intelligence profession, who are always behind the scenes seeking truth, confirming, vetting, and confronting those that seek to harm us. My wife is one of those silent warriors.

Table of Contents

About the Author

Henry H. G. Mungle is a highly decorated Vietnam combat veteran after multiple tours and has been awarded the Silver Star, Purple Heart, and Legion of Merit and several Intelligence medals. He retired from the US Army Criminal Investigations Command as a Chief Warrant Officer. A retired federal law enforcement supervisory special agent and polygraph examiner working for the Department of Defense IG (Tailhook Investigation), and US Customs (Office of Professional Responsibility), as well as the Central Intelligence Agency and Defense Intelligence Agency. He has served in Iraq and Afghanistan and a host of other countries throughout his 47-year career. He completed a Bachelor of Science in Psychology at The State University of New York, Albany, and a Master of Science in Criminal Justice at The George Washington University, Washington, D.C. He is retired and lives in Arizona with his wife.

CHAPTER ONE:
Afghanistan

* * *

He lay awake, thinking over the worst and deadliest dilemma of his life. He was now in an impossible position by his decision. He went through the motions during prayer as his mind rejected Allah. Who was Allah, a god who wanted complete obedience. Allah did not give anything back, there was no hope, no love, no compassion, nothing! His struggle was believing Islam stood for good. He decided it did not ... blasphemy, the thundering inner voice yelled at him! His mind tortured over his thoughts.

The room lacked modern conveniences that would make life comfortable—no air conditioning. The walls painted a dingy yellow long ago were peeling from wear. The paint placed over mud, straw, and most likely farm animal dung to form the interior walls bore the pock marks of use throughout the interior and looked like bullet holes. The air in the room smelled of long ago burnt wood absorbed into the mud walls, along with the animal dung gave off a disgusting odor. The small village had nothing.

His mind wrestled with his decision. The insects buzzing about his head were as busy as his mind. His soul demanded an answer to why warfare was necessary to establish Islam. His intellect was stunned by the complexity of what he thought was the truth. The man he used to admire was insane with his recent pronouncement of wanting to build a nuclear device to use on the enemies of Islam.

Ibn Abbas was not a large man, standing at five foot seven and slim. However, he was a brilliant mathematician, he earned his doctoral degree in Great Britain, his birthplace. He initially struggled to accept Islam as a young and inexperienced man, eventually being won over by the Iman of his Mosque in London and decided to join the fight against everyone who was not a Muslim. The lesser Jihad was crushing his humanity while fighting everyone until they succumbed to Islam. Now he was in the greater Jihad, fighting against the spirit of himself.

His rise in power as second only to the master bomb maker of Afghanistan was explosive and quick.

His recent discovery of the bomb maker's insanity raised questions concerning his faith and allegiance to his understanding of Islam. Abbas instinctively understood he had made a mistake in his evaluation of Khan. The problem loomed large in his mind; what to do about it?

True to his natural intellect, Abbas involved his in-depth analysis of everything he thought he knew and understood. Abbas arrived at his conclusion earlier in the day, and his decision shocked him. He was about to do two things, give up Islam, and betray the bomb maker, the mad man, Khan. Also troubling his soul was the idea he had been part of killing so many people. He never killed anyone directly, but since he was helping the master bomb-maker, he felt responsible. The last bomb exploded unexpectedly, killing over thirty Muslims at a wedding party, and he was sick with despair, while Khan shrugged it off. Abbas was a dead man walking. Khan was gleeful.

Alexandria, Virginia

* * *

Special Agent Jack McGregor was operationally orientated and hated to be back at headquarters. Vetting spies, working counterintelligence, and being on the tip of the war's spear on terrorism was the apex of his career, and he was more comfortable in the field. Jack was one of those rare people, a polygraph examiner. He became the consummate skilled professional honing his abilities by unraveling secrets that hide the truth from fiction. A knowledge few people have in life.

Originally trained at the CIA, he had a strong disagreement with assignments and left the agency. The Defense Intelligence Agency quickly offered him an appointment as an operational examiner supporting the polygraph requirements for jobs and the Defense

Clandestine Service (DCS) operational matters. The DIA is the Department of Defense equivalent of the civilian CIA. The DIA smoothly absorbed him.

He decided he needed a break from thinking over every detail of his last assignment by driving across the Fourteenth Street Bridge to his favorite tavern in Old Town Alexandria, The Horse and Soldier. Located on a side cobblestone street, it offered some parking along various streets. It was popular with many of the Northern Virginia crowd. What he liked about it was he could be alone in a group and benefit from both. However, tonight was not going to turn out that way.

He was deep in thought about his last trip to the sandbox, Iraq, and his assignment. In his latest excursion into the fantasyland of the human mind, Jack uncovered a source known in the trade as a "dangle." The routine polygraph was covertly conducted in Iraq; Jack discovered the asset worked for Iranian intelligence and identified American intelligence operations. Six months of operational work exposed to the bad guys. His anger was not at the spy but at the case officer for believing the Iranian supplied reliable information. In true fashion of his skills, Jack obtained information exposing the source's true nature when he lied about meeting a known Iranian assassin two nights before running the test.

The case officer, a young woman, allowed her asset to mislead her, and to add insult to injury, she allowed him to enter the meeting with Jack carrying a hidden nine-millimeter pistol tucked into his middle back. Jack discovered the gun during preliminary security questioning by merely asking him if he had a gun. Jack removed the weapon, dropped the clip, and took the round out of the chamber. Jack quickly disassembled the handgun in front of the spy. The case officer violated routine safety procedures.

After the failed test, he chewed the operations officer's butt for being gullible and sloppy. Jack uncovered information showing the asset was working with a known assassin to kidnap her. Jack just saved her life and, at the same time, felt betrayed because the spy could quickly have shot him. His internal meter of tolerance pegged out. His quick temper hurt his ability to remain entirely professional, but he got the job done.

He had settled in at a small table facing the bar and was oblique to the front entrance. The bar mirror gave him an advantage of watching the front door in case of a threat.

The waitress, a middle-aged woman with a pleasant smile, tight jeans and sandals that did not match the rest of clothing approached his table and asked, "What would you like to drink, sweetie?"

"MacCallan's, twelve or eighteen year will be fine, neat please."

A few moments later she delivered the drink sitting it on the table, "Is there anything I can get for you?"

"No, thanks." Jack said. He picked up the glass and sipped on it for a moment and put it down. The golden liquid gentle caressed his tongue as it slid down his throat giving him a nice glowing feeling.

Then it happened so unexpectedly, breaking his chain of thought; she was an obvious distraction. He watched her and her friends disrupt the entire tavern with their presence.

Jack could not keep his eyes off her since she walked in. She had the right look Jack appreciated. The woman was tall, he guessed, five foot eleven with auburn, shoulder-length hair. Jack could not see her eyes due to the dimmed lights but noticed she held her head up and looked directly at everyone. He liked that. She was confident, self-assured. But what he like the most was her chosen attire. It looked like she decided her clothing specifically to be different. She was wearing Levi's, and a white blouse opened at the neck adorning a white pearl necklace and, best of all, cowboy boots. She also wore a short style black leather jacket. She presented an image and combination of country girl and sophistication. She stood out in a bar of business suits and others dressed up for the Washington D.C. attire but matched him in his faded blue jeans, dress shirt, and sports jacket.

She had glanced his way twice, as he was deciding if it was worth the risk of being publicly trashed and rejected.

He evaluated his chances of rejection deciding it is not like he has not been rejected before approaching a beautiful woman; he often had like most men. It is a dance, and you do not want to step on her toes. His ability to read people was ingrained in his every thought process because that was the type of work he was involved in, interrogation, but a special kind.

Everything about her body language told him she was approachable, but he strongly suspected only by the correct type of man. Was he the right type? He was unsure. He slowly sipped on his scotch, watching her in the mirror hung over the nearby bar. It was almost too perfect to see her in the mirror, framed like a picture. He watched her sneak a glance his way again, slightly twirling her hair with her two middle fingers. Her nose somewhat wrinkled when making a point in the conversation, with a generous smile. That was his sign. He noted how she dispatched two luckless guys that walked up to her table. Their dejected look was a warning. He was not going to be the third.

* * *

The bar was noisy, with glasses clinking together and low talk. The interior was warm on a chilly Autumn night. Amid the soft noise, Paige engaged in a discussion utterly unaware of the furor around her she created, well, not completely unaware, but ignoring it. Her presence had all the men looking, wondering if they should approach her to give her a try. Others had failed spectacularly, sending them away with their tail between their legs.

Her reddish auburn hair and statuesque build made her stand out like no other woman in the bar. Her two girlfriends at the table were happy about the attention she drew because maybe, just maybe, some of it would rub off on them. She had noticed the lone guy sitting several tables away, seemingly not looking her way. That made her curious.

She wrinkled her nose as she often does when curious and smiled about her private thoughts.

Paige's girlfriends had intentionally chosen a table in the center of all the action. Not to attract men, but to observe them make fools of themselves. Her girlfriends were just as beautiful as she knowing sitting there was driving men crazy. She had already rebuffed two attempts when approached. Not out of meanness, just they were not her type. She knew what she liked, and she did not substitute, not anymore.

"How come you rejected that guy in the gray suit?" Claire asked.

"No pride in his dress. I just felt he was a smarmy type. He reminded me of my ex." Paige responded while looking at the lone guy ignoring them while she played with the ends of her hair.

"His suit was rumbled and dirty. A businessman or a lawyer, just not at all to my liking."

Susan absently said, "I get why you did not like the second guy. I did not like him at all. Too much swagger."

Paige's keen instincts with her analytical observations identified the second guy as a loser. A cowboy of sorts, much like where she grew up in Montana. Seeing his wedding band, she quickly dispatched him with a cold stare. She turned back to her friends with a sharp eye to the lone guy. He looked interesting. Slightly older than her forty-four years, dark brown hair, broad shoulders, and obviously, he took care of himself. Besides, she might have seen him at her workplace, which was important because that made him vetted uniquely.

Her analytical mind rationalized how she was viewing this guy. The bar scene was not about a one-night stand. She did not function that way. This was about meeting someone for a long-term commitment, if that was even possible, in Washington, D.C. Then he stood up turning toward her table. His body movement was confident, straightforward, and if he was nervous, it didn't show. In a nanosecond, she evaluated, liked, and did not object to him. Her heart skipped a beat giving her face a nice even blush causing her to smile.

* * *

Jack screwed up his courage, downed the last of his scotch, getting up from the table. He intentionally got up in a way to catch her eye, and he did. She was smiling, showing her perfect white teeth. He held his stare looking her straight in the eye as he walked toward her.

Everyone was watching him. He overheard a couple of guys at the bar, betting that the gorgeous redhead would smack him down. Not once did he avert his gaze.

With his best broad grin, he said, "Hi, my name is Jack. I would like to buy each one of you ladies a drink. I have never seen three ladies cause so much rise in testosterone in one place. You are doing a fantastic job of making all these guys act out their secret desires and turn them into dysfunctional lumps of humanity."

This unexpected opening line left the three women laughing. "My name is Paige; this is Susan and Clair. Please have a sit before you become dysfunctional."

Jack appreciated her quick wit while he engaged the three women in conversation, blending his discussion so that each felt like he was talking to them individually. His sometimes-slight sarcastic humor created laughter from the three and eased his presence at the table. As if on cue, another man walked up and introduced himself to Clair starting a dialog of meaningless talk. Jack recognized his position at the table allowing this other guy a chance like the alpha male wolf. He turned his attention to Paige. Moments later, Susan was engaged in conversation with the table directly behind theirs. Jack had broken the ice naturally. A balance struck.

"Paige, this is going to sound a little trite, but I almost think I have seen you before. Not here, but somewhere else."

"You have because I recognize you from our place of employment. I saw you several days ago getting a cup of coffee in the dining area. I recall you looked deep in thought. There was another person with you, not as tall as you, older, with blondish hair."

"You work there also?"

"I do."

"Where do you work?"

"On the third floor on the west side of the building."

"Oh… you are one of those, an analyst," Jack said.

"How about you, Jack? Where do you work?"

"Polygraph Division, on the first floor. The guy you saw me with is my boss."

"So, you are one of those guys. You rattle the skeletons in my closet," she said, smiling.

Jack smiled in return. Careful to understand what she was saying. Polygraph is a sensitive issue with some employees. "Yes, we rattle some people, but you have to know we go through the same process ourselves in a lot more rigorous test than you would. We all have closets with skeletons. We are human."

"Are you?" she said with a broad smile.

"Stop analyzing me," Jack said with a grin.

"Stop reading my body language and sitting there thinking you have it all figured out; you don't," her quick wit punctuated the conversation. Jack smiled.

* * *

The early fall night air was chilled. It was warm and happy in the bar that two people slowly came together cautiously. Jack felt the burst of cold air hit them as they walked out of the bar and noted the dry leaves scattering in the wind across the sidewalk in Old Town, making the noise only dried leaves can make on cement.

Jack cupped her elbow in his large hand and started to walk her down the sidewalk. Catching her look, he said, "Let me walk you to your car and make sure you are safe."

"OK, I will allow that. I'm parked right there, about fifty feet from where we are standing," Paige said with a smile.

That smile melted Jack's heart, and he almost had weak knees. Jack straighten out his legs as he moved toward the car.

"I enjoyed our conversation tonight. I would like to call you later for lunch, dinner, or whatever I can do to see you again," he said.

Smiling with a hint of a twinkle in her hazel eyes, slightly tilting her head, she said, "Let me think that over, Jack. I will call you in the morning now that I know where you work. I will give you, my answer."

Somewhat deflated by her answer, he nodded in agreement. Smiling, he said, "Goodnight then. I hope to hear from you soon."

Paige got into her car, started the engine, turned her head with a slight tilt to look at him as if doing another appraisal. She drove away, leaving Jack standing in the road with his heart beating hard. Somehow knowing she was suitable for him, asking himself *what the hell happen, Jack?* He walked across the street, slid into his 750i BMW, heading back to his apartment in Washington D.C.

* * *

Jack stared at his empty glass, wanting another drink and fighting against it. He intentionally left his apartment dark on this Saturday night. The bottle of twenty-five-year-old McCallan's sat on the table alongside the empty glass. He watched the reflecting multi-colored neon light passing through an outside window as he thought about himself. He often sat brooding in a quiet, dark room somewhere in the world, like this one, reflecting on his past to the one defining moment that transformed him.

Half asleep in a comfortable, easy chair caused Jack to finally drop into a deep troubling slumber like a tortured soul dreaming about the first human he killed, some forty years earlier. In his dream, once again, Jack confronted this man. At that moment, both knew they would fight to the death with only one surviving, with a distinct possibility both could die at each other's hands.

Jack's phone rang sharply, pulling him back into the here and now. Fumbling, he picked it up and grunted, "Yea, what do you want?"

Stan Kaufman's deep booming voice replied, "Jack, this is Stan. We have an immediate action alert concerning bombs and bomb makers. I need you to go to Pakistan."

"Nuclear or conventional?" Jack sarcastically joked.

"Don't be a smartass, Jack, conventional, of course."

Stan Kaufman, Jack's boss at the super-secret Defense Intelligence Agency, always called him at the worst times. It meant someone with DCS, somewhere had high-value intelligence needing vetting through an operational polygraph test.

Jack croaked, "When do I have to be there?"

"Yesterday, get your ass over here so the HUMINT collection team can brief you. You can pick up your tickets for your flight. You are leaving tomorrow afternoon out of Dulles to Minneapolis, Tokyo, Bangkok, and into Pakistan."

"Fine, can't someone else go? I just returned from the sandbox two weeks ago."

"Nope, you're the flavor of the month, get moving. The team in Afghanistan specifically asked for you." Jack realized early in his career that being the best at his profession was a double-edged sword. Working with potentially devious and challenging assets made every assignment dangerous, one way or another. Case officers and analysts want the best vetting possible.

"Crap... I will see you within the hour."

Wearily, Jack got up walking into the bathroom to freshen up before making the short drive to DIA headquarters. His right hip throbbed because of an old combat wound, but he was unsure if exercise helped him anymore.

A ragged man with hollowed eyes stared back at him from the mirror. Jack pulled his mixed thoughts together muttering to himself; *the pace of traveling the world on short notice is killing me.* The death of any polygraph examiner is losing his psychological edge and being tired eroded his abilities. His job already cost him his marriage several years ago. He blamed himself. What upset him most was she got his dog. Whispering under his breath at the thought, *Damn, I loved that dog, and I miss her.* His pup brought comfort on nights like this one.

* * *

Maneuvering, slightly drunk, through the Washington D.C. traffic, brought him to Bolling Air Force Base and DIA headquarters. The Security Police at the main gate inspected his blue intelligence community badge, allowing entrance to the base. Jack parked his black BMW in the parking garage, away from other vehicles, so he would not suffer a ding from cars in the lot. Instead of a long walk from a large parking lot on a cool humid night, the covered garage provided a more direct entrance to the building. Getting out of the car, he pulled his blue intelligence badge on a thin chain back over his neck. The blue badge slid over the reader, creating a clicking sound igniting a green light on the panel. He entered his passcode, allowing him to enter the building. He was on the opposite end of the vast DIA complex to the Polygraph Division as he started his trek toward his office.

The hallways were empty this time of night. He heard his footsteps echo in the hall as the sound bounced off the walls, like a basketball hitting the hardwood. Passing through a large sitting area near the building's front doors, the floor directly in front of him gently descended, making it easy for anyone in a wheelchair. Arriving at the bottom of the slope, he turned left entering a small corridor with a single door. The sign read 'Polygraph Division Level Six Access Only.' Jack swiped his badge over the reader, waiting for the green light to enter, and joined his division. He walked around the outer waiting room down a small hall arriving at his boss's office.

Kaufman looked up, "About time. Before you go to your briefing, we need to discuss the information you developed in Afghanistan several months ago on some Pakistani building a nuclear bomb."

Jack said, "I recall that information. It came from an Iranian I tested at one of the safehouses in Kabul. That test took place at two in the morning due to the asset's availability. As I recall, he characterized the information as 'old woman's gossip' but felt it was important enough to pass to us. He said a Pakistani might be involved. Has the analyst developed anything more on the information?"

"Sort of, but not conclusively. As you know, collection efforts go on continuously, and it is a tough puzzle to put together. However, the analyst showed that the Pakistani might be from Great Britain. But that is not certain. There is information suggesting this mysterious Pakistani was educated there. He may be hiding somewhere in Pakistan or another nearby country. Other sources have reported he is the bomb maker of all bomb makers directing operations in Afghanistan for al-Qaeda and the Taliban. No one is sure of his name, but there is a big push in the theater to get a name and find him."

Kaufman was a hard man and always fair with Jack. He recognized Jack's PTSD but kept it to himself, deciding that if Jack was working, he did not have time to focus on his past. He was correct. Kaufman intentionally ignored Jack's sarcastic attitude. A break he gave to no other examiners on his team.

* * *

Self-perception is often deceiving, as the saying goes. Jack ignored his shortcomings that battled with his confidence. Jack's self-worth lived in constant fear of discovery and recognition by others of his forever aliment, post-traumatic stress. Jack's damaged psyche was a mutation brought about because of multiple combat tours. Jack was brutally honest with everyone except himself. He lacked the courage he needed to recognize the truth about himself or reveal it to his superiors.

Jack stood at six foot two and weighed in at two hundred pounds. His broad athletic shoulders gave him the appearance of strength. His wild and unkempt brown hair with penetrating emerald eyes punctuated his handsome look. He was a sophisticated weapon few people knew how to handle or relate to at any level. His distrust of authority, manufactured by post-stress or not, made relationships with anyone complicated.

* * *

"OK, what does travel to Pakistan have to do with this guy?"

"A case officer Peter Bennett, I think you know him, is reporting he may have a lead on some bomb makers that have evaded capture so far."

"Yea, I know Pete. He is usually spot on when he has information. Is he the one that requested me?"

"Yes. Peter sent a request to headquarters, suggesting an analyst tied these bomb makers to this mysterious Pakistani. He suggested you are the one that could best determine if this is all the same package. The analyst's name is Paige Anderson. Do you know her?" Kaufman asked.

Jack was not smiling. "That is strange. I just met her tonight at a bar in Virginia. I had no idea she was the one putting all this information together."

Kaufman Ignored Jack's response, "Get yourself across the hall to the third floor and get a briefing and review the file of the asset you have to test. Pick up your tickets at the Travel Center. Get some sleep if you can. I'll talk to you after you have completed your mission."

Jack endured the HUMINT briefing, collected the airline tickets after complaining and moaning over not being able to travel in first-class for such a long flight. He headed back to his apartment to pack. Time to find a nuclear bomb.

* * *

Paige had to learn how to trust again after marrying the wrong man. Coming from a ranch in Montana, she was naive about Washington D.C. She had fallen in love hard as the young often do marrying too quickly at age twenty-eight. She failed to see the warning signs of a profoundly flawed man immersed in himself. Her husband's narcissism left her hurt and almost destroyed when she discovered his obsession with other women. So, she was careful in her evaluations of men. She liked Jack and did not see the damaging traits in him as her ex-husband had deciding to call him.

In the morning, she called, "Good morning, Jack, I thought it over. I would like to see you again. How about a lunch today in our cafeteria at 11:30?"

"That sounds good. I'll see you at 11:30. I need to talk to you anyway about bombs."

"What do you know about my work?" she asked.

"More than you think, we'll discuss it over lunch. See you then."

"I am looking forward to our discussion. I'll be leaving in the morning for an assignment." Paige said.

* * *

Jack, on the other hand came from a different background. Jack grew up in rural Colorado on the Western Slope of the Rocky Mountains. He hunted, fished, and spent most of his time outdoors. Jack often took off for days, camping and sitting by a fire, watching the stars and meteor showers. He learned from his father, who always gave him plenty of room to roam and grow. Reaching eighteen, Jack wanted to experience the military and joined the Army. Like his father, he went into the infantry, became a paratrooper, and took the grueling US Army Ranger course. He also completed several combat tours in Vietnam.

He boarded the Delta flight later that day, around six in the evening. Quickly finding his seat in the enhanced economy section, he stowed his carry-on gear in the overhead. The flight would take him to Minneapolis, and there he would catch a flight for the long haul of his trip to Tokyo. Not wanting to talk to anyone, he closed his eyes, withdrawing into himself.

CHAPTER TWO:
Qureshi, Uzbekistan

* * *

Imagination is the wellspring of creativity or demise. Born from one's needs and desires, its application for good or evil is inherent in nature or moral fiber. Abdullah-ibn-Khan was born in Lahore, Pakistan, the second of nine children. Khan's brother was the oldest. Therefore, heir to all the good things that come out of a Muslim family and left him with picking up the trash. That would not do. His brother, Monhammed, cruelly rubbed it in Abdullah's face that he was inferior and not entitled to any of the oldest son's benefits. He devised a plan when he was fourteen, and his brother was sixteen. Khan lacked the moral fiber that made him good, or for that matter caring.

During a heated argument, Monhammed said, "Your place in this family is not relevant, I am the oldest and will inherit everything that will rightfully be mine. I will receive the best education and eventually have the best women in my life. You will be herding goats."

Abdullah responded, "That is not true. You have no say in how our family will treat me." The hate burned hot in his eyes and heart, searing the depth of his emotions.

Enraged, he planned to follow his brother as he went to meet his friends. Waiting patiently in a dark alley that he knew was the route home, he prepared himself for what he was about to do. Monhammed bragged about using hashish. This evening was no different as he stumbled down the dark alley. As Monhammed approached his brother hiding in an alcove, Abdullah Khan allowed his brother to pass and then pulled a sharp knife approaching his brother from behind. Quietly he slipped the knife around the front of his brother slicing deep into his throat. Monhammed dropped to the dirty floor of the alley, Quickly, the gash in his throat allowed him to bleed out.

Abdullah dropped some hashish around his dead brother and made the scene more believable into the pool of blood gathering around his

24

head. In a final gesture, spit on his dying brother before fleeing. Along the way, he dropped the murder weapon down an outside toilet.

No one discovered his murderous deed, and his parents were told by the authorities their son was involved in illegal activities with drugs. Most likely, murdered over a lousy drug transaction. In his parent's shame, Abdullah Khan gained promotion in the family hierarchy.

Abdullah Khan inherited the benefits making his parents proud, allowing him to gain an education in England. His educational efforts led him to be a brilliant physicist. Now he was a bomb maker for al-Qaeda and the Taliban. The pinnacle of his career happened to coincide with the 911 catastrophe. He planned to destroy the world in the name of Islamic Jihad. He fervently believed in the Koranic verse, *"O Prophet, make war upon the infidels and unbelievers, and treat with severity." Qur'an Surah 66.9.*

The Al Qaeda attack's success sparked his imagination and reinforced his belief that Islam was the path to greatness for "The Base," known as Al Qaeda, as well as for himself. He pulled strings behind the scenes as the "puppet master" on all bomb makers. His acute paranoia not only made him dangerous but cautious. His hate for the infidels fueled because he blamed all of them for the death of his wife and children in a bombing near Karachi just prior to the attack on America.

Khan's uncaring attitude extended to those that did his bidding. Recently, he used an impressionable youth, Mohammed, named after the prophet, as a courier and instructed him, "May Allah be with you on your secret mission against the infidels. Deliver this message to our friends in the south so we can prepare the way to victory." Obedience was never in doubt, nor was it ever questioned.

Mohammed's journey was dangerous and, more likely than not, fail due to the crafty infidels who may capture or kill him. Khan protected himself by demanding the message to be memorized and verbally delivered.

To protect the message to the Taliban terrorist, he secretly dispatched another courier carrying the exact words two days before. Per Khan's prearranged orders, Taliban commanders will reward the first courier to arrive by welcoming him to the fight. The second courier would be killed to protect the message making sure he is not an informer for the Americans. Khan did not care how it worked out, as long as the message was delivered.

The message to the Taliban commanders was twofold; begin their fall offensive in September, and the location of stockpiled IEDs necessary for the attack against the infidels. The latter part of the message had much greater importance as the prearranged location of stockpiled IED'S was known only to him and his lead bomb maker Ahmed.

His admiration for Al-Qaeda helped further his reputation as the "chief bomb maker" by his unique improvisation of explosive devices used against the infidels in Iraq or Afghanistan. Each success led to his culminating desire and sinister imagination to create the ultimate nuclear weapon to explode them in the heart of Israel, or the great Satan, the U.S. - preferably both.

Khan avoided those hunting him by quietly hiding in Qureshi, Uzbekistan, north of Afghanistan. He utilized that unique location near the American encampment, K2, the war zone, and his Pakistan village. This locale gave him additional "inner" proof he was doing "Allah's bidding, as he plotted the destruction of infidels. His callous disregard for human resources reflected his desire that no mission was too dangerous.

* * *

Ibn Abbas was summoned to Khan's office to suffer through Khan's daily self-praise of his alleged superior intellect, once again interrupted Abbas's thoughts.

Abbas bowed slightly and, with servility, replied, "I am at your service."

"Is there any word from the commanders in the south about the first courier I dispatched?" Khan asked.

Abbas answered in an intentionally, barely audible response, "No, it has been quiet,"

As expected, Khan launched into his plan's daily rehash just as soon as he entered the room. Abbas listened patiently, as Khan said, "Obtaining the fissionable material for a nuclear bomb and the placement of my dedicated operators in the Americas is vital. I know we have talked about this before; do you see any weakness in my plan?"

Abbas supplied his usual, none challenging answer, "No. All support your plan for the delivery of a nuclear bomb to America."

Abbas already discussed the Iranians with Khan, and to a lesser degree, the Russians, and the new terrorist group on the international scene, ISIS. The slippage of al-Qaeda from the world stage created a vacuum in Iraq, allowing ISIS to prove themselves as more violent than their predecessor as they bid for the leadership of Jihad across the world. The American President's miscalculations, naming ISIS a "Junior Varsity team," made it all possible.

Abbas had complete disdain for Khan. Until he put his plan into motion, he suffered a secondary role to this madman. Khan said, "Bring me the last message from the Iranians and some tea."

"As you wish."

Abbas hurriedly left the room, headed to his office. He unlocked a safe to retrieve the documents that outlined the Iranian proposal. He peered into the nearby kitchen saying to Amul, "Prepare some tea for your master." The large building, they operated from comprised nine rooms, a courtyard, and a newly constructed wall surrounding the house, more for privacy than security.

While waiting for the chia tea, he silently took out his tiny camera, photographing the Iranian document. Then reinserting the camera into a hiding place underneath the desk in a cutout compartment, Abbas understood discovery was certain death and in the cruelest of ways. He could lose his head. He only photographed documents he brought to Khan so he could hide his deception. Opening the safe at any other time caused suspicion.

Abbas collected intelligence on Khan's operation for a year. Abbas's dilemma was how to provide the data to the right people to reveal the nature of the attack. Instinctively he knew he must approach the infidel Americans. He could not condone the actions of a madman's intent to set the world on a path of nuclear fire. Conflicted, Abbas turned away from Islam's ideology he thought was at the top of the world's pecking order during his realization of his pending betrayal. Islam was a sham.

Returning to the room, Abbas watched Khan standing at the window. As was his custom, he gently placed the tea on the table and waited for Khan to turn around. Abbas intentionally followed Khan's instructions about never leaving a document lying on a table. Khan demanded the materials handed to him. Abbas presented the Iranian papers to him without comment. Abbas felt the tension between Khan and himself. He feared, at times, his betrayal has been discovered but was unsure as Khan derisively waved his hand dismissing Abbas.

In the failing light of the day, the sun set over the valley, Abbas recalled the discussion with Khan. The documents revealed the logistics and procedures for transferring a small amount of processed plutonium to make a nuclear device. The plutonium, about large softball size, was just enough to wipe out a small city or a large city section. There were specific safeguards to take to avoid contamination exposure.

Abbas had listened to Khan explain all the transportation requirements and contingencies involved. The location for the exchange of material and the amount of money donated by ISIS benefactors for this service would be twenty-five million Euros. Khan had agreed with the Iranians in Turkmenabad, Turkmenistan, just off the M37 route across the border from Uzbekistan about eighteen months ago for the plutonium.

Deep in thought, Abbas shuffled from one room to another, lighting the oil lamps. A generator would be excellent, but they are hard to come by in Uzbekistan. Besides, a house with a generator attracts attention as someone with money. Until then, oil lamps will have to do. He ignited each light, stared for a moment into the flame, deciding how he would escape from Khan's unrelenting control. The window for action had shrunk feeling the pressure of time collapsing like a large stone on him. Abbas had a small window of three months before the Iranians supplied the plutonium, and then it may be too late.

Abbas asked Khan, "What is your plan of attack against the infidels?"

"I will use a nuclear bomb and whatever other methods I can devise to destroy the infidels. The world will fear me like no others before me. I will cleanse the world of infidels."

Abbas felt a chill run down his spine.

CHAPTER THREE:
Lahore, Pakistan

* * *

The never-ending clicking noise of a window air conditioner rattled, interfering with Jack's thought, as he waited on Peter Bennett and his asset at a nondescript apartment in the middle of Lahore, Pakistan. The walls painted a pale color of something he didn't recognize—the furniture old but functional, served his immediate needs in the apartment. Although the paint was peeling off the cabinets in the kitchen area, it was clean and worked for the intended purpose. Thankfully, the ceiling fan was smooth and working without noise.

The safe house, carefully chosen by the case officer and rented through a third party, ensured Pakistani intelligence services, ISI, did not know they were in the country. There was always a risk conducting operations that could or could not be against ISI interests — still guessing each day if ISI is pro-US intelligence services or against the US intelligence services fighting terrorism.

The SDR, surveillance detection route Jack used to get to his location, had taken him all day. Making sure he had not picked up a tail, Jack wove in and out of various locations looking at the sights on a sweltering, humid Lahore day. The last complication Jack needed was ISI rolling him up in a raid while in the middle of conducting a polygraph test on a Pakistani national. ISI would be extremely upset, and he would be in some hot and muggy jail cell for an undetermined time.

The polygraph, often referred to as a lie detector, is not a lie detector, but popular culture and urban myth keep the jargon alive. The polygraph does nothing except, in question format, record the physiological responses of the examinee. Jack was the lie detector, passionate in his analysis. He interpreted the collected data deciding if the truth had been concealed or not, based on his interpretation of the collected charts.

The DIA asset claimed to know the location of five terrorist bomb makers. The terrorists had evaded multiple attempts by special operations forces to capture or kill them. Returning recently from Afghanistan with information, Abu Omar had an excellent record of reporting reliable intelligence. His detailed information hit the matrix, a sophisticated alert system used to filter data, making sure only the most critical secrets get to the United States president. Not everything hits the matrix, but Abu Omar's information did, causing Jack to travel 8,000 miles from Washington, D.C. to Lahore, the quickest way possible in three days. Now he sat and waited. The air in the room was still moist and hung like a wet blanket on him. The humid air was trying to cool to an acceptable level; however, Jack felt rivets of sweat rolling down his back.

Assets are recruited, trained, and used by intelligence services to spy on their country, their tribe, or their friends to collect intelligence to use against all of them. A source voluntarily provides information to an intelligence service for a reason or motivation that is sometimes hard to determine. Jack was highly suspicious of both.

Jack allowed his thoughts to wander through his relationship with Paige. Since they both worked at the Defense Intelligence Agency, they did not have to worry about slipping up and telling secrets they were not supposed to talk about, even though there were some secrets.

They were both exceptionally bright people with healthy egos subject to assignments that took them both to other parts of the world unexpectedly. How to make a relationship work would be a problem; under those circumstances, the separations being an issue. This time, however, she would meet him in Kandahar due to the information being developed.

* * *

A slight knock on the door interrupted Jack's thoughts. His Sig Saur 9 mm pistol gripped in his hand for the last half-hour; he held it securely against his leg as he approached the door. Lahore, known as terrorist central in this part of the world, and Jack wasn't taking any chances and standing to the side of the door opposite of the door handle, in a low voice, "Yes," As he brought his weapon up and pointed the muzzle at the door.

Waiting for a response and feeling anxious, he heard, "Scorpion seven."

Jack waited for two heartbeats moving to open the door. Standing in the hall is Peter Bennett, a DIA case officer he knew, and another man dressed in typical Pakistani clothing. Abu dressed more formally for this meeting than Jack expected. He was wearing a white Kurta displaying a traditional length with slits up the side starting at his knees with a Sherwani collar with a blue waist coat. Both entered the room quickly. Jack quickly closed and locked the door. Jack never used his real name when meeting an asset, and he introduced himself as "Bob."

Turning to Peter, Jack asked, "Were you followed?"

Peter played along with the name change, knowing Jack and how he operated, "I am not entirely sure, Bob, but I think not. For a while, some guy seemed to be following me. I managed to lose him in the bazaar in the train station before meeting with Abu."

Since this was the first meeting with Abu Omar, Jack asked, "How is your English?" since there is no interpreter with Peter.

"My English is good, and I have taken your tests before with no problems."

He keyed in on his pronunciation and syntax use and decided an interpreter was not necessary. Excellent, he thought, because most tests in this part of the world need an interpreter. Using an interpreter typically caused a three-hour test to turn into a six-hour one. It also means finishing sooner and leaving the area if ISI learned American intelligence was running an operation without their knowledge or permission.

Jack never forgot about the Muslim ritual in this part of the world. Jack provided cookies with a fruit center in preparation for the meeting, and Peter brought some chia tea. As the tea heated on an electric hot plate, and cups magically appeared from the meager cabinets. All of them sat around the coffee table and had a small meaningless talk about life, family, and the future, all while sipping tea. Jack didn't care for the chia tea. It tasted a little bitter to him, and no sugar made it barely drinkable. He watched the small tea leaves float about his cup. Turning his attention to Abu, Jack watched him as he spoke slightly, bowing his head while speaking of family, a sign of humility, and that is good. Abu openly explained his hopes for the future of the region once the Americans leave.

Jack asked, "What do you expect from this never-ending war in Afghanistan, Abu?"

"Freedom to be who we are. I do not want my government to tell me what I can and cannot do. I want to be able to choose. But secretly, I find Islam restricting me, and I have a conflict I need to work out."

"That is a tall order Abu. You run a risk; I suspect."

"Agreed, I do run a risk," he said, thoughtfully sinking back into the chair and sipping his tea.

This protocol was necessary to help break the ice while building rapport in the Islamic culture. Americans succumbed to this tradition to avoid offending Muslim assets. In America, it would have been a handshake; let's get down to business, run the test, and kick them out the door, but that does not work in Islamic culture. Jack did not mind as he gave him a chance to evaluate Abu.

Jack's first exposure to this ritual was comical. In the middle of Baghdad, a well-established asset had allowed the conduct of the polygraph examination upstairs in a vacant room. The asset was running a ring of spies. Testing each one was necessary. Not understanding the protocol, Jack jumped right into testing. In the middle of the test, a house servant entered the room with tea and cookies and served them to the examinee and Jack as he asked questions. The unintended interruption destroyed the entire test. He had to start over again.

Before running the polygraph test, Jack set up his computer with the attachments in an adjacent room as Peter waited in the apartment's living room. Jack had already run a listening device from the "polygraph suite" to the living room so Peter could listen. The listening device placement was kept secret from Abu.

As he put down his teacup, Abu inquired, "Bob, are we testing in the other room?"

"Yes, we are, and Peter will provide protection and privacy for us." Jack knew that Abu realized the risks of helping the Americans, and if discovered by ISI, a beating would inevitably occur. Abu would be in jail in the murky world of Pakistani intelligence, eventually released from custody into the hands of terrorists. Abu's freedom would cost him his life, and at the request of ISI, the terrorists would do their bidding. Trust was always an issue.

"Abu, do you have any weapons on you?"

"Yes," Abu produced his own FN 9 mm pistol and showed his four magazines. Abu knew the drill, no weapons in the polygraph, and laid the gun on the coffee table, looking at Peter.

"I will get it back?" he asked Peter.

"Of course, my friend. I have no intention of depriving you of your protection."

Jack led the way into the adjacent room, where the polygraph computer sat on a table. Jack's weapon was secured in the small of his back, and his shirt covered the gun since he does not trust any asset. Abu followed him into the room and took a seat near the table. The door closed; Jack settled in for the lengthy process of the polygraph.

Jack knew Abu had taken multiple polygraphs before, three to be exact. The DIA was always cautious when Abu brought them information. Others before Jack and Peter explained to Abu that if he lied or misled the Americans, they would abandon him in less than a heartbeat. DIA paid very well for the information Abu provided. It is a matter of building trust by supplying helpful information, or Abu would lose his income source. Jack constantly reinforced the trust aspect of the relationship throughout testing.

Jack's inherent distrust came from his demons and issues from many years' experience of testing a person who had already betrayed their country, tribe, or employers. It is a short step to revealing a secret relationship with US intelligence, putting intelligence officers at risk. Case officers usually fall in love with their assets, metaphorically speaking, because the case officer is all about building relationships and using the asset to obtain the information they cannot. Besides, the better the report, the better the case officer looks to his superiors. A symbiotic relationship, nonetheless.

On the other hand, Jack met an asset once, sometimes twice, and then never sees them again. He was a lot more skeptical, but that is OK. His role was to be that way, so he was good at pulling the truth from people. Jack functioned more like an apex predator, always searching for a weakness in a source or asset.

Before leaving Washington, D.C. to conduct this examination, Jack read the extensive file compiled by the various case officers on Abu Omar, known officially as Case# 10-876-A. He read with interest about Abu's past polygraph examinations by three other examiners. Jack's approach will be one of familiarity and friendliness to maintain crucial rapport.

"How do you feel today?" To start the process of setting up the sound dynamics of the test, Jack queried.

"I am feeling well. Last night I was upset because I had a dream about this machine and could tell if I was lying. I am better now after thinking it over."

A perfect segue was presented to Jack to explain the polygraph. Jack reminded Abu, "The last time you took a polygraph, I think you can recall that when a person lies, it comes from the heart, and you cannot cheat the heart. Your brain may know the difference, and you can hide your deception there, but your heart gives you away. That is why we record your heart rate."

Abu nodding his head, replied, "My heart is always true, and Allah knows my thoughts, and my heart bears the truth."

Jack paused for a moment and continued, "Your heart also impacts your breathing. If you run for a mile, your heart beats faster as you breathe harder. Your lungs and your heart work as one, and then you sweat for relief and cool off." This simple explanation of how the body works is enough and will work in this circumstance without getting too deep into physiology.

Abu acknowledges with a nod. To drive the point home, Jack asked, "You heard similar things before from the others that tested you. You understand and know how your heart works?"

"Yes, I know," replied Abu.

As he eased into the discussion, Jack decided to start on the most basic of questions and asked Abu to explain his trip to Afghanistan, "Where did you go? Did you speak to anyone? How did you return to Lahore? What information did you learn? Why do you feel this information is important?"

Jack knew Abu wanted to be thorough and listened to his story, "It took many days to get to Afghanistan from here. I traveled by motorbike. I took a taxi and walked for many days. I avoided the Taliban, as they are merciless and do not believe anyone passing through the borders. I managed to walk with a family crossing the border as they accepted me as one of their own, since they are from Pakistan also, and protected me from the inquiries."

"Did you say anything about American intelligence to anyone during your travels? Did you try to impress any young girls about working with the Americans?" Jack inquired.

"No, absolutely no. It would mean my death. Girls cannot keep secrets they talk too much. I cannot trust any woman about such important things. I tell no one."

He questioned Abu some more, "Did you perhaps spend money too easily creating questions and inquiries about the source of your money?"

"No. I keep my money hidden acting poor, just like the people around me. One traveler, an older man, asked me if I could give him alms during Ramadan, as the holiday was upon us during my travels. I gave him little money. Nothing else."

Understanding alms was a gift of money typically given to street beggars during Ramadan, he followed up, asking, "Did you enjoy the services of a woman at any time in your travels?"

Abu remorsefully looked down as he started talking, "Yes, in Afghanistan. I was away from everyone I had traveled with; it was only for an hour in temporary marriage. I never saw her again. I told her nothing about me or the Americans."

"Where did you travel to after you left the woman?"

"I walked for several days to the south, looking for work. I came to a village and asked about helping with their goat herd. I was surprised when a family needed help telling me the Taliban had taken their sons away and could not manage. Several days passed when I heard the men talking about strangers in their village, who I learned might be trouble for them. They were not the Taliban but acted like them."

Alerted, Jack specifically asked, "How many men were strangers in the village?"

Abu replied, "Six, I think, one was a teacher, called Ahmed. The others listen to him. One was different because he carried a pack with him every place, he went never leaving the backpack by itself. The village men stated there were riches in the bag believing these men stole from other towns, which scared them.

"One day, I sat nearby them observing the men, including the one with the pack. He opened it, pulling out a computer, a laptop. I knew these men were not who they say they were because of how they dressed and spoke. Their clothing was not the traditional dress of these mountain villagers. I also heard one of the men speak English on the phone, which I recognized as a satellite phone. They all carried weapons and knives and did not seem to be afraid of anything. Their weapons and manners caused me to believe they are dangerous."

"What did you do to find out who they are?" Jack asked.

"I decided it would be best to sit near them, to listen, because they spoke Farsi. I understood everything they said, but nothing made me suspicious. One day, the one they call Ahmed was on a cell phone and speaking English. I understood everything he said."

Jack listened intently. "What did he say?"

Abu paused to recall the exact words replying, "He said, 'Khan will get his material from the Iranians.' Ahmed then switched to Farsi and stopped speaking English. He talked about bombs in Kabul by September."

As he told the story, Jack carefully noted the expression on Abu's face. Abu showed every sign he was thoughtful in his response. There was no distinct body language indicative of deception.

Jack, also trained in neurolinguistics, evaluated each word and its context carefully. Barring for cultural and language differences, Jack's evaluation of Abu indicated he was telling the truth at this point, but that was just preliminary in his thinking. He would verify the information through a polygraph. Jack surmised Ahmed switched from Farsi to English and back to Farsi as a security precaution to prevent anyone listening to know the discussion's nature. Jack thought *Ahmed had just made the biggest mistake of his life.*

The languages of Pashto, Farsi, and Urdu, all spoken in that region of the world, had enough similarities that the more intelligent and traveled person could communicate across tribal and country boundaries. English was the oddball language not typically heard, except in Pakistan, which had been influenced by the British.

In the other room, Peter listened carefully. So far, the information Abu gave matched his earlier debriefing by Peter's team.

"I need a toilet break, Bob."

"Good idea, let's take a short break before I review the questions with you."

As Abu left for the water closet, Jack quickly stepped into the outer room asking, "Peter, what do you think so far?"

"He is right on target with everything he said to my team earlier. I did not hear any deviations in his story."

As Jack turned and reentered the room, he mused aloud, "Excellent."

CHAPTER FOUR:
The Recruiter and Insurgency

* * *

Abdul Rahim Ayyub was a crucial operative in the Khan network and excelled as a trainer. Sternly looking over the group of young men and women, he said, "We are winning against the infidels and will continue to win as long as you each carry out your assignments. We've been infiltrating the United States through Mexico since 2010 in groups of three, sometimes individually." Pausing for effect, Ayyub, originally from Indonesia, understood the necessity in inoculating a group for a dangerous mission, "Do not be fooled by the propaganda the infidels put on the radios and televisions about making the crossing of the border into America, it is secure with many different obstacles.

"Your assignments are secret from one another. Your mission will be to infiltrate the country first, get to your target cities second, and third to find a way to employment with the government agencies I have explained to you. The most influential are American spy agencies, border guards, and policeman positions. If all else fails, try running for public office."

The recruits for this dangerous mission shared standard abilities; educated, young, and dedicated to Jihad. No one doubted their resolve to carry out the assignment. Still, there were temptations in America that could be distracting seducing them into Satan's liar with all its perceived freedoms in a moment of weakness. Ayyub hammered on prayer to reinforce their will and build their determination to succeed.

"Operatives, with the help of Islamic agencies already established in the country, demand Sharia Law be recognized, and they are trying to develop self-acclaimed "no-go" zones, much like Europe. You will live in these no-go areas for your protection and away from prying eyes."

Ayyub once again reinforced the Islamic concept that no-go zones are areas that Muslim populations have set as their exclusive turf, no matter which country they are in, as part of their stealth migration and eventual takeover of any landmass. Once an area is occupied and controlled by a Muslim population, it is theirs for eternity. No one, including the government of that country, has any rights in that zone to enforce laws of that land because the only supreme law they recognize is Allah and Sharia Law. The Islamic agencies worked hard to manipulate the media and all Americans to conceal the true nature of Islam's stealth invasion into the United States. But, like Lemmings, the population followed along.

A young woman in the group raised her hand for a question. "Yes, what is your problem? Ayyub asks.

"Please explain those people we have to depend on in Mexico to enter the United States, who are they? Are they part of our brotherhood?" she asked.

Ayyub decided to go into more in-depth detail about the Mexicans, "They are not part of our brotherhood of Islam in any way. They are infidels. They are the worst kind of infidels. I will tell you a story so all of you may put this into perspective and understand the dangers you will face in Mexico.

"Khan's contacts had arranged for his operatives to be smuggled into the United States by the drug cartels. Using "coyotes" who prey on the poor souls looking to better their life, did not work well for Khan. Discovering his operatives taken advantage of, killed, and in several cases raped by rogue coyotes, his assassins revenged their honor and blood. The coyote with their families in the name of Jihad and Islam were punished by beheading, sending a message that harming Islam warriors had consequences. Do not trust any of them. Be prepared to kill them if you must. Let that be a final warning."

Ayyub did not bother to explain the drug cartels took more direct control for a price. The cartels offered an enhanced protection plan to bring operatives into the North American countries without any harm through Mexico. Khan sent agents first to Venezuela for false identification to avoid any further complications, then onto Nicaragua to begin their journey north.

* * *

Abbas listened to Khan, in one of his many moments of grandeur claims, "Praise is to Allah, we managed to breach the interior of the infidel countries with the help of the political party that encouraged open borders. Just like Europe. It is my destiny and Allah's wish."

Abbas had severe doubts about Khan's dreams. Dreams, for the most part, have meaning and structure. Dreams speak to the ego in a language requiring an objective interpreter. Abbas is that interpreter. Abbas knew Khan's analysis was subjective, highly flawed, and recognized his mind's pure evil.

Dreams shape history in dramatic ways — thoughts can give birth to empires or bring them down. An idea or a meme can inspire hope. Khan dreams of grandeur and expectations of greatness, yet it clouds his belief.

Abbas knew how to manipulate Khan's ego for his survival, "Khan, I know your anger with how the West controls and influences the rest of the world, and you are entitled to the mantel of power of Islam. I see you as the next Caliphate."

A smile spread across Khan's face, as Abbas continued, "You are the Muslim warrior of the ancient past, thrust into the modern world, and you will not conform and will tear it apart and reshape it."

Khan said critically, "Why did our Jihadist brothers focus on New York and Washington, D.C., for the attack? Their assumptions the country's financial network and the government would collapse with an attack on these cities were wrong."

Abbas agreed said, "Your analysis of the infidels over their concern of threats of attack motivated large financial institutions to move their electronic data was correct. Our operatives rightly discovered established *Cool* and *Hot* sites to control the data. You knew this would be the Achilles Heel of the United States. You developed plans accordingly."

"That is all true, my analysis was correct. Now I know where and how to destroy them. My elaborate plan will throw off the infidel's intelligence inquiries misleading at each step of the attack," Khan said.

Abbas walked out of the room to make Khan his afternoon tea before throwing up over Khan's gloating face. He had done enough to pump Khan's ego keeping Khan on the other side of his upcoming betrayal.

After instructing the house cook to prepare tea and lunch for Khan, Abbas recalled one of the rare moments of conversation with Khan, prompting him to explain the nuclear bomb.

Khan's detailed response was chilling in its concept and insane in his description, "For me to build this bomb, I need plutonium. The plutonium will be approximately the size of a small ball. I choose to have plutonium because it is a fissionable material and will explode with conventional explosives' proper triggering device, difficult to build. Until that happens, it is almost harmless as long as you do not inhale the fumes emitting from the plutonium because this will certainly cause lung cancer."

"How can this plutonium be transported safely by our brothers?" Abbas queried Khan.

"It does not take much to shield us from the fumes of the plutonium and can be safely carried in an appropriate container that will not allow the fumes to escape since it is not radioactive."

"What types of conventional explosives are needed, Master Khan?"

"Perhaps shaped explosives that the Americans, called C-4. that is triggered electronically. However, the use of C-4 and its triggering mechanism requires further scrutiny. The timing of the explosive is critical to creating a nuclear explosion, and since it is a delicate and complex operation, I need assurance it works as planned."

"Will this small ball be sufficient for our purposes?" Abbas pressed.

"It is enough to destroy a city. When the conventional explosives ignite in the outer shell of the first case, it causes the plutonium pit to implode, causing neutrons to penetrate the plutonium, creating x-rays to detonate the weapon."

Abbas recalled this chilling conversation often. However, his most disturbing memory was Khan's eyes. Lifeless and soulless eyes; eyes when searched reflected the embers of hell. Deep shudders ran throughout Abbas' body as he recalled the memory.

His Islamic beliefs are more rational than Khan's, and Islam's spreading in a more traditional non-violent method is the better path Abbas decided. Abbas's abrupt turn away from Mohammad and the Sword made him an apostate for holding this belief. Abbas was an astute reader of history and understood how Christianity spread throughout the Western world, the violent and the peaceful. Abbas understood the good, evil, and spectacle of religion. As he grew older and wiser, a more moderate path for Islam was desirable.

Now, betrayal by Abbas was absolute. His risky plan was to contact the only people in the world that can stop Khan's madness, the Americans. To get to the Americans, all he must do is be free of Khan for at least half a day or longer and determine the route to the next town, Kazan, where he can approach them.

Abbas knew al-riddah, apostasy, was his death sentence. His upcoming association, once arranged, was one of the acts necessary to label him an apostate. His actions were interpreted as disrespect towards Allah, and Islam condemning him to death. He has resolved to move ahead anyway.

* * *

Khan had an inherent distrust of everyone and caused him to plant misinformation about the attacks and targets. His discussion with Abbas was misleading just in case his suspicions were correct. Abbas had slowly withdrawn from him, and he started to have reservations concerning Abbas. Only Khan knew the exact destination of the target city. Khan had directed a boat to be purchased in the United States.

* * *

The motivation for choosing a trawler was to blend in with the regular river traffics favorite fishing vessels cruising the waterways. The trawler's draft was two and a half feet, well under the five feet recommended for the river to avoid obstacles.

The marina in Florida had boats for sale, all kinds of boats, and the inventory always was in a state of flux. Currently, the largest boat was a trawler. An interested party had shown up. Phillip Stowers, the owner, handled the deal personally because lots of money was involved.

The man wanting to make the purchase looked over the boat, walking around it, making some kind of inspection by poking at the hull with his cane. That was odd all by itself.

Stowers walked over saying, "So, what do you think. Is this the type of boat you want to buy?"

The man only introduced himself as Raul speaking with a foreign accent that Stowers did not recognize, "Is there any damage to the hull, and is it seaworthy for a long trip?"

Raul Two years ago, had joined a secret group of terrorists currently operating throughout the United States and was given the assignment to purchase a trawler for no more than $200,000.

"Yes, it is seaworthy on calm waters, and there is no damage to the hull at all. However, the engine will need refitting, and the crew quarters will need to be cleaned up."

"OK, I will buy it, the price you advertised for was $200,000, and I will have some of my men pick it up."

"We have a deal then if you want to pay the price." Stowers thought the whole transaction was odd. Raul did not even ask a question about the boat's seaworthiness in calm waters versus rough seas. He did not seem to care about the shallow draft of the boat. No matter the boat was sold.

Kamal, an electrical engineer, and Abdul, a mechanical engineer, arrived the next day at the marina with a flatbed trailer truck. The boat was hoisted onto a ready-made platform on the trailer, secured and driven off by the two men without any conversation. Stowers money was electronically deposited in his account. He was satisfied and could not care less about how the boat was moved, as long as it was off the marina.

The boat was delivered to another marina in Mississippi, where the two engineers started refurbishing the vessel. There were lots to do before the mission advanced to the next level.

At the boatyard in Biloxi, Mississippi, specifically, the trawler underwent extensive refurbishing for this operation. Abdul fitted two new Volvo Penta diesel engines, each giving off 330 horsepower. In addition, two expanded fuel tanks made of aluminum, containing 191 gallons of fuel, extended the cruising range giving them 764 gallons of diesel. Unfortunately, the route chosen created the necessity for extra tanks with only two gas stops within 800 miles.

The trawler held two cabins and two bathrooms to accommodate travelers. Additionally, an enlarged freshwater tank holding 200 gallons allowed plenty of water for cooking and showers. This trawler's cruising speed was determined to be 17 knots with a maximum speed of 23 knots. The two terrorists on board, both engineers, decided for maximum fuel usage; the cruising speed will be 15 knots. They acquired the Corps of Engineers and US Coast Guard nautical charts and data to plan their route and journey.

It took a solid eighteen months to refurbish the trawler, sparing no expense. Kamal made sure the cabins were fully air-conditioned and the kitchen well-appointed with a microwave, gas oven, and stove. Hot water was abundant for cooking and showers. Sea and freshwater bilge pumps with battery chargers were replaced, a 12-volt generator installed, and solar panels added to help with the trawler's energy needs. The two engineers did an outstanding job preparing the trawler for its deadly mission into the heartland of the Great Satan. "*The Wind*" became the new name of the trawler.

CHAPTER FIVE:
The Asset Test

* * *

Abu returned taking a sip of water from the bottle on the table as he sat back down in front of Jack nodding his head, "I'm ready to continue."

Conducting a polygraph examination is a challenging task of balance and continuous assessment. Jack had to ensure during the test that there was a complete understanding of the question. The questions must be specific, on target, with the issues at hand, making sure Abu understands clearly, while Jack kept rapport as his goal.

The pretest's first question was introduced, which was not characterized by Jack, but just read, "Do you intend to answer each question truthfully about that information you told me about?"

"Yes."

"Let's go ahead and review the additional test questions. Then, I will ask you the question: Have you ever told anyone you are working with American intelligence? How would you answer that question?"

"No, absolutely not," Abu said sternly.

Jack explained, "Please just answer No or Yes, truthfully, nothing else."

"No," Abu stated.

"Another question: Did you fabricate any of the information you have told me about today?"

Abu replied, "What is fabricate?"

"That means to lie." "It is another word for lying or making up a story."

"No," Abu replied.

"Are you comfortable with the word fabricate, or would you rather I use lie?"

"No, no, I understand the word now. It means have I lied to you or Peter about the information."

"OK, I will ask this question again: Did you fabricate any of the information you have told me about today?"

"No," Abu said soundly.

Jack said, "The next question: Have you ever told anyone Peter's identity?"

"No."

Needing to set the psychological hook, Jack explained, "The next series of questions concerns your character and integrity. We value high integrity and high character, or we would not have asked you to be our friend and help your country fight terrorism."

Abu understood and remarked, "I love my tribe and my country. The Taliban have hurt my people many times, even murdering my father and mother. I am true to my word!"

"Excellent, the next question will be about those issues: Have you ever violated the trust of any of your friends?"

Abu hesitated, thinking, and slowly muttered, "No."

He observed and listened to Abu's response carefully, knowing the question would create conflict in a truthful person.

"The next question will be: Have you ever done anything in life you are ashamed of?"

Again, Abu slowly started to answer, then stopped and looked around the room, "I think so."

"What is that?"

Abu hangs his head and slowly stumbles through his answer, "I have had desires to have sex with my friend's wife. I know this is wrong, but the desires are strong."

"Have you acted on those desires?" Driving home, the psychological impact.

"No, but I want to," Abu replied.

"Let me modify the question and read it this way: Besides, what you have told me, did you ever do anything in your life you are ashamed of?" Jack questioned.

Slightly hesitating, Abu croaked out, "No."

Jack was pleased about the question's conflict, and Abu's reaction was a robust psychological hook, showing a sign of a truthful person.

"Another question I am interested in asking you will be: Have you ever done anything that will dishonor your family?"

"No," with a raised voice from Abu.

Inwardly, Jack smiled; his raised voice was another indicator of concern over his answer. "Please answer in a normal tone of voice." Jack then introduced some irrelevant questions used to stabilize Abu's physiological responses. "Now some questions that will be very easy to answer:" Is today Thursday? Are you now in a room? Were you born in January? Abu answered, "Yes," to each of those questions.

Looking directly at Abu, Jack finished reviewing all the questions, "Do you understand the meaning of all the questions I will ask during the test? I am asking about the information you have given to Peter and me, his identity, and working with American intelligence. I am also asking questions about your integrity and character that are important to our continued relationship. Lastly, I am asking questions about you and our location today."

Abu's concerns appeared on his dark, rugged complexion, "I understand Bob, and I will be truthful."

"We're going to start with a simple test to make sure all of the components are working correctly. I want you to pick a number between 2 and 8 and tell me your choice."

"I pick 6."

Jack told him to write the number 6 on a piece of paper. Then he taped the paper to the wall in front of the asset and, at the same time, instructed, "When I ask you about the numbers, I want you to answer with only 'No.' Do you understand?"

"I think so. Say no to all of the numbers except 6." Abu replied.

"Incorrect, I want you to say 'No' to each number, including 6. You will lie about 6. I want to see what a lie looks like from your body. Say 'No' to each number."

"I thought I was to be truthful on all the questions."

Jack patiently explained, "On this test only, I am permitting you to lie on the number 6. You must say 'No,' so I can calibrate the computer to your body signals."

Abu said he understood as Jack attached the pneumographic components to his chest and stomach area, the cardio cuff to his left upper arm, and the electrodermal plates to the palms of his right hand. Jack explained that each component would record Abu's body responses when he answers. He did not go into any depth explaining fight or flight physiological responses, other than to say that his heart is the bearer of truth during the test, and his brain is the bearer of choice in lying and telling the truth.

A polygraph with Americans allows for a more comprehensive explanation of how the physiological and psychological meld of fight, flight, and freeze works. Still, because of language comprehension issues, Jack decided not to confuse Abu and made it simple.

He instructed Abu to sit still and look straight ahead at a blank wall with a piece of paper and the number 6 written on it. Jack started the computer and inflated the cardio cuff at the same time. The screen reflected a chart slowly moving from right to left, across the monitor. The four components move and record Abu's physiology, leaving a tracing of his breathing, cardio heart rate, and the electrodermal activity from his palms. After waiting about 25 seconds, Jack asked the first question, "Regarding the number you wrote, did you write the number 3?"

Abu answered, No. The next question is: "Did you write the number 4?"

Again, the answer is No, as instructed. Abu answered "No" to each question on the numbers, including 6. The response at 6 was as expected. The cardio rate climbed two chart divisions; simultaneously, the electrodermal component quickly traveled to the chart's top by five chart divisions. The breathing showed a slight change in inhalation exhalation followed by mild apnea. Compared to the other numbers, six stood out as the question of concern because he knew he lied, even with permission, yet there were no other physiological changes on the chart when he told a known truth.

Jack explained the results without showing Abu the chart. "I am pleased to see that when you lie, like at number 6, even though I permitted you, it stands out and is easy to read because lying bothers you. It is equally clear when you answer a question truthfully."

Abu gave Jack a defeated look, "I tried not to allow my body to respond to 6, but it still did not matter how hard I tried to stop it. I am a truthful person. Lying has caused me great pain."

Jack smiled and agreed with him, setting the tone for the test. Jack reminded Abu to be truthful to all questions on the test.

Without hesitation, Jack got up pulling the paper with the written six from the wall and sat down, declaring, "Please sit still, look straight ahead." He turned on the computer, hit the start button, and the chart slowly moved across the screen. He inflated the cardio cuff to 68mmg with a slight adjustment on the sensitivity dial as the components are engaged and, after waiting 25 seconds, stated, "This test is about to begin."

The questions' presentation was not in the same sequence as the review process, and timed delivery of each issue depends on physiological responses. Jack read each question in a moderate low tone of voice with no increase or decreased voice level. Jack started the test by stating, "Please remain still. The test is about to begin."

Once the collection of charts is complete, Jack declared, "The test is now over. Remain still." He allowed some 15 seconds to pass and released the air from the cardio cuff and turned off each component, instructing Abu, "You may move. This portion of the test is now over." Abu moved slightly in the chair. Within a minute, Jack repeated the same cycle and presentation of the test questions additional times in mixed order, so Abu has no idea what question came next.

At the end of the test, he removed the components and told Abu to step into the other room and talk to Peter.

Jack used the standard scoring system to evaluate Abu's responses on the charts to decide his truthfulness.

As he reviewed the charts, he could hear Abu discussing the test with Peter. After receiving a thumbs-up signal from Jack, Peter told Abu they are satisfied with the test results and instructed him to leave and meet him at another location in several weeks. Peter handed him an envelope of money, which Abu stuffed in his pants. The hallway was eerily quiet except for the echoes of Abu's footsteps bouncing off the walls as he departed.

Leaving the room, Jack announced, "He passed with flying colors. No deception indicated."

Peter inquired, "Jack, can you go to Forward Operating Base Snow Leopard outside Kandahar in two days?" Jack nodded as he watched out the window in the late evening darkness as it swallowed Abu walking down the damp and foggy street outside the apartment. Abu Omar is the only person on the road, and Jack recalled the final scene in the old movie *Casablanca* as the two main characters walked away from the hangar onto the airstrip in the fog.

The two men prepared to leave the apartment. Jack quickly rolled up the polygraph attachments, turned off the computer, disconnected the various cords, placing everything into his backpack. Before leaving the room, both men checked their weapons to make sure a round was in the chamber.

As Jack started his two-block walk, he noted his skin was immediately wet as he stepped from the vehicle. The humid air caused a trickle of sweat to run down his back. Jack's clothing was suddenly moist, and he was grateful for the ride. To avoid compromise of their mission, Peter dropped Jack two blocks from his hotel. He did not have to hunt for a taxi but was hyper-alert stepping out of Peter's vehicle.

Jack felt a slight satisfaction as his Sig Saur pushes against his waistband. As Peter pulled away, Jack was left alone in the darkness and started his slow walk along the damp street to the hotel. Lahore is a dangerous city at night for any Westerner walking the streets.

Jack mulled over the evening and the test. Everything looked good, but a persistent uneasiness gripped him. Jack's sixth sense had alarm bells ringing loudly, which he could not ignore; it worried him to his core. Something is coming!

CHAPTER SIX:
A Border Village in Pakistan

* * *

The deadly group of men moved along the ravine of a small canyon. The narrow defile took them to their objective, still 5 kilometers out. The team dropped at the landing zone by two MH-6G Pave Hawk helicopters far from the target to avoid detection. The ancient Chinese had a saying that described skillful warriors as swift with precision, and their force derived from releasing a trigger like the force of a catapult. These men were of such caliber.

Operational Detachment Alpha-647 was an exceptionally skilled Special Forces team trained for precisely this mission, thrust upon them by events. Detachment leader and commanding officer, Captain Joe Miller, expected his team to operate as one large weapon that can be highly destructive, if needed, and just as quiet when called for in any given situation. All his men were highly qualified professionals with skillsets for peacetime or war and were all melded into one, moving quickly and quietly through the darkness.

Several sources had initially produced actionable intelligence. A DIA polygraph examination then vetted the information to verify the story, and the internal directorate, known as J2X, authorized the mission. Their mission was to find, capture, if possible, or kill the targets. In this case, the targets were a group of five or six men, all experienced bomb makers who had managed to avoid capture repeatedly by special operations.

The last attempt was by a SEAL Team, and the bomb makers evaded them by leaving their secured positions a day ahead of the raid. Command believed that one of the assets might have warned the bomb makers. A quick go for action was issued, backed by another spy; the information looked compelling. Abu Omar did not know that several intelligence agencies were tracking him. Verifying his operational information and location through debriefings followed by polygraph supported his intelligence as being correct. The polygraph results also confirmed the team was not walking into an ambush.

Captain Miller and his team fully briefed before departure from their forward operating base, Snow Leopard, outside of Kandahar, Afghanistan, knew actionable intelligence has a short window for tactical forces to respond. The US Special Operations Command analyzed information in this environment, making decisions within hours to move forward to a target. Accordingly, they flew north along the mountains to engage their assigned target in the Pakistan-Afghanistan border region.

As ODA-647 approached the small village, they slowed their pace and then stopped making sure their night optical devices or NOD's were fully charged and in place. The soldiers rechecked their ammunition pouches and any backup weapons such as a knife or handgun and medical supplies.

This brief check served two purposes, a moment of rest and a moment to focus on each team member's objective. Each man knew this action could turn highly violent in the first minute of contact. Their primary aim was to capture these terrorists alive. No matter which way it unfolded, the team prepared to function by deadly brute force.

If they were extremely fortunate, they could capture all the targets sleeping, and subdue them by sheer force, if they were not expecting any Americans.

Captain Miller whispered into his comms, "Sergeant Hart, move your men to the alpha point near the southeast side of the village and eliminate any sentries." Sergeant Hart moved with his three-man team; all had suppressors on their weapons held in the ready position as they advanced. They split left and right as they approached the village edge and, within 50 meters, stopped spotting a sentry.

Sergeant Hart whispered in his comms to his teammate, "Kill the sentry." Without another word, one of the men moved forward slowly and deliberately. Darkness still covered his movement on this moonless night. Tim stalked the actions of the sentry just long enough to get a sense of his slow-moving direction. Since the sentry was moving toward the SF soldier, he waited silently. The sentry approached within 20 meters of the SF trooper, and the slight pop from a silenced weapon announced his death.

Without hesitation, the advance team moved quickly to the side of the hut containing the bomb makers. Sergeant Hart whispered, "Alpha point is secure." The rest of ODA-647 moved to the mud hut, leaving a sniper and spotter overlooking the building from a small hill allowing the sniper team to see clearly down the village's only street.

Inside the hut were six men. It was quiet. The only noise heard was the faint sounds of sleeping men with an occasional movement. The little light in the room, fueled by a lamp, was running low on whatever energy fueled the fire.

Captain Miller spoke quietly to his sniper, "Any movement near us?"

"No," came the response.

Captain Miller said, "Check the door to see if it is locked." Quietly, one of the team members reached up and tried the door. It was unlocked. Captain Miller gave the team a hand signal to form on him as they prepared to enter the hut.

Captain Miller was the first one through the door and moved left out of the way of the next man, who stepped right, and the third man walked straight into the sleeping men. The entry was intentionally loud and fast to disorientate. The fourth man into the room was Sergeant Hart, who headed straight for the furthest sleeping man, trying to close the distance to prevent him from raising his rifle, an AK-47, into action. The weapon went off, hitting Sergeant Hart in the left arm. He returned fire with his silenced M-4 striking the terrorist in the mouth. The AK-47 awakened the rest of the village, and as expected, lights started to come on.

The sniper watched and prepared to engage anyone with a weapon. The rest of the team members fell upon the remaining sleeping terrorists pinning them to the ground. One fought back with a knife stabbing one of the Green Berets in the leg. The terrorist was not so lucky as the trooper who engaged him; the terrorist died with a gagging sound; the trooper's knife stuck in his throat.

Four terrorist bomb makers were still alive, and two ODA-647 troopers were wounded. Captain Miller ordered the men to set up a secure perimeter around the house. He asked for his sniper to give a situation report or SITREP and then commanded his intelligence officer, Chief Warrant Officer Taylor, "get busy!"

The sniper called in a SITREP to the Captain of several people looking around down the village street, and so far, no one was armed. The entire team was on the alert to all movement. Most villagers stood and looked at the heavily armed Americans they barely could see and did not approach them.

CWO Taylor, an exceptionally skilled interrogator, needed to quickly learn if any of these men were the long-sought-after bomb makers that had been killing and wounding US and allied forces throughout Afghanistan. CWO Taylor also could speak Pashto, at least to a degree, to make himself understood.

The first terrorist looked like the one described in an intelligence report and was pulled immediately into another room where CWO Taylor and Master Sergeant Danny Lopez questioned him.

Lopez's dark complexion and an elongated scar along his right side of his face from a hunting accident many years previously, and his single gold front tooth exposed when he smiled, gave him a menacing look. Lopez was a very intimidating soldier who seemed to take up most of the small room space. Perfect Taylor thought. The visual aspect of this was what they needed for a short and productive interrogation. Lopez pulled out a long knife, sat in the corner with a sharpening stone, and slowly sharpened his blade while staring at the terrorist.

Wasting no time, Taylor spoke in English, "What is your name? What can I call you?"

His interpreter presented the question directly to the terrorist. No answer.

Taylor stated, "I will ask once more than my friend with the knife will be asking." The terrorist looked at Lopez before the question could be translated, thus giving away the fact, he understood English. The translator repeated the question anyway.

The terrorist replied, "Ahmad Durrani, and you will die for the violation of this village," speaking perfect English with a slight British accent.

Taylor and Lopez looked at each other, and both smiled. Taylor responded, "Right, and you will also die if we choose this as our best course of action."

Taylor asked, "Ahmad, we do not have time for the niceties of your tradition of tea and cookies, bringing me right to the point of this forced meeting. You make bombs, and you and your men are responsible for killing many Muslims, Americans, and other allied forces. There is no doubt you have the expertise to make and fashion weapons of destruction. We have known of you for several years; it's no accident we are here. As we speak, other forces are entering your home in Lahore and seizing your family for a thorough interrogation." Taylor monitored Ahmad's reaction.

Ahmad gave Taylor a stern look. To add to the pressure, Taylor informed, "We also plan on removing your sons to a different area of the country, and you should count on them gone for many years." Ahmed's eyes started to water, and his rage grew. Taylor and Lopez patiently waited on him to fully grasp his predicament. Then Taylor spoke. "Your chances of seeing your family again will increase with your cooperation, and it will decrease with your silence. Your chances will increase with your truthfulness and decrease with each lie."

Taylor knew he would get nowhere with physical abuse or threatening to kill Ahmed since he expected to die anyway. Psychological pressure and manipulation were so much better than physicality to extract information. It is a game played with sincerity and strength, and it must have consequences. With the help of analysis, Taylor and Lopez had studied Ahmed's profile and noted his Achilles heel was both of his sons.

Telling Ahmed information about his family, life, and friends' locations substantially impacted how Ahmed handled his betrayal to the Islamic fight.

In the other room, Miller's team pulled all the documents and laptops together, getting them ready to be carried to the extraction point. CWO Talbot was the team's physician's assistant. A super medic could perform medical procedures anywhere in the field, including some operations that doctors typically perform.

Talbot went to work at once. Hart's wound showed a bullet had passed straight through his upper arm. Talbot examined the wound because it was an AK-47 round that typically leaves about a 25cm path of minimal tissue disruption. Some muscle damage and tearing occurred, but he would survive.

Talbot said, "Hart, you will live, and the wound is not as bad as it looks."

He stopped the bleeding with a powdered substance known as a quick clot and applied a dry dressing to help prevent the narrowing of arterial blood flow associated with ischemia. He then cleaned and treated for infection with an antibiotic.

Another teammate was attending the trooper with the knife wounds to ensure the leg wound had not severed an artery. Talbot immediately irrigated and debrided the injury with clear sterile saline to prevent infection and started an antibiotic of cephalosporin via IV. No artery damage or leakage was detected. He wrapped dry bandages around his wound. He would be able to walk short distances, with help, to the extraction or exfil point.

Talbot would go into the surgery room to assist the doctors when they returned to the base camp. His team knew this about him. It provided a certain level of comfort to the wounded, knowing they were in good hands.

The dead terrorists were photographed, searched, and discarded. The remaining three terrorists in the room underwent a search, and plastic handcuffs placed over their hands behind their backs and a burlap bag placed over their heads completed the necessary security steps to transport them to the exfil location. One terrorist was so scared he was visibly shaking and throwing up. The other two just sat there on the floor.

Taylor left the room and pulled Miller aside.

"Sir, I confirmed the guy in the room is Ahmed, and he does speak fluent English. Our ploy worked as he gave up the others as bomb makers. These are our guys, no doubt. Also, he is holding something back that we need but refuses to explain it. I think it is his big bargaining chip for his sons, but I am not sure. Whatever it is, it's crucial to him. He tried to bargain with me asking us to leave him behind."

Miller said, "No way, he is going with us. Let's keep him interested in his sons. Do the other three understand English?"

Taylor shook his head, "No'.

Miller checked with his sniper. "All clear, boss," came the reply.

Taylor re-entered the room and placed plastic handcuffs on Ahmed's wrists, a burlap bag on his head, and stood him up. Taylor gave him a stern warning about talking to anyone but him, as it would cancel his deal and his son's whereabouts. He was then guided into the other room.

Miller instructed the security element outside of the hut, "Each man take one of these guys, keep them upright, moving and no talking. We are heading 220 degrees southwest to exaction point Bravo and wait there for the exfil." He then instructed his communications NCO to contact Snow Leopard for exfiltration from the Bravo point and tell them they had four Tango's in custody and two wounded in action to transport.

Three exfiltration points predetermined operational decisions and needs. Bravo was the closest with two wounded men and four prisoners of war. With their POWs and one interpreter in tow, the twelve-man Special Forces team moved out two hours after entering the village. Miller's team had managed to eliminate five bomb makers and one technical guy, killed by Hart, who was sitting on laptops full of intelligence.

The team arrived at the exfil site without incident, security was set up, adjusted their NOD's and separated the prisoners. The entire group sat in complete silence in the dark.

The stars in this part of the world blanketed the sky from horizon to horizon but offered no light; it was ink-black, Miller noted. Without the NOD's, you couldn't see anything, not even your hand in front of your face. In the distance, the low thumping of the MH-6G's coming for extraction was heard. No navigation lights, and suddenly, the helicopters were there and set down. As the doors opened, the interior red glow was visible, and all ODA-647 with their prisoners boarded in a matter of seconds, lifting off, returning to Snow Leopard.

CHAPTER SEVEN:
Forward Operating Base Snow Leopard, Kandahar

* * *

The hood and plastic cuffs' removal left Ahmed sitting on a hard bench observing his surroundings, his senses heightened. The only sound he heard was distant and muted. A single lightbulb high above his head burned intensely. The door to the cell was heavy and locked, and the air was dry and crisp, with only the hard bench to sit or lay on for rest.

Footsteps approaching alerted Ahmed, and he braced for what he believed would be the first round of torture. The door creaked open, displaying a small viewing area through three bars. An American face filled the small opening. Food was placed with water onto a small shelf on the inside of the door. The American waited and finally barked in English, "Take the food now, or it will be on the floor when I close the door."

Without a word, Ahmed removed the food. The port closed with a loud bang and a noise like a rusty lockset from the cells inside shelf. The clop, clop of footsteps diminished as the American walked away, followed by silence. Ahmed felt the pangs of hunger as he ate and drank his water with abandon in the stillness of the cell. His mind was tortured by not knowing what would happen next.

The helicopter ride and a scratchy burlap bag on his head disorientated him, and he didn't know which direction they were traveling. Ahmed sat for what seemed like hours on a hard bench when he heard footsteps, coming closer, then silence. He strained to listen to voices. Minutes passed as he started to feel like another pair of eyes observed him. He looked around the small room discovering a tiny camera lens in the ceiling corner of the cell. The walls are at least 15 feet high, and the camera is out of his reach. The plaster walls give no place for a foot or handhold to climb to break the camera.

A familiar voice of the American who captured and questioned him in the village broke the silence, "Ahmed, it is now your turn. Stand away from the door and keep your hands in front of you."

Ahmed complied and stood rock still, barely breathing. Suddenly, he felt his throat constrict, his heart raced, as fear enveloped his body. Silently he prayed to Allah for guidance.

The large door opened with a thud, and his tormentor stood there with two other Americans, one who placed metal shackles on his wrist, keeping his hands to his front. The other put a burlap bag on his head. Hands gripped him hard pushing him forward toward the door. His legs weak and shaky, but he managed to walk. The Americans firmly grasped his arms on either side and walked him out of the room, but to where he wondered, his senses working overtime?

The four-minute walk felt like a long time when you cannot see where you are going. Ahmed forced himself to notice the smells and sounds around him as he shuffles along in his blindness. He smelled different odors as he walked into what he thought was a hallway. Ahmed's senses picked up the smells of food and distinct noises as vehicles move outside. The guards pulled him up hard stopping. The door creaked open, and Ahmed was propelled forward with a shove, brushing against a door frame, into what he sensed was a room. Roughly turned around and forced down into a chair.

The footsteps fell away, as the door banged closed. Underneath the bag, only silence and his labored breathing against the burlap. Ahmed sensed someone was in the room with him. He could smell the musk of sweat, a slight tobacco aroma, and he does not smoke.

The burlap bag was removed in one quick uplifting motion, causing him to pull back as the course material assaulted his skin. His eyes started to adjust almost immediately to the brightness. He squinted his eyes against the light, slowly making out three figures standing in front of him. He recognized the American who initially interrogated him, the interpreter, an Afghan, who had spoken to him first, and another American he had not seen before.

The man with the scar and knife was not present, and he felt a specific relief for not seeing him. A small table decorated the room, which has one window high up, allowing dusk's fading light. Ahmed noticed the walls, made of the same pure white plaster as in the previous cell. He was barely breathing in anticipation of what will happen next.

The American softly greeted, "Ahmed is there anything I can do or get for you; are you thirsty?"

Ahmed, shocked and put off balance by what he heard, was momentarily confused by the gentleness in the American's voice and stumbled in his answer, "No."

The American interrogator pulled up a chair sitting directly in front of him. The other two men in the room stood behind him silently, increasing tension, making him nervous even more because he cannot see them. It's the unknown creating terror in his mind. The American must-see concern etched in Ahmed's face, the nervous twitch under his right eye, and he knows he is off balance.

* * *

Taylor watched the terrorist closely as he started the process, "Ahmed, we are going to have a productive conversation. You are going to follow my rules since you are now in my house. Will you please tell me if you understand the importance of what I am saying to you?"

Ignoring the American, Ahmed started to look around the room as if measuring what he sees. Taylor magnified his voice to get his attention, "Look at me! What is your answer?"

"Yes, I understand," refocusing on Taylor.

Taylor surprised Ahmed again by saying to the other men, "You two may leave now." Without another word, both men depart the room. As the door closed, Taylor used keys to the shackles and released Ahmed's handcuffs, placing them into his pants' large cargo pockets.

Once the restraints disappeared, Taylor noticed a slight change in body posture as the terrorist relaxed.

"Ahmed, as you recall, when we captured you at the village, I made it clear that you must not lie to me about anything. I know you have no reason to trust me at this point, but let me assure you, I have only your best interests in mind. Your health and your life are critical to me. Your failure to cooperate will keep you separated from your family and lead to a long and extremely uncomfortable life in captivity."

As Taylor spoke, he adjusted his body to communicate a non-confrontational posture but in complete control. Sitting erect in the chair, his legs comfortably open, he placed his hands in his lap and peered directly and intently into Ahmed's eyes. Taylor's body language conveyed confidence, directness, and empathy.

* * *

Ahmed listened to this strange American, and his apprehension started to ebb. He could feel his posture begin to relax. His concern over torture abated while he evaluated this American. Perplexed, Ahmed's expectation of violence was not evident from the American sitting opposite him.

Ahmed replied, "I remember everything you said," as he found himself off-guard, relaxing, less frightened, and more attentive.

The American continued his passive onslaught. "May I get you anything to make your situation a little more comfortable? Perhaps some hot tea may be nice to help warm you in this cool room?"

Ahmed replied, "Tea, yes, it would be good."

The American smiled, "Sounds good to me also." If on cue, the door opened, and a soldier brought in a tray with cups, tea, and fig cookies, placed them on a table, and walked immediately out of the room.

Ahmed again looks around the room, noting a small camera in the corner by the ceiling, and looks back at the American with a questioning look.

The American had noticed his look and smiled slightly, "Cameras are visible for yours and my safety; they are continuously monitored acting as reminders for everyone's safety.

* * *

Jack viewed the interrogation from an adjacent room with Peter and the interpreter, recognized the process Taylor used to build rapport, the most critical first step in any elicitation process.

Paige had arrived two days before he finished his test in Pakistan. This was no surprise since she was critical of the data being analyzed. Nevertheless, DIA wanted her on the ground collecting the raw data as it developed. Jack and she shared the information over lunch and informed each other where they were going and why. Paige watched the exchange, asking, "Why the tea and cookies?"

Paige grew up on a ranch in Montana with her three older brothers. She always had dreams of traveling away from Montana and the ranch. Her brothers wanted the ranch life, the hard work, and the rewards, as few as they were in that life. Her escape was going off to the University of Montana in Bozeman. She discovered she had an interest in analyzing situations, politics, government, and business. Her mathematical abilities were off the charts. She went to seminars starting in her third year, and members of the intelligence community promptly recruited her. She was awarded her Ph.D. in Political Science and told her family she was leaving for Washington, D.C., and life in intelligence. Her family was stunned, and she was excited about all the possibilities.

Jack explained patiently, "Paige, it is an important step in establishing trust and rapport. In Islamic culture, one does not charge in on a conversation. That is only done in Western culture, whereas this culture considers it rude. Listen to the conversation and understand everything that is happening is for a purpose. Look at the body language, listen to the tone, and evaluate his response."

Jack was attracted to her beautiful five-foot-eleven inches with shoulder-length auburn hair and hazel eyes. Her ability to put people at ease when they recognized her intelligence overshadowed her stunning looks was a pleasing plus for Jack. Sitting next to Jack, making continuous entries into Ahmed's intelligence file, she was unaware of Jack staring at her.

Jack was like a storm on a distant horizon. Quick flashes of lightning reflected in his gaze. Rolling thunder in his mood, and at times tears like rain shed in private. The hot and humid air of the Washington D.C. area aggravated him, especially when he smelled diesel, then throws in the sound of a passing helicopter, and Vietnam images came back to him in a flood that was hard to dismiss. He was tormented by his ability to recall precise details of his early life as a combat soldier. He suppressed his rage and made his condition worse, not better. He understood it would be a barrier in his relationship, but like most who suffer from post-traumatic stress, he believed he could handle it, not fully recognizing how he looked to others.

Peter impatiently responded, "If we are going to defuse those bombs in time, we need to find them."

"Have faith, brother. He will get that information shortly, and we can compare the information obtained from the other three terrorists we captured." Jack said.

The interpreter looked at Jack, smiled, and said, "I've seen this tactic many times. I am going to get some chow. I will be back later."

* * *

Taylor carefully poured the tea and offered Ahmed some cookies, "You have a long journey ahead of you. You need to understand what is required of you before you take that first step to see your family again."

Taylor knows trying to deceive another person takes a certain level of energy and time to construct a story the deceiver thinks will stand the test of an interrogation. Upsetting that timetable through counter moves was his goal.

Taylor noted Ahmed's immediate response with a change in his body language, which is closed and resistant. Protecting himself, he holds his legs together with his chin up and defiant. His arms lay across his stomach; his hands are in a fist. He is prepared to fight, verbally, at least. Taylor's words caused Ahmed to focus.

* * *

Ahmed violated his faith by cooperating with the Americans when captured he felt shame and guilt. Mentally, he resisted the words spoken to him. He already acknowledged his fellow Jihadists and himself as bomb makers. He couldn't change what he'd already divulged. He remembered the Korans instructions are to be deceitful in the hands of the enemy if it would lead to victory. He was deceptive thus far in his dealings with this American.

The Americans' questions were going to be about the bombs he assembled, and they will want to know where the stockpile of IEDs is. Ahmed knew the location of the stockpiled IEDs for the next attack on American forces in Kabul. So even though he feared the Americans, Ahmed decided he would only divulge the information in parts to confuse his enemy and try to work a deal for his sons.

Unknown to Ahmed, one of his fighters admitted he was an "apprentice" bomb maker just learning his craft. The terrorist who had been the one shaking and vomiting under his hood in the village denied making any bombs. He was not allowed to touch them because of his overwhelming fear of making a mistake. The Americans already had extracted some information on the stockpile, but not enough.

The American did not start his questioning directly but instead inquired, "How did you meet your wife?"

"We attended the same school. She would be walking home to our village, and one day I addressed her. She was shy like a good Muslim girl; she did not talk to me and ran home."

"How old were you at that time?"

"I was 12, and she was 10."

"How old were you when you married her?"

"I was 20, and our families were delighted for us to be married."

"What was your age when your first son, Mahmud, was born?"

Surprised that his son's name is known, Ahmed cautiously responds, "I was 22 years."

"Your second son with the cleft pallet was born two years after that, and his name is Muhammad."

Surprised at how much information this American knew, Ahmed nodded. Racing, through his mind, is the information the Americans have on his family. Many questions loom large in his thinking, making it difficult for him to lie when answering questions.

Ahmed studied the soldier watching his facial expressions trying to gain an advantage, like in a high-stakes game of chess. Words and body language have an impact cutting into Ahmed's mind like a razor.

Ahmed hid his despair poorly, revealing to the American how he felt. The psychological wedge of the American's words registered on Ahmed, causing him to feel helpless, torn by his family, and what he perceived as his duty to Islam. The conflict crushed his will.

Again, the American started, "Your lovely wife, Amira, put up a good fight to protect your sons. You should be proud of her bravery." Ahmed stared in disbelief.

"Amira, is she hurt? Is she alive?"

"Yes, she is fine. So are your sons. No one was injured," the American said.

Ahmed's level of fear and concern increased as he realized his family's danger with the Americans. His heartbeat severely against his chest wall; his breathing became shallow as he tried to control his fear. Ahmed knew he was slowly caving into his terror; the Americans knew more about him and his family than he thought possible.

The American disrupted his thinking, "Please finish your tea, have something to eat."

Ahmed's predicament was direr than he thought. The American was just sitting in silence, studying him with confidence. Ahmed felt the heavyweight of pressures over family, his duty, truth, and lies. Trying to construct the lies was becoming difficult. Ahmed's inner tension was building. A sheen of sweat appeared on his face as he calculated his options.

* * *

Paige broke in, "Jack, what is he doing?"

"He is allowing Ahmed to think. His silence will force Ahmed to speak. Ahmed must respond to the silence as this would be a natural human response to address the conversation gap."

"How long will this take?"

"It depends on Ahmed and how he assesses his problem," Jack teased. Without waiting for Paige to respond, "There are no real-time limits here, but what is important is the first one to speak loses the superior position."

Jack fully understood Taylor's methodology. Language is a critical component in the construction of a lie, and the deceiver always leaves clues. It is vitally important to listen carefully to answers and stories.

Jack observed Taylor. *He is good.* Jack thought, not as good as himself, but good as one gets without doing this daily. Jack took note of Taylor's body language, recognizing a relaxed position, staring right at Ahmed, waiting patiently, unmoving. Ahmed looked at the floor, a sign of defeat. Jack noticed his legs still closed together, a symbol of resistance. Slowly, Ahmed's legs opened. He removed his hands from across his stomach and placed them open-handed on his legs. Lifting his head, he looks right at Taylor, then drops his head, looking at the floor. Jack knew the moment had arrived!

* * *

Ahmed was feeling the combined crushing weight of betrayal, guilt, and concern for his family. The feeling of a thousand stones upon his chest crushed his resistance, and slowly he acknowledged his defeat, "What do you want from me?"

The American said, "I want you to reveal the location of the two storage areas of your bombs. We have already flooded the general area of the impending attack with our forces. Our silent aerial aircraft carrying missiles are hovering above the battlefield, waiting on orders to strike the first Taliban movement we detect." Ahmed is listening to the low-keyed tone, "Your cooperation saves lives on both sides of the fight. You and your family have an increased opportunity to be back together.

"Your Jihad is over because the three other men captured with you have surrendered all their information identifying you as the chief bomb maker in Afghanistan. Your apprentice bomb-maker was the first to divulge everything about you." Ahmed now understood the betrayal by his men. The American's words hammered home the final nail; any lingering thought of resistance was no longer a straightforward option. Ahmed knew he was defeated.

Ahmed listened carefully to the proposition. Looking at the American, Ahmed's calculations ran amok, knowing what must happen and how he will handle his betrayal, placing his family's interests over theirs. True to his beliefs, Ahmed was not about to give up entirely. He reasoned about divulging the least amount of information, using a mixture of truth and lies, as the best way to stop the pressure of guilt.

According to Shari'a law, consistent with his Islamic beliefs, he can lie under these circumstances to his enemies.

Ahmed gave up one location but withheld the second of his stockpiled bombs. That was the wrong decision, but he ignored its potential impact on him.

"The house's location containing the bombs is four kilometers outside of Kabul to the East, a small house behind the larger house with red shutters and trim. The second location is closer, in the ruins of the old capital, the one the Russians destroyed."

* * *

Taylor watched the expression and facial changes on Ahmed's face. Ahmed hesitated to tell the second hiding area's location, looked up and to the right, and then down at the floor as he spoke. Taylor decided Ahmed just lied to him. He also chose not to press the point currently and moved forward with his next question.

"Ahmed, do you recall the conversation about your truthfulness and helping you reunite with your family? Failure to fully tell the truth will increase the distance between you and your family and make life very uncomfortable. We have ways to determine if you tell the truth."

Taylor watched him nod his acknowledgment of his statement and heard him lie again, "I tell the truth, even though I do not want to, I did." Convoluted answer. Taylor recognized another lie just presented because a truthful person's response would have been a simple "Yes." Ahmed's linguistic style changed in his answer, another clue.

Jack, in the other room, also knew a lie when he hears one.

* * *

Paige was busy transmitting information to forces on the ground outside of Kabul, with a description of the house and ruins to be searched. She unnecessarily gave a warning about watching for boobytraps when the soldiers enter the structures.

Jack was already at work structuring a polygraph test by writing out possible questions he would ask to verify Ahmed's information.

Two hours later, the phone rang, and Paige answered as Peter, Jack, and Taylor listened to half the conversation. "Which location? How about the other location? Right. OK. Thanks," Paige explained, "Some IEDs have been found at the house with red trim. But nothing at the ruins of the old capital."

Ahmed placed himself in an impossible situation, and Jack knew it as he prepared the room to conduct a polygraph test. The computer sat on the table with the polygraph components attached to the computer and laid in an orderly fashion as part of Ahmed's mental picture. Taylor escorted Ahmed into the room where Jack waited patiently, guiding Ahmed to a chair with arms near the table. Taylor instructed Ahmed to sit in the chair and left the room. Jack stared down at a psychologically beaten man.

CHAPTER EIGHT:
Ahmed's Decision

Jack, Peter, and Taylor discussed what they believed was the lie Ahmed concocted during the interrogation. Taylor was concerned about what other information Ahmed possessed since he tried hard to negotiate his way out of capture in the village. Peter had concerns over how vast the web of bombers is within the Taliban.

Jack wanted to engage with Ahmed about his deceit and impress Ahmed that lying will hurt his family's chances of reuniting. Psychologically breaking Ahmed into full cooperation, Jack wanted Ahmed to be at an impasse by exposing his lie.

* * *

For two hours, Ahmed studied the two young Americans in the room with him, both large and intimidating. On their uniforms, each one had two letters: MP. Ahmed was unsure of the meaning, not knowing it stood for Military Police. Not a word passed between the three of them. Ahmed sat quietly, staring at the American's posture. The message clear; do not test us. He feared their response might be violent.

The American inquisitor entered the room and instructed the MPs to escort him down the hallway. The two MPs moved as if one, roughly grabbing his arms, lifting him out of the chair as if he was a feather, pushing him toward the door.

Entering a second room, he noted bare-walls, and Ahmed was looking at yet, another American. His eyes landed on the table containing a computer with strange wires coming from it. The MPs left the room, and his interrogator introduced him to the other American, calling him "Bob," Then his tormentor departed the room.

* * *

Jack's six feet two-inch two-hundred-pound frame towered over Ahmed, "Ahmed, sit in the chair with the arms." Jack noticed Ahmed

75

could not take his eyes off the components lying on the table and kept glancing back at him. Jack instinctively understood questions and concerns are probably racing through Ahmed's brain, wondering if the Americans will torture him. By staying silent, Jack increased Ahmed's level of fear dramatically.

Jack studied Ahmed's reaction to him and the room as he started the polygraph process. Jack explained in some detail that the computer could record his physiological responses. Jack told Ahmed about his heart betraying him if he lied, and in general, made Ahmed aware that his attempt at lying would be futile because Jack would know.

Jack's green eyes were penetrating, and hard as emeralds as he stared at Ahmed. The uncontrollable constant tick of Ahmed's left eye was a telltale sign of how very concerned he must be over his lie about the ruins. He noted tiny beads of sweat broke out on Ahmed's forehead. The noises coming from his stomach could be heard in the silent room betraying his stress. Jack intentionally held his gaze, knowing Ahmed's fear was working against him. It is true; you can smell fear. It has a pungent odor; it radiates from one's pours and their breath. Jack could smell it all over Ahmed.

Breaking the silence, Jack reviewed the test questions with Ahmed and made sure he completely understood the nature of the test, "Do you have any questions?"

Ahmed, with a slight tremor in his voice, "No, I understand."

The two relevant questions that interested Jack were: Did you lie about the bomb's location at those ruins? And: Did you lie about the exact location of all the explosives?

During the test, Jack could see the cardio tracing was at a faster rate than average. The dicrotic notch in the cardio tracing disappeared, a sign of deception. Ahmed's heart was beating out of rhythm, increasing blood pressure and peaking each time he heard those two questions: Jack could almost read his mind, *"it is a lie, and my body is giving me away."*

Jack administered the test collecting four charts with the same questions asked in random order. At the end of the examination, Jack analyzed the tracings on the charts, Ahmed failed, and he failed hard!

Jack rose from the chair as he already formulated how he would approach Ahmed on his failure. He decided the best way under these circumstances was to DPC him, "direct positive confrontation."

Jack removed each component from Ahmed's body, arm, and hand and stated directly, "Ahmed, you failed the test because you were dishonest with me. I am disappointed because I had faith in you. Your failure places an obstacle between us, a lack of trust."

Ahmed's fear was etched on his face, quickly evaluated by Jack. He also knew he was trying to think of how to justify his lies. Without realizing it, Ahmed placed his arms across his chest and looked to the side. He crossed his legs. Jack fully understood Ahmed's blocking body language to escape from his lies. The chess match was on!

Lying is complex and places demands on the deceiver that are different from a truth-teller. Liars try to be imprecise as possible, and a person telling the truth is telling their stories in a way that explains what they did and what they did not do in a direct narration.

Not waiting for Ahmed to present his lie verbally, Jack stated, "Ahmed, we are trying hard to work with you on this problem. Your lack of faith in helping us is bothersome because you know it will also impact your family.

"As we are talking, your family is being moved from Pakistan to another location for their safety. We are the only ones that will know the place of your family. You are making their situation worse if you continue to lie to us; the decision to remove your children to a different site from your wife will be your responsibility.

"Ahmed, your Jihad is over. You are no longer involved in the fight. Your men have betrayed you, not once, but three times, as each one has given us information about you, your family, and the bombs." Jack stopped abruptly, for impact, increased tension, and sat back to wait for

Ahmed's response. Jack's move was designed to increase Ahmed's growing internal pressure.

Ahmed attempted a strong response, but it was all bluster, "You Americans think you will win, you will not. Allah is on our side, not yours, and he tells us we shall win in the Holy Qur'an."

"That's odd Ahmed, our Holy Bible informs us we will win, and we will. We're at a stalemate when it comes to our God's, and right now, you are not winning." Jack intentionally shut the religious debate down because he did not want the interrogation to turn into a circular religious argument on God.

Jack intentionally continued by describing a book, "I know about your book and manuals on Shari'a Law, permitting you to lie in certain circumstances and to give misleading impressions to deceive your enemies. I have read the playbook of your sacred laws. I allowed a measure of margin for such tactics, but that is over. Your attempts at lying are falling on deaf ears, and my patience with you is running out.

"Ahmed, I want to help you, not hurt you. I want you to know I am your only friend right now. The truth is in your heart; I know this as I could see when you lied because your body betrayed you. I could see your heart almost explode in your chest. I know you felt it."

Jack understood how the human mind and body worked in tandem to stress and observed Ahmed feeling his lie's pressure. He watched as Ahmed's body transformed, opened, and his hands come off his chest, a good sign. However, he was still holding back, blocking, and defiant in his answers. Jack was sensitive to the fear, rage, and inner conflict Ahmed felt.

Jack observed him twist in his chair, double over as if his stomach hurts. The emotions are raw. Ahmed's fear and resentment were crushing him, pushing him one way and then another.

Jack increased the palpable tension in the room, "Ahmed, you are at a crossroads. Your choices at this moment are going to place you far away from your family, never again to be able to visit your family. We may have to tell your wife to search for a new husband and a new father to your sons, or you can help us save lives of innocent Muslims that your bombs will surely kill."

Jack pushed the emotional buttons to pressure Ahmed. His eyes are tearing up; he wrung his hands; he uncrossed his legs into an open position. The moment arrived, and Jack reached over, gently touched Ahmed's forearm, and said in a low tone, "Let me help you."

Jack's touch has the desired impact. Ahmed dropped his head, drained emotionally, and defeated psychologically. Looking at the floor, "The bombs are at the Kabul Golf Club."

Jack asked, "In the foothills just above, Kabul?"

"Yes"

"Where at?"

"They are buried behind the restaurant, on the side of the hill in several containers."

He almost collapsed in his chair. Psychologically defeated, his energy gone. Ahmed played his last card.

* * *

In the other room, Peter, Taylor, and Paige watched and listened. Paige took notes and reached for the phone to call the field commander in Kabul.

Taylor looked at Peter, "He is good, do not leave me alone in a room with Jack; he'll have me telling all my secrets."

Peter smiled and quietly thought the same to himself.

Paige ended the phone call, "Elements of Company C, 5th Infantry moved to the golf course." All three of them looked at each other and burst out laughing. The idea of a golf course in Afghanistan was alien to their way of thinking. Ridiculous! But the on-ground commander said he knows the golf course.

* * *

Jack watched Ahmed cry. Jack understood war and combat, yet he felt no compassion for him; he had killed many Americans and NATO troops.

Just as Jack often does, he waited for Ahmed's opportunity to compose himself. He always asked one more question. "Ahmed, what else did you want to tell me?"

Ahmed looked up from the floor, "You have been righteous and not lied to me. I am compelled to tell you about someone extremely dangerous. I will tell you in exchange for my family. This man wants to use the big bomb, a nuclear device, in your country and knows how to build one. He told us about it when he showed us how to construct the bombs for Kabul. He plans to bend the world to Islam and has scared all of us."

Jack, alert now, looking at Ahmed and in an even voice, ordered, "Tell me his name and where I can find him?"

"His name is Abdullah-ibn-Khan. I do not know where he is living or where he hides. He will build a nuclear bomb and will detonate it on America."

CHAPTER NINE:
El Golfo de Santa, Mexico

* * *

Concerned about getting into the United States, the three Jihadi fighters hid in El Golfo de Santa, Mexico's sunbaked town on the Gulf of California forty-three miles south of the border. They were thousands of miles from the world they knew as they endured the uncomfortable, agonizing wait for the drug cartel coyotes to show them how to navigate the vast Southwest deserts of Mexico and the United States.

They struggled for over two months traveling from Yemen to Africa to Venezuela to Nicaragua into and through Mexico. They were close to their Jihadi goal and an end to their dangerous journey. The little three-room house lacked any accommodations to make their stay comfortable. The largest room contains four chairs, a table, no beds, no other furniture to sit on. The toilet facilities are primitive. The dwelling was dirty with low airflow through the house, making the rising heat uncomfortable. Scorpions scurried across the floor, ignoring the latest intruders.

Each terrorist carried a secret with them to assist Khan in building a bomb to destroy a city. Without naming the secret targeted location in the United States, Khan mysteriously implied that the town would evaporate under a nuclear bomb explosion. Their most immediate concern is how to get into the United States without being detected. Traveling through a desert is not alien to them since they are Berbers who know how to survive in the high Saharan Desert environment of North Africa.

Al-Hazam looked at his two companions with admiration. Both Ibn Tabari and Muhammad Ahmad have been involved in Jihad for over three years before they volunteered for this dangerous assignment, two and a half years longer than he had been on Jihad. Al-Hazam was impressed. Their stories of fighting in Iraq against the Americans were inspiring, and he had not had the honor to be in combat. For that, he is jealous of his friends.

Al-Hazam asked once more in his native Arabic, "How much longer before these pigs show up?"

Muhammad Ahmad chastised him once more, "Speak English, brother. We must speak English more to improve pronunciation so we will be successful on our journey."

Both men listened as Tabari slowly spoke as if forming the words in his mind first, "These drug dealers will speak English. We must show them that we're ready to travel to America. At the same time, we must also be prepared to kill them because they are the worse kind of infidel for the drugs they sell."

All of them felt the heat of the day as it slowly climbed to one hundred degrees, and the morning coolness faded away.

The ocean, located just a few miles from the house, created a temptation, inviting them to go wade in the coolness of the Gulf. It is only the discipline of Tabari, their leader, that they did not seek relief in those waters. "Relax and drink water; the time is coming soon for our journey across this desert. We do not understand creatures here and the strange vegetation we need to know for our survival. The hard part of our journey is going to be on the American side of the border." Tabari explains without further elaboration.

In the distance, Al-Hazam heard a vehicle and listened. Quickly going to the window and watched dust rise in circular swirls on the other side of low hills hiding the road, "They are coming."

* * *

A few moments later, a severely dented and faded blue Ford pickup truck arrived at the house's front. The driver, Enrique Cruz, yells at the other two men in the vehicle, "Get out now!"

Looking sinister, all the Mexicans armed with AK-47's, with belts of ammunition and long machetes dangling from their hips, took up positions to the rear of the truck.

Entering the house, Enrique carefully eyes the three Arabs, and not seeing any weapons, tells them, "My name is Enrique. Tonight, about midnight, we will travel to the border for the crossing." His English is better than the Arabs but broken.

* * *

Looking over the Mexican leader with his weapons, Tabari slowly replied in stilted English, "We are ready to travel and are well-rested for our journey. Do you have the maps we requested of the United States?"

"Yes," producing a well-worn map folded many times with the word Esso on it. "Here is your map, which I have marked with your route into the United States through the State of Arizona, where you will meet our contact on Highway 8," said Enrique.

Tabari unfolded the map and laid it on the table upside down. Enrique reached over and turned the document around, appropriately orientating it to a North-South direction.

Listening, the Mexican quickly explains as he points to the border, "Here is where we cross near these mountains. The fence is minimal, but the Border Patrol is everywhere. They have motion detection devices. We will be moving quickly down the mountain before they can arrive."

Tabari carefully studied the map. The names of towns on the map are unfamiliar, and his concern about the crossing was evident in his voice, "This area to cross is the best?"

"Yes, it is rough terrain and difficult to travel through, not only for us but for the gringos."

"What happens if discovered?" Tabari asked.

Enrique smiled, "We have two choices. We fight or run. Your choice is your own. I will make our choice when that happens."

Tabari's companions focused on him as he decided, "We will fight, or we will die to accomplish our mission." Tabari believed the Mexicans would abandon them if it were in their best interests.

Enrique said, "As you choose. Everyone needs to rest before we start tonight." Looking at Tabari, "You will need to listen to me as we travel the desert. There are snakes and other creatures that can be very unpleasant for you and your men to meet, so listen to me when I instruct you to do anything."

Tabari nodded in agreement. Unfamiliar threats at night in the desert are his concern. He understood Enrique's comment, but doubts still linger hard in his mind about trusting the drug cartel members entirely.

Finding space on the floor, both the Mexicans and Arabs were not concerned about the scorpions, brushing them away. They settled in for the long wait as the Mexicans started preparing a typical peasants' meal of beans and rice, with tortillas, enough for everyone. It would be the only meal they have before the long walk to the United States.

* * *

Enrique grabbed Tabari's arm shaking him awake. He had slept through the heat of the day. It was now twenty-one hundred hours and almost entirely dark outside. He noted Enrique and his men were moving about and picking up their cooking utensils; blankets shook out and rolled into tight bundles. Al-Hazam and Muhammad Ahmad were packing their rucksacks while adjusting straps so that the backpack will ride comfortably on their backs.

Enrique looked at everyone declaring, "It is time, everyone, in the truck, Montoya, you will ride in the back with our guests, Ramos ride upfront with me." There was a quick exchange in Spanish between Enrique and Montoya, who nodded his head.

Tabari did not like the exchange in the Mexican language. It sounded too much like a betrayal to his ears even though he had no idea what the Mexican leader said, and that was the problem. He decided to test his feelings, "What did you say to your man?"

Enrique looked squarely at the Jihadi, grunting, "None of your business!"

Tabari now turned to his men and told them in Arabic to beware of the Mexican's treachery. Kill them if anything goes wrong.

Enrique started the truck, looked back to make sure everyone was in, then pulled forward to the road leading away from the house. As the vehicle picked up speed, he turned the headlights on catching a glimpse of a coyote running from the dirt road; the night was alive with desert creatures. The stars are out, but there was no moon, which made it best for the crossing.

CHAPTER TEN:
Sonora Desert, Arizona

* * *

On the other side of the border from Mexico, a team of US Border Patrol Agents, part of the BORTAC or Border Observation and Reconnaissance Tactical Team arrived by helicopter dropping into the desert. Team leader Michael Baines signaled the men to gather around him for one last briefing before going to their assigned sectors. Baines' job was to ensure everyone understood the latest intelligence and how the operation would unfold.

The highly trained team was comprised of six men. Their previous experience in the military, along with their current training with special operations elements, enhanced their training. Skills hone to a fine edge enabled the men to conduct operations like the present improving their odds. They will divide into two-man teams covering three sectors along the border.

Baines began his briefing, "Gather around men. Tonight, we have some new intelligence. The drug cartel will move a large load of cocaine through one of the three sectors we will be covering, but no one knows exactly which sector. Make sure all of your equipment is working; does anyone need batteries for NODs or flashlights?"

As proven law enforcement officers, none needed to be reminded at the briefing to check their equipment. Team members were issued standard M-4 rifles and 9 mm pistols. However, against the rules, Baines carried a .45 caliber pistol as a backup weapon in the small of his back. The only thought Baines had is, *"Can we locate the bad guys?"*

Baines read off the two-partner pair up. "Ruiz and Rojas, you will be in sector one. Billings and Garcia will be in sector three. Torres and I will be in sector two." Baines strategically chose sector two for command-and-control purposes as his sector was equally distant if he had to travel in either direction for backup. "All of you have about three hours to arrive at your setup locations at the foot of the Angelo Mountains; before the sun goes down, move out!"

Baines' BOR Team headed south as each member checked compasses and orientated their maps in slightly different directions, slowly spreading out from the others as their line of march took them into the heat of the desert and shadow of the Angelo Mountains.

The terrain was tough with the rising midafternoon heat of the scorching desert. The men were used to it. After two and a half hours, Baines called his team members on their comms, "Team One, are you set up?"

"This is Team One; we just arrived and will be set up within the next 10 minutes."

"Roger that."

Team Three, are you set up?"

"This is Team Three; we are set up and ready."

"Roger that, Team Two is ready."

Setting up was a unique procedure for each team, as the terrain dictated their choices. The landscape chosen was elevated and decorated with shrubbery for cover. Each unit selects a spot located on top of rocky terrain, raised to give them the advantage of seeing the mountainside's base one mile away. The teams are looking down well-worn trails.

The night was pitch black; night vision devices were a necessity to see any movement. They could hear on their comms some soft chatter of other Border Patrol Agents operating in different areas. Those patrols were with vehicles and horses along Interstate 8, running from the East in Arizona to California.

All the teams fell into a comfortable waiting period as they believed the cartel would not make any moves down the mountain without checking for their safety first. The cartel typically sends scouts out to make sure trails are clear. Knowing this, the BOR Team sits quietly, not moving.

Billings suddenly whispers, "Shit, a rattlesnake just crawled across my boot."

Garcia looks around apprehensively, trying to spot the rattlesnake, but it has slithered away and disappeared into the brush, "Man, I hate when that happens." They both lapsed into silence.

Coyotes are howling in the distance, most likely because they have a kill they're rejoicing over. The desert birds give a hint of movement as Nighthawk's cruise through the darkness devouring insects as they compete with bats for food. The stars are beautiful, and Baines wondered if there was intelligent life out there because there are times, he doubted there was any creative life on this blue ball called Earth.

Ruiz and Rojas managed to find a sweet spot to view their sector. Rojas looked around with his NOD's and whispered to Ruiz, "Bobcat, at 2 o'clock, moving laterally to our position."

Ruiz replied, "I see him, nice. It looks like he is hunting." A coyote speaks again in a yipping howl causing the bobcat to stop for a moment and look around.

"I love the desert," Rojas proclaimed as he studied the silhouette of a Seguro cactus against the starry skies.

"I know what you mean," Ruiz said. Silence descends over them as they focused on the mountain to locate drug mules.

CHAPTER ELEVEN:
The Mexico/United States Border

* * *

Enrique drove the truck for one long hour along the vacant road before turning off onto a dirt road. The dust flew from the soft earth leaving behind a cloud as the truck moved directly north to the mountains. He hoped his plan to foil the Border Patrol would work, and if not, he was prepared to sacrifice the Arabs. Enrique viewed the Arabs as just another business arrangement assigned to him by El Jaffe and rid himself of them as quickly as possible.

* * *

Already tired of the ride, Tabari felt every bump in the road. He looked at his companions, noting their expressions assuming they felt the same. The Mexicans seemed to be oblivious to the dust and bumps as he stared off into the darkness.

The truck started to slow and turned to the left as it slowly negotiated a curve coming to a halt, causing the dust cloud to envelop them. As the dust cleared, Tabari saw Enrique standing about 25 feet from the truck.

"My friends, it is time for us to walk."

I do not see a path." Tabari grunts.

"The path is in between the rocks. That is why you paid us so that we can show you the path up the mountain and down to the other side into the United States."

Al-Hazam and Muhammad Ahmad jumped out of the truck, straightened out their packs, and beat the dust off their clothes. Muhammad looked at a tall plant and turned to Enrique, "What do you call that plant?" nodding at it.

"Seguro. It is a cactus. It takes 50 years to start growing its arms. This one looks like it is at least 100 years old."

Tabari watched Al-Hazam walk over to the plant, place his hand on the cactus. At once, one of the needles penetrated his skin. Cursing in Arabic, he withdrew his hand as the sound of the men's laughter is heard in the silence of the darkness. Enrique extended his hand, "Give me your hand and let me look."

"The needle is well embedded. Montoya, your pliers," ordered Enrique.

Montoya handed the pliers to Enrique, who grabbed Al-Hazam's hand and unceremoniously ripped the needle from his palm.

"You mother of a pig," Al-Hazam yells out in surprise and pain.

Ramos produced a bottle of Tequila and poured it on Al-Hazam's hand. "This will help with any infection," Ramos explained, as Al-Hazam jumps around from the stinging alcohol.

Ignoring Al-Hazam's comments, Enrique wrapped the wounded hand with a dirty bandage to stop the bleeding and turned to Tabari, "This is why I told you to do as I tell you. There are things out there that will harm you and can be deadly. We may meet rattlesnakes, Puma's, Gila lizards, and scorpions. Do as I say and do not touch anything."

The waves of heat from the desert night radiated all around them and laid heavily on the six men. Tabari, in a stern voice, warned, "Do as he says. Do not put your hands anywhere unless the Mexicans do it first. Walk in their footsteps and listen to them."

Ramos was designated as the scout leading the way into the rocks and up to a hidden trail.

Enrique followed Ramos up the path, followed by Tabari, Al-Hazam, and Muhammad Ahmad in a single file, Montoya, in the rear.

Pushing forward in the darkness, the climb up the trail on the Angelo Mountains' Mexican side was strenuous. The men leaned into the steep mountain trail as their feet slipped on the loose rock and dirt. The heat of the desert and the darkness made the trek harder. The ground was unfamiliar to the Arabs, and their muscles burned in their legs, feeling their efforts as they struggled to keep pace. The Mexicans seem to be totally at ease with the climb. After two hours, Enrique signaled for the group to stop for a water break.

Tabari instructed his men, "Drink some of your water and be careful not to waste it by drinking too much." However, his advice was not needed as his men are inhabitants of the desert and understand the necessities of drinking water and conserving it.

Tabari asked Enrique, "What type of rattlesnakes do you have in Mexico?"

"Our snakes are called Mohave Rattlesnakes and are considered the most venomous rattlers in North America."

"Will the venom kill you?"

"Yes, it can; it is very deadly to humans. It causes most people to swell badly in the bitten area, and then they die. It is best to avoid the bite."

"What about this lizard you mentioned?"

"They are called Gila Monsters, and they are very poisonous. When they bite, they lock onto the body and inject poison into you. You have to cut their heads off to release them." Enrique replied, smiling.

"What about the scorpions?" Muhammad interjected.

"Scorpions hurt like hell when they bite. They will not kill you unless you have an allergy, like to bees. It hurts bad; I know as I have been stung several times, and I am still alive."

Montoya chimed in, "Puma is what they call a mountain lion, and they will kill you. Since Puma's are shy, we do not typically spot them.

We do see bobcat's that are smaller than Puma's, and if we leave them alone, they leave us alone."

Al-Hazam asked, "The noise we hear now, what is that?"

Enrique replied, "Coyotes calling to their mates or maybe a kill. They are like small wolves. They are nothing to worry about."

Rested, the men lifted their packs, placing them back on as Enrique moved up the trail. The stars in the sky offered little light; each insurgent could only see the man in front of him. The sweat on their clothing had already dried after their brief rest. All they could feel was their rough, salty skin.

The men slowly made their way up the side of the mountain, and as they came around a bend in the trail, Tabari saw the top of the mountain silhouetted against the spiraling Milky Way. The faint outline of rocks and large boulders filled his vision as he neared the top. His attention turned to Enrique, who was leaning against a large stone.

"What time is it?" Ibn Tabari asked as he neared the boulder supporting Enrique.

"One thirty, we made good time. It will be all down the mountain now. We need to take precautions because the Border Patrol is everywhere."

"Where is the border between Mexico and the United States?" Tabari asks.

"Right there, next to the large boulder. See the metal stakes in the ground. On the other side of those stakes is the United States."

Tabari could barely see the stake next to the boulder and walked over to it and noticed wire curled up on the ground. Many have passed by here.

Enrique instructed everyone, "Once everyone rests, we will start down the trail. Do not place your hands on the rocks because snakes will lay on the rocks at night for warmth. Watch the trail for snakes. If you hear that rattling noise, stop and do not move. Call out quietly to me. If you try to run, you may run in the wrong direction."

Tabari stared out into the night in the United States' direction, seeing lights on the horizon and movement far below; all can see what looks like headlights of a car, or maybe it is a truck, driving on an unseen road. The pin dots of light are so small it is hard for them to determine the distance. A sudden feeling overtook Tabari that was hard to define. He decided it was the fear of the mission and, almost at the same time, he was excited about entering the lair of the Infidels.

The descent into the United States started smoothly, but not without pain to their toes being crushed in their boots, as the men slowly shuffled down the trail. About halfway down the mountain, Tabari heard a rustling sound and froze automatically. He spoke softly, "I hear a snake! I have stopped."

Al-Hazam, not seeing Tabari stop, crashed into him, knocking Tabari forward. Tabari fell to his hands and knees, finding himself face to face with a giant snake, coiled and ready to strike. The serpent's tail raised, vibrating loudly. The trail's steepness caused Al-Hazam, like a domino falling forward, over and beyond the top of Tabari, landing face-first just past the rattlesnake. Suddenly, Al-Hazam felt a sharp pain in his right shoulder; the snake recoiled from the strike, preparing to strike again.

"I'm bit!" screamed Al-Hazam, and before he could move back, there was another bite in his right cheek.

Instinctively, Tabari moved slowly backward, away from the rattlesnake. At the same time, Enrique slammed his machete into the snake's coiled body, slicing off its head.

Al-Hazam, was in a total panic, as poison pumped through his body as he felt the side of his head going numb and pain beginning to set in. His shoulder started to hurt badly.

As Tabari scrambled backward, Montoya stepped over Tabari and is next to Al-Hazam, pulled his knife, and started cutting into Al-

Hazam's cheek, causing him to scream out in pain. "Hold still. I need to get the poison out." Ibn Tabari quickly crawled to his fellow Arabs side and held him down as Montoya continued to use the knife to cut deep into his cheek to open the wound for drainage. He hooks his fingers inside the Arab's mouth and squeezes, causing the blood to flow from the puncture wound.

Enrique yelled at Tabari, "Rip his shirt off by his shoulder."

Tabari did as instructed. Another knife came out from Enrique and cut open the wound around the two puncture holes in the shoulder. The injury was now draining with copious amounts of blood.

"Will he live?" demanded Tabari

"I do not know, perhaps he will, but he will be very sick and unable to travel," claimed Enrique.

"We must leave him here. Once we get you down the mountain, we will come back this way and pick him up and return to Mexico. It is in God's hands now."

Enrique's answer was unsatisfactory to Tabari, but he knew it was the truth. He bent over whispered in Al-Hazam's ear in Arabic, "Allah has you now. Your fight is over. Go in peace, my brother," as he slid the sharp knife across Al-Hazam's throat.

* * *

Enrique watched in amazement as one Arab slew another. His companion may or may not have lived. Enrique had already decided to kill him on his return if he found him still alive on the trail because he had no intention of carrying him back up the mountain. So, it's done.

Enrique said, "Everyone on their feet, our rest is over," as they resumed the trek down the mountain, leaving Al-Hazam to Allah and the hungry hunting creatures of the night.

* * *

Border Patrol Agents Rojas and Ruiz suddenly looked at one another as both men placed their hands on their weapons; Rojas asked, "Did you hear that?"

"Yes," Ruiz replied. "It sounded like it came directly ahead of us."

Rojas and Ruiz knew the sound, especially at night in the desert, can be confusing, and makes the exact location exceedingly difficult to tell.

"It sounded like a man yelling something."

"I think it was a scream," Rojas replied, his senses now on high alert.

Ruiz depressed his button on his comms and called Baines, "Team Two, this is Team One, over."

Baines responded, "Team One go ahead."

"We heard a man scream, we think, it came from the base of the mountain. Did you hear anything? Over."

"Team One, we believe we heard something but thought it might be a coyote howling. Over."

"Team Two, we are pretty sure it was a man yelling out, not a coyote."

"Roger, let's keep listening. Who or whatever it was will be coming toward us soon enough?" Baines replied.

"Roger, Team Two, out."

Baines decided to call in a SITREP to his command post if contact with cartel thugs happened, so a helicopter could be ready to aid in search of the desert when needed. He also checked with Team Three, "Did you hear anything about five minutes ago coming from the mountain?"

"This is Team Three. That would be negative. The only thing we keep hearing is coyotes, over."

"Roger that, stay frosty. Keep your eyes and ears open. We may have some activity," Baines responded.

* * *

The Mexicans and the two remaining terrorists arrived at the base of the mountain, firmly within the United States. Compasses checked; they walked single file, following Enrique across the desert landscape, maneuvering around giant cacti. Enrique looked at his watch, it was three-thirty in the morning. The desert heat had cooled down to a comfortable eighty-eight degrees, and the terrain flattened out, allowing their pace to quicken. Confident that they had eluded the Border Patrol, the Mexicans unknowingly, in their Northward trek, walked right into the BOR Team ambush, exactly between Team One and Team Two.

* * *

Ruiz depressed his mike button, whispered, "Team Two, we have some movement to the right of us, about six hundred yards out, over."

"Team One, Roger, we heard them to our left. Coming between us, I think."

"Roger that, will move towards them in five minutes."

"Roger Team One, break, break, Team Three, we will need your help, move towards my northern exposure, and set up a blocking position if they get by us."

"This is Team Three, Roger that, moving now," Garcia responded as he picked up his rucksack and weapon, indicating to Billings to move.

Team Three walked in a fast-paced northeast direction to be positioned right behind Team Two; the sky was starting to brighten on the horizon as the sun rose in about thirty or forty minutes.

Baines contacted his headquarters and requested helicopter support. It would take them some 20 or so minutes to arrive at the sectors they were covering.

Baines and Torres moved east to intercept the group. Rojas and Ruiz moved west so they would meet with Team Two.

Baines picked up his binoculars and, from a squatting position, scanned the terrain. The shrubbery sporadic enough to give him cover yet see patches of open ground. He looked to his left, and he saw Rojas and Ruiz approaching and hand signals for them to halt and take up a position.

Baines watched and observed a man walking alone, carrying an automatic weapon. Baines warned all team members, "Single man with AK-47 walking toward us about 400 yards out."

Ruiz came over the comms, "I see four men walking, two with automatic weapons, AK-47 and two without any apparent weapons."

Baines held his hand up to Torres, Ruiz, and Rojas in a clenched fist, meaning maintaining their position. Baines knew his men would respond at the right time; they trained many times for this exact situation.

The Mexican on point had no reason to suspect an ambush and presumed the route was clear. He was alert for any movement and was confident he would easily spot the Border Patrol's green uniforms. Ramos's real problem was that the BOR Team was wearing desert camouflage uniforms, blending with natural surroundings, making the team virtually invisible until they revealed themselves. If you were not looking for them, you would not see them until it was too late.

For Ramos, it was too late. Baines stood up with his M-4, pointed directly at Ramos, and, in Spanish, yelled, "US Border Patrol. Stop! Drop your weapon. You are under arrest."

Baines, anticipating a firefight, was prepared with the weapons safety off, raised, and aimed center mass at the unsuspecting Mexican;

on the other hand, Ramos was ill-prepared with his AK-47 pointed at the ground.

The Mexican cartel coyote, hearing the command, stopped, looked to his left, saw only one Border Patrol Agent, made a fatal mistake raising his weapon to engage the Border Patrol. Baines, an Iraqi and Afghanistan combat veteran, was more than prepared for the Mexican's move. Baines fired three shots center mass into him in a split-second, dropping him straight to the ground.

Before the echoed sounds of gunfire faded away, Rojas and Ruiz made straight for the other four men. The first to see the group leader, Rojas, screamed at him in Spanish, "US Border Patrol, drop your weapon." Enrique, not being the type to easily give up, turned his weapon on the Border Patrol Agents opened fire. Ruiz fired, hitting the Mexican in the legs, dropping him to the ground; however, Rojas took a bullet in his right shoulder, also falling to the ground.

Montoya, in the rear, ran back down the trail. Tabari immediately rushed forward and picked up Enrique's dropped AK-47, opened fire on Baines, missed him, and hit Torres in the stomach. Rojas lying on the ground, rolled over, bringing up his M-4, and shot Tabari in the legs and chest five times before losing control of his weapon and dropped it.

When the shooting started, Billings and Garcia ran to the sound of gunfire. As they arrive, they saw one man in the process of picking up the AK-47 lying on the ground, dropped by the dead Tabari. Billing's training kicked in and acted first before the assailant could bring the weapon to bear and fired several rounds at Muhammad Ahmad, hitting him in the ankle and right arm, knocking him back into a sitting position on the ground.

Baines, now on the radio, requested a medical team and instructed the helicopter pilot to search for one perpetrator on the run and heading south, carrying an AK-47. Within moments, the aircraft flew screaming past their position, heading south. Baines and Garcia apply first aid to Torres, trying to control the bleeding.

Billings approached the man he shot, sitting on the ground, and shouted in Spanish, "Lay on your stomach" as he points his M-4 at him. Unmoving and just sitting there looking at Billings, who once again repeated his demand in Spanish. The man wincing from pain replies in broken English, "Please do not shoot."

Billings, in English, "Lay on your stomach, now, hands out."

Muhammad slowly complied; as he rolls over, he pulled his knife from his belt, placing his hand up under his chest.

"Put your hands out now." Billings demanded.

Approaching from the rear of Muhammad, he placed his weapon against the back of Muhammad's head and set his right foot in between Muhammad's legs. Again, he demanded, "Put your hands out!" Muhammad started to roll over, and Billings recognizing a knife in his right hand, kicks Muhammad in the balls, hard enough to make three points at any football game. Muhammad screamed in pain, dropping the knife. Billings quickly kicked the knife away and snapped plastic cuffs to secure Muhammad's hands in the small of his back.

Ruiz applied first aid to Rojas to control the bleeding from his shoulder. As he was securing the bandages, a Blackhawk from the aviation branch landed with a medical team and stretchers.

The medical team took over and started transporting Torres and Rojas to the helicopter for a flight to Yuma's nearest hospital. Baines gathered Billings, Garcia and Ruiz around and informed them they were going after the one who slipped away. Other Border Patrol Agents arrived in another helicopter taking Muhammad and Enrique into custody and providing medical attention. Baines inspected the area where the firefight started and noted there were no large packages of drugs that he expected to see. Lack of drugs is highly unusual, raising questions in his mind, why?

Baines contacted the helicopter pilot and asked if they had spotted the Mexican yet. "Nothing yet, we are still... Standby."

"Roger."

Baines heard distant automatic rifle fire, sounding like the familiar crack, crack of an AK-47, a sound he knew very well from his combat experiences.

The helicopter pilot came back on the comms, exploded, "We found him, and the son of a bitch opened fire on us. We pulled back. He is running directly south to the mountain. He is about a half-mile from your location."

"Roger, on our way." Baines and his men started running in the direction of the fleeing Mexican.

The Border Patrol Agents closed the distance rapidly, and as they climb up a slight hill, they could see the Mexican slowly running up a small hill, heading for the rocks and boulders at the base of the mountain. Baines saw the Mexican trip and fall, with his AK-47 tumbling away as he instinctively used his hands to break his fall. The Agents rushed forward, trying to shorten the distance.

* * *

Montoya decided he was fighting the gringos no matter what happened. He heard the helicopter and knew it was a matter of time before they would capture him. His whole life dedicated to the cartel and sworn oath to never leave except in death; made him stand. Montoya struggled to get off the ground taking several steps, and retrieved his weapon. Looking over his shoulder, he saw men in camouflaged uniforms running toward him.

* * *

Baines saw the Mexican stop and turn around, hoping he would give up; Baines was mistaken. The Mexican instead raised his AK-47 firing. Baines and his men scrambled for cover. Rounds ricochet off the rocks near them as Baines directs Billings and Garcia to move to the left and flank the Mexican. Baines and Ruiz pushed forward from boulder to boulder. Baines watched the advance of his men and experienced déjà vu, *"Crap, I'm back in Afghanistan."*

All four of the Border Patrol Agents positioned in an "L" shaped standoff with Montoya boxed in against the rocks. In Spanish, Baines demanded Montoya's surrender.

Montoya replied, "Never, come and get me."

Baines, concerned with his men's safety, contemplated their next move as they were in a standoff when the Mexican started shooting again. This time he was standing out in the open, away from cover. Billings and Garcia seizing the opportunity, open fire on Montoya, quickly sending him to the other side of life. Montoya died just like he lived, hard. Baines and his men survived the firefight so that they could fight another day.

Baines asked for more Border Patrol Agents and a Supervisor to come to the latest deadly location as his men secure the new crime scene. Again, no indication of drugs. Who in the hell are these guys, Baines's thought? All operations with fatalities require an internal investigation, but this one was uniquely different; it does not fit the mold. Listening intently on comms, Baines replied, "Roger that."

Garcia was looking intently at Baines and asked, "What?"

"Torres died on the way to the hospital. Rojas will live. They think one of the captured guys is an Arab. Strange combination, drug cartel, and Arabs." Baines's gut was in a twist; losing Torres and learning the latest Intel knew this investigation would take them into new unchartered territory.

CHAPTER TWELVE:
Operational Detachment Alpha - 647

* * *

Jack saw no other way around the issue. Valuable intelligence was collected and analyzed in detail and revealed a specific threat. Moving forward with the Intel required his level of expertise; the Colonel placed the responsibility squarely on Jack's shoulders as there wasn't anyone in this theater of operations with his skills. Secretly, he was concerned over how he would function in a combat situation and if he could hold his end up in an encounter with the enemy. He came to the realization his PTSD worried him.

"Colonel, it's been a while since I've been in a position of direct combat. Seriously, I may be a liability versus an asset to the operation; hell, I am considered an old man compared to a Special Forces team."

Colonel Davenport, Commander, 10th Special Forces Group (Airborne), listened intently to each word spoken by Jack. "Between you and me, none of us are spring chickens, and we all have our aches and pains each morning. I see you every day doing workouts and running miles around the base camp. You look fit, and besides, I have your military records in front of me. You are no cherry when it comes to combat, as you proved multiple times in Vietnam. Besides, the simple fact is we need your expertise in this operation, and DIA has cleared you to go. Since you are a civilian, I cannot order you; I have to ask."

"Have you told the team I will travel with?" Jack asked.

"Can't, not yet; I need your response! Well? Yes or no! I need to get this show on the road."

Jack looked at Peter, the case officer from DIA, sitting in the corner, smiling. Peter was 15 years younger than Jack and just as fit but lacked the in-depth experience required for the mission. "OK, Colonel, you got yourself one polygraph examiner for the mission."

"Great, and thanks! Your decision will make things a lot easier for all of us." Colonel Davenport replied.

"What does that mean?" Jack asked.

"It means I do not have to postpone a mission, nor do I have to explain it to my boss at the Pentagon."

"I guess I miss the point about this being easier on me," Jack replied with a grin.

With plans now finalized, Colonel Davenport left to brief the ODA team about the mission and Jack's addition to the group. Although technically a civilian, he ordered Jack to follow, "Jack, in 30 minutes, meet us at the team house for a brief introduction to the team."

Jack piped up, "Peter before I go to meet the team, let's go over this intelligence one more time to make sure I understand the importance of traveling to a country without the permission of that country."

"No problem. The information Abu Omar collected leading to the village's raid and the bomb makers' capture is a considerable success. You verified all that information making everyone feel comfortable to give it the green light." Peter retorted.

"Glad everyone was happy with the work, but it would never have happened if you had not worked so well with Abu," Jack teased.

"Right! We are in this favorable position because we captured Ahmed, who had a come to Jesus' moment, metaphorically speaking, with you, when he gave up this guy named Khan." Peter continued, "Our checks on Khan are a little slim, but he appears to be real. We have crossed checked his name in multiple ways. We are certain he is a physicist, a nuclear physicist, educated in France and England. He also schooled at Harvard, where he was awarded his Ph.D. after his schooling in England."

Jack queried, "How do we know he is behind anything at this point? Only Ahmed knows a name, but nothing else."

"This is where you come in, my friend. We have records of odd one-sided telephone dialogues. Although they were one-sided conversations, their oddity piqued our interest," Peter chuckled, "if you call it a conversation in the normal sense."

Jack said, "That is strange; go on."

"We recorded the following message: "I am Ibn Abbas; I need help from the Americans because my master wants to build a nuclear bomb. His name is Khan." Peter continued after checking his notes, "This message coming from Uzbekistan repeated no less than five times. The signal seems to move around; on one occasion, it came from Turkmenistan."

"How was that done with one phone?" Jack asked.

"Our intel analysts think he used two phones. He had control of both phones calling the other phone for a connection, then just started talking. At first, they thought it was one phone because the two phones used were so close together. They finally figured it out." Peter confirmed.

Jack guessed, "Smart and resourceful, this is the guy we want to meet; somewhere on planet earth, correct?"

Peter acknowledged, "Yep, that is why you are needed. We cannot capture this guy if he has any contact with the mysterious Khan because we would expose our hand. At the same time, we cannot ignore the message. We need verification of his information."

"That is going to be tricky, if not impossible. Many variables come into play, such as where we are, time, and power for my computer, to name a few. Maybe I can borrow one of the battery-operated polygraphs if they could get it to me in time." Jack snickered.

Peter laughed, "Well, my friend, that is why you are going with a Special Forces team to keep your butt safe."

* * *

Colonel Davenport entered the team house and requested a meeting with ODA-647 commanding officer, Captain Joe Miller, his intelligence officer, CWO Mike Taylor, and intelligence NCO, Master Sergeant Danny Lopez.

"Captain, I am giving you an alert notice to respond to a high-value intercept of intelligence that needs verification for the President of the United States. No one outside this room, except for the personnel I will inform you of, will need to know about your mission. Is that clear?" directed Colonel Davenport.

"Yes, sir." All three acknowledged.

"Captain, after I layout this mission, you will decide and inform me of how many of your team will be necessary for the mission. A civilian will be traveling with you, whose expertise is needed to help assess as well as confirm the information from the source you will contact. His name is Jack McGregor. He is a DIA polygraph examiner, an expert at elicitation and interrogation."

Looking directly at Colonel Davenport, Captain Miller asked, "Is this guy in shape for this mission? What's his background?"

CWO Taylor broke in, "Captain, I worked with Jack after the last raid and watched him at work with the terrorist we captured. He is indeed an expert. Smooth as silk, retrieving information from people. He appeared fit, but I do not know his background."

"I was just with him, and he volunteered to join this mission after DIA approved it," declared Colonel Davenport. "He is as fit as any 50-year-old. I see him running and working out every day around here. I also have a military file.

"Let's get this out, so you understand him. He is a US Army combat veteran of Vietnam with three tours. He completed Airborne School at Fort Benning in 1968, just before his Vietnam tour. He also is Ranger qualified, a course he completed after his second Vietnam tour. He has three Purple Hearts, two Bronze Stars with "V" for valor, and two Silver Stars. One of his Silver Stars started as a Distinguished Service

Cross and was downgraded, which often happens to enlisted folks."
Colonel Davenport explained. "He is no stranger to hardship or combat.
He has multiple tours in Iraq as well as Afghanistan. Unless you have
some concrete reason why he should not go, he is going, and it is your
responsibility to make sure he gets there and comes back."

"Sounds like he is going. I have no concerns." Captain Miller
replied.

Colonel Davenport grinned, "Good, let's discuss where and why
you are going."

"The location is on or near the border of Iran and Turkmenistan.
There is some ambiguity in the exact location. We'll get the exact
location soon. Both sides of the border are dangerous to US personnel;
make no mistake about it." Colonel Davenport lamented.

"We believe the town of Serekhs, just south of Meana, is the
location where we will meet the source. We are trying to confirm that
now. That is the where. Why is another story."

CWO Taylor interrupted and asked, "Who in Turkmenistan is
helping us?"

Colonel Davenport confirmed, "Excellent question, Chief, but
wrong country. The person or persons aiding us are Iranian resistance
fighters. As you know, this raises the stakes for us being there. Our
mission is twofold. Of course, we want the information, and at the same
time, we need to show goodwill towards the Iranian resistance. Nothing
is straightforward for us on this mission."

CWO Taylor absorbed this added information as the Colonel
continued, "The reason we're going is a result, through a rather
ingenious way, a source-identifying himself as Ibn Abbas. He is
reaching out to us about a guy named Khan, explaining to us this guy
has or will acquire a nuclear device. The polygraph test conducted by
Jack, the one you witnessed Chief, started the wheels turning in all
corners of the administration and the Pentagon."

Master Sergeant Lopez asked, "How do we know the Iranian resistance isn't Iran intelligence, and this is a trap. This guy Abbas may be bait?"

Colonel Davenport looks at each man in the room, slowly saying, "We do not know for sure; it is a risk. The information you are after is definitely worth the risk we'll be taking."

For a couple of minutes, there was complete silence in the room as each man mulled over the impact of the dangers. Colonel Davenport broke the silence, "There is more. US Border Patrol had a firefight a week ago on the Arizona side of the Mexican border. A Mexican cartel member and an Arab identified as Muhammad Ahmad survived the ordeal. An interrogation has revealed that he was on a mission for a guy named Khan. Is it the same Khan, referred to by Ibn Abbas, we do not know?"

Captain Miller mused, "Looks like we have a major problem, sir."

"Yes, we do. That is why everyone has concerns over this. We need answers, and this team with McGregor will have to get them regardless of the risk." Colonel Davenport said, driving home the point of the dangers involved and the importance of intelligence.

"Captain, get me your plan of action by 1800 tonight and how many men are going. Here is the alert order with specifics on what equipment you may need. I am going to see if we can nail down the location of this meeting."

"Roger that, sir." Captain Miller replied, coming to attention as the Colonel departed the room.

"Chief, you and Sergeant Lopez work out an intelligence operation plan on the area for infiltration, then choose a spot or two for the exfiltration."

The three Green Berets immediately morphed into operation mode, figuring out the necessities of such an operation logistically.

* * *

Jack jogged around the complex as best he could, tried to get some distance in before the day was out. Jogging gave him time to think and work out problems with Paige.

As he completed five miles, he saw Colonel Davenport and terminated his run.

"Colonel, what's the verdict? Will your team be OK taking a civilian with them?"

Smiling and looking intently at Jack. "No problem at all. I just read ODA-647, your military file. They are fine with the extra baggage."

Not missing the "extra baggage" comment, but ignoring it, "What time do we meet for an informal hello?"

"How about 1800, after chow at the team house?"

"Roger, that I will see you there." Jack trotted off, picking up speed heading to the showers.

* * *

Entering the small dining facility for the compound to grab a quick cup of coffee and a sandwich, Jack saw Paige sitting alone at a table reading a book and drinking a bottle of water.

Walking up to the table, he quietly said, "Mind if I join you for a couple of minutes?"

"Not at all. I am pleased to see you so soon." She smiled.

"We have not had too much time to talk, but I will admit I am strongly attracted to you if you do not mind me laying everything on the line here."

"Jack, I do not mind at all. I have had the same thoughts about you. Your different from a lot of men I have met. The differences are refreshing for me. I like the idea of working together because it gives me a chance to see how you operate around others. Most men are all into trying to impress, and you do not engage in that behavior. You are more in the mode of what you see is what you get. That is the part that is refreshing to me."

"Paige, that is nice to hear. I don't put on any pretenses and try to be honest in my encounters with everyone. I can't stand lies; I have always been like that. This profession I am in is well suited for me."

"What are you doing this evening?"

"I have a meeting I must attend with the Special Forces team. It looks like I am going on an operation with them. I will be gone for several days. How about we get together when I get back? I'll take you to dinner at the Hard Rock Café."

"What café? I do not know about anything like that here." Paige said seriously.

Laughing, Jack said, "I am referring to this dining hall. It is just a hard place with lots of rocks. If a Hard Rock Café existed, the Taliban would have burned the place down by now."

Laughing, Paige said, OK, you got me. I will see you in a couple of days and be careful on this operation. You know those Green Berets can get into some serious situations."

"Yes, I know. I'll see you soon." Jack said as he got up with his coffee and made for the door.

CHAPTER THIRTEEN:
Hi, I'm Jack

* * *

Approaching the team house, Jack saw slivers of lights through the curtains. The meeting was going to be necessary to establish relationships. No special operation team likes to have a "stranger" join them; it interrupts the group's dynamics. If the fit was not good, it creates unnecessary tension on the mission.

Knocking on the door, Jack heard, "Come in." from Colonel Davenport. "Gentlemen, this is Jack; he is now your responsibility." The colonel made individual introductions around the large table located in the center of the room. The table acted as a briefing area for all operations.

Jack recognized Chief Warrant Officer Mike Taylor, "Chief, how are you doing?"

"Great, and it will be good to work with you again," Taylor replied.

Jack did not know the other seven team members and decided he would do his best to talk to each one making them feel more comfortable about him. However, penetrating a team is complex, and he needed to initiate the process.

Colonel Davenport looked around the room stating, "This mission will be tough. Not because you will necessarily be in combat or contact with terrorists, but because you will have to restrain yourself from being noticed or captured by anyone."

Colonel Davenport let that sink in for a moment, then continued. "We have confirmed the meeting will take place in the small town of Serekhs, Turkmenistan, within a mile of the Iranian border. Typically, this area has low traffic; these two countries co-exist in a general way, with most of the suspect activities on the border's Iranian side. One of the advantages will be a large population of former Russian ethnic people in the area, removing any white men's suspicions. An estimated 4,000 people of mixed demographics are living in and around this town. Trade is extensive, and people cross back and forth over the border. That is good news."

"What is the bad news, sir?" Captain Miller inquired.

"The bad news is Iranian intelligence operates freely around the town. Your presence there needs to be low-profile. Captain Miller, do you have that arrival worked out yet?" said Davenport.

"Yes, sir. We will arrive late at night or early morning hours when it is still dark entering the town in pairs. We were discussing the location of the safe house when you showed up; maybe I can continue with that and get your thoughts."

"Go ahead, Captain."

"We identified a field about five miles east of the town between two low ranging hills. The hills will muffle the sound of our helicopter in addition to the reduced noise inhibitors. We can walk the five miles easily into town from the landing zone."

"Sounds good so far." Colonel Davenport said.

"Yes, sir. Each man will have a 9 mm with suppressors, backpacks with extra ammo, knives, and several grenades. Our team medic will be carrying a full complement of medical supplies. Our signals NCO will also have his gear. Jack, what weapons are you checked out on?" Miller asked.

"9 mm, 45 calibers, M-4, and just about anything you have," Jack replied.

Miller asked, "When is the last time you were at the range or used a weapon?"

"Last week, my detachment did standard close quarters shooting qualifications with M-4's set to malfunction or run out of ammunition and switching to handguns to finish the target."

Captain Miller smiled, "Excellent."

Jack interjected, "I will also be carrying a small computer and polygraph attachments if that opportunity arises for us. The weight is inconsequential for me. I see no issues at keeping up with the team at all."

"Sergeant Lopez will be going along for the ride to K2, our departure point for this mission, but he will remain there because there are no Mexicans in that part of the world." Captain Miller explained. Everyone laughed as Master Sergeant Lopez gave a wide grin displaying his gold tooth.

" I will stay at K2 to monitor radio traffic and coordinate the extraction from the area with Nighthawk Seven Zero," Lopez replied.

Lopez continued, "The location of Serekhs' is just over one mile north of the Iranian border. About five miles east of the town are some low-lying hills and a flat pasture ideal for a landing zone. I have identified three areas where a helicopter can land for extraction. One place is to the north of the original landing zone by one mile, one to the south of the original landing zone, about one-half mile, and one in an unexpected area right between the town and the Iranian border. The Iranians would least expect this LZ.

"The last area is on a slight hill, not the best area, except in an emergency. I intentionally chose this site as it would be an unexpected move if you are on the run; to run towards Iran." Lopez finished his briefing.

Taylor asked, "How about radar in the area. Are the Iranians going to be able to monitor or see our choppers coming in or leaving, and how about anti-aircraft batteries?"

Captain Miller responded, "No anti-aircraft guns we know of now, maybe radar. CIA and DIA analysts scrubbed the entire area. The Iranians have nothing there we are aware of, as far as anti-aircraft. It is a sleepy little place in the world of sleepy places. Our biggest concern is Iranian intelligence getting wind of our activities."

Colonel Davenport asked, "Have you taken any other precautions, Captain?"

"Sir, I have. Sergeant Bradley Lee, my team sniper, will be the only one with a long gun on the mission. He will insert ahead of the team to cover our arrival and extraction when we leave." Nodding toward Sergeant Lee, the only Chinese ethnic in the room.

"OK, to recap, you are taking a total of eight men with you to K2. You will depart K2 with seven men. One man will go ahead of the team for security, and one man will remain at K2. How is Sergeant Lee getting into the country?" Colonel Davenport asked.

Sergeant Lee spoke up for the first time, "High Altitude Low Opening, sir. I will depart K2 four hours before insertion. HALO in at about 30,000 feet. I should be on the ground in position way before the team arrives. I will move to our primary extraction point while the team completes the mission. If the mission is compromised, I will make my way out of the country any way I can by escape and evasion."

Colonel Davenport noted Sergeant Lee's special skills badge. He was the only one in the room qualified to do a HALO insertion, a true warrior, and nodded his approval of the plan. "Captain Miller, I am done here. You have an official green light for your planned mission. Report to me when you get back." Colonel Davenport quickly left the team house, headed for his office.

As the Colonel shut the door, Jack asked, "What do you know about the information developed in Arizona by the US Border Patrol?"

Taylor spoke up, "I can do that, Captain, since I got the intel from the States directly."

"Go ahead, Chief," Miller said.

"After the firefight in Arizona, the Border Patrol thought they had stopped a drug smuggling operation based on their intelligence. They discovered there were no drugs. When they tried to talk to one of the two men left alive, he did not understand Spanish. He spoke English with an accent, of course. The two survivors of the firefight were treated for their wounds. One enterprising Border Patrol Agent, dressed in civilian clothes, managed to get himself covertly admitted to the same hospital room as a patient and acted like he was an illegal alien involved with the cartels, smuggling drugs."

"Looks like he was thinking ahead, or he smelled a rat," said Jack.

"Correct. The BP agent started talking to the cartel guy named Enrique. It was clear Enrique was in pain, so the Border Patrol Agent was encouraging Enrique to escape along with him, knowing damn well he could not walk on legs with bullet holes in them. He offered a car to make their escape.

"During the conversation, Enrique let it slip that ISIS hired him to get the Arabs into the United States for some terrorist's mission. He also revealed he thought they were going to St. Louis as their destination because he was supposed to hook them up with a guy on Interstate 8 in Arizona who would transport them." Taylor explained.

"That is good intel. Was there anything else?" Jack asked.

"Yes. Border Patrol notified the FBI since they would have jurisdiction on terror-related matters, and someone told a contact at CIA about the conversation, which pissed off the FBI guys. The FBI and the CIA arrived at the same time in Yuma to talk to the Arab. I guess there was an argument of sorts about who should talk to him first. Border Patrol just stood back and laughed at them." Taylor said.

Jack already understood the argument without even knowing the details. Law enforcement and intelligence agencies do not always mix well. They had a whole different train of thought on how to get the job done. It boiled down to law enforcement wanting to read them their rights, collect enough information for an indictment and conviction, then put them in jail. Intelligence folks wished to discover additional information and to identify other players, like who is in St. Louis or whatever their real destination is and what exactly their mission is. They want to look at the whole scenario, work it by uncovering the cell. Incarcerated or dead spies help no one.

Taylor continued, "Looks like they both spoke to the Arab and agreed not to give him a rights warning. It took a little while, but he finally admitted he was on a Jihad and received instructions from a person he knows only as Sheik Khan. His destination is a little vague. Something was going to happen in St. Louis, and after that, his story fades."

"We are now back to the discussion on the mission and the source, Ibn Abbas. If Abbas is for real, we may have a bigger problem than anyone fully appreciates. But just the same when you talk nuclear device, it is big." Jack said.

Captain Miller said, "Get some sleep. We have a C-130 taking us to K2 at 0900 in the morning. I want everyone packed and ready for an inspection of equipment by 0700, and that includes you, Jack."

"Looks like I am back in the Army." Jack joked, and the team chuckled.

CHAPTER FOURTEEN:
HALO Over Serekhs, Turkmenistan

* * *

Sergeant First Class Bradley Lee, ODA-647, his oxygen mask in place, stood on the lowered ramp of the C-17, flying at 31,000 feet. His faceplate firmly down on his helmet made sure his oxygen was flowing correctly. His M110 sniper rifle broke down, with the attached scope and suppressor securely tucked away tight against the left side of his body.

Lee's rifle was snug against his body by the D ring of his reserve chute, yet out of the way of his parachute so it would not interfere with the opening. His attention was riveted on the lights located on the inside of the aircraft to his immediate right. He watched a yellow bulb burning brightly in the darkness. He waited on the bulb beneath the yellow one to light up green. All he could hear was the roar of the jet engines. A momentary glance at the jumpmaster, also wearing an oxygen mask, gave him three fingers up, signaling he has three minutes until he steps into the dark void.

As Lee waited, he contemplated his Chinese ancestors. Warriors of remarkable skill and stamina steadfast in their purpose. Cautious yet dangerous as they focused on their mission, the horde traveled from one hazardous land to another. He had resolved to honor this tradition with his heritage by joining the best of America's special operations.

One finger and then the jumpmaster pointed at him, thumbs up, and the light turned green. Sergeant Lee shuffled toward the darkness, and with no hesitation, went over the edge of the ramp into free-fall, heading to earth at a terminal velocity of 180 to 200 mph. Lee smoothly transitioned his body into the classic Delta shape, bending his head and chin down against his chest to avoid the force of the wind snapping his neck, the cold air biting his face, pushing it out of shape.

Quickly knifing through the night sky with air buffeting his body, his wrist altimeter continued to glow red and green, indicating his elevation has just reached 20,000 feet. However, the height counts down feet per second, which showed his free fall was too fast. His GPS also indicated a slight course correction to the left was needed. Spread eagle slowing his descent, he slightly pivoted his body, affecting the necessary course correction, then returned to a Delta position picking up speed.

At 2500 feet, slightly below mission dictated SOP, Sergeant Lee deployed his MC-4 Ram Air parachute; at the count of four, Lee looked up to make sure his chute was correctly deployed. Observing the horizon to judge his descent, he confirmed the accuracy of his GPS coordinates of the landing zone.

In the distance, he saw lights from towns in Iran, assuring the location of the border. As he landed, he quickly collapsed his chute, dug a shallow hole, and buried it, adjusted his equipment. He assembled his sniper rifle screwing on the suppressor. His GPS reflected he must move slightly to the west and then straight to the low-lying hills in front of him. He pulled his night optical device down beginning his short hike.

Lee reached his destination at the crest of the hill, set up his comms, and called, "Nighthawk seven-zero, this is Rocker two-two, in position."

"Roger Rocker two-two."

Then silence, under the night sky, his only companion the stars above. Lee did a time check, 0045 hours, sitting back under the dome of darkness.

* * *

The C-130 landed at the K2 base in Uzbekistan. All the men loaded onto trucks and were immediately driven to a secured building on the airbase to begin their final preparations for insertion into Turkmenistan.

Jack listened to the ongoing conversation but did not ask questions or interrupt since he was an outsider to the team.

Captain Miller gave final instructions to Sergeant Lopez, "Danny, if something goes wrong on this mission, make sure we can get air cover for our extraction."

"Got it already covered, boss. I made arrangements coordinating with the Air Force Combat Controller on K2 before we left Kandahar for extraction and air cover if needed."

"Jack let's see your pack again. I want to see your 9 mm, so I can switch out barrels for a silencer."

"Right here, Captain," as Jack cleared and handed him the weapon.

Jack watched the Captain disengage the slide on the weapon removing it, and then pulled the barrel out, handing it back to him. Then the Captain placed a barrel with threading on the front for a silencer, inserted it into the weapon, replacing the slide into the receiver, locking it in.

"Here is the silencer for your weapon." Captain Miller said, handing the long black cylinder to Jack. "Screw it onto the barrel, finger tight only. You will find the weapon slightly heavy on the front end, causing you to fire before adjusting your aiming point up to hit your target. Just keep that in mind."

"Got it. Fired weapons before with suppressors, and you're right; it takes a moment to adjust to the weight." Jack replied.

Miller said, "Gather around men. Let's do this check one more time. Jack and Chief Taylor will walk together into the village first. Staff Sergeant Tim Conyers, the team's heavy weapons NCO, and CWO Billy "Doc" Talbot will be the second team. I will be with the signals and communications specialist, Sergeant Bud Thomas, as team three. Chief Taylor, it is up to you and Jack to blaze a trail into the town without arousing anyone's interest."

"Describe the safe house again," Conyers asked.

Taylor once again went through the description, "We are aware there aren't any street addresses, and the house looks ordinary, with one distinction. The house is gray with red-colored brick about 6 feet up from the foundation, just to the main entrance's right. Since it will be dark, the house color is not relevant. Your best clue to finding the house will be looking for the red colored brick to the right of the entrance. Also, according to our contacts, the door is unlocked."

Captain Miller added, "Get inside as fast as possible, do not turn on interior lights. We'll wait in the darkness until the sun comes up." Miller looked around at each man asking, "Any other questions?" Scanning the men, "OK, saddle up, and let's get to the chopper." All the men grabbed their rucksacks and equipment moving in silence to the vehicle waiting outside. Jack placed his handgun in his ruck as it was now too long to fit any holster.

Within minutes they rolled onto the tarmac and were dropped near an MH-60 Blackhawk designated for the mission with reduced noise baffles to fly for purposes of this nature. Each man found a position on the floor, hooking into the cargo straps attached to the floor rings bolted of the Blackhawk for the 55-minute ride to the landing zone.

The crew chief moved next to Captain Miller yelling as the engine noise steadily increased, "We're flying the nap of the earth; it is going to be a roller coaster ride." Captain Miller gave a thumbs up.

Miller bent over and yelled something to Taylor, who, in turn, told Jack, "Hold onto your butt, we are riding the nap of the earth, a real roller coaster ride." Jack thought, oh shit, we are hugging the curvature of the terrain as the rotors picked up speed, and the whine of the engines drowned out any further conversation.

The MH-60G Pave Hawk rolled down the tarmac for 300 yards then lifted, dropping its nose, as it picked up speed and altitude. Just outside of the lights of K2, Jack observed the pilots pull their NOD's down, shutting off all lights in and outside the helicopter. Jack saw the shadow of some low mountains coming into view. The Blackhawk lifted and dropped over the hill. When he looked out the door, he barely made out what appeared to be trees screaming by, just under the belly of the helicopter. Jack's first thought was, *"Hope there are no power lines out there."*

After 45 minutes, the engines' tone changed to a muffled sound, and the noise was significantly reduced. Just like jump school, the Captain raised his hand, gave the signal, 5 minutes! All the Green Berets locked and loaded their weapons, putting them on safety. Jack pulled his from his ruck doing the same.

The Black Hawk made one final swooping up and over the hill, then a belly dropping dive into a shallow valley heading straight for another mountain. All the men unfastened their harnesses grabbing onto their rucksacks. Jack knew the routine as this action was all too familiar from his tours in Vietnam.

Just as the helicopter touched down, all the passengers immediately jumped out, headed in a straight line away from the aircraft's side. Within moments the helicopter lifted off and disappeared into the darkness. Silence descended on the small group.

"Rocker two-two, this is Rocker six, over." Captain Miller whispered into his comms.

"Rocker six, I have you directly east of my location and identify seven targets."

"Rocker two-two, there should only be six, over." Miller looked around immediately, adjusting his NOD's.

Sergeant Lee stated, "Roger, Rocker six. Target seven is about 100 yards east of your location. Target seven showed up about one hour ago. I have target seven in my crosshairs waiting on your go signal."

"Stand by," Miller ordered Conyers and Talbot. "100 yards," as he pointed east, "one unknown, find him, Lee has him in his crosshairs." Both men adjusted their NOD's and moved off.

Miller turned to the other men and gave an arm signal to lay down and hold the position.

A few moments later, the comms crackled, "Rocker six, we have the individual. He is wounded, need you here at once, Talbot is working on him."

Miller instructed his men to hold a position and trotted to Conyers and Talbot. "What do we have?" Miller asked.

Talbot explained, "Gunshot to the chest. He has a sucking chest wound; I think I have him stable for the moment. He wants to tell us something."

Miller crawled over to the wounded man and identified himself, "Who are you, and what do you want to tell me?"

Whispering and struggling to get his words out, "I am Fahad, Iran Resistance Group Three, your mission may be compromised. Iran's intelligence killed my team. I escaped."

"Has the safe house location been compromised?"

"I do not think so; everyone is dead." Fahad started coughing up blood and struggled to breathe. Then he stopped moving.

"He is gone, boss," Talbot declared.

"Take his weapon and search him and remove any papers he has on him. Cover him with brush and get back to the LZ."

"Roger that," Talbot replied.

Miller headed back to the LZ, and several moments later, the team assembled in a circle around Captain Miller. Miller had already explained the problem to Jack, Taylor, and Lee. Everyone opined the mission was too important to stop. Miller mulled over his decision and ordered, "Taylor and Jack go to the safe house. We will follow in 30 minutes."

"Rocker two-two, this is Rocker six. The mission is a go. Watch this area until tomorrow night and then leave for extraction point at grid 337255944."

"Rocker six this is Rocker two-two, affirmative."

* * *

Jack started across the valley with Taylor, their NOD's on, and their weapons secured. Jack followed Taylor at a brisk walk. Aside from their NOD's only the stars showed some light. In a matter of three hours, it will start to be light as the sun peaks up from the east.

The village eerily quiet as they approached the house. The streets were empty. Taylor pulled a small flashlight out to illuminate the door. The light exposed the red brick. Immediately Taylor turned off the light. The house looked like the one they needed to locate.

Taylor reached the door first, trying the handle. They quietly moved inside, shutting the door and conducting a room-by-room search, finding the house was empty.

Taylor spoke into his comms, "Rocker six this is Rocker one-one. We located the house and are inside. The front door is unlocked, and all appears to be secure."

"Rocker one-one, this is Rocker six, Roger, see you in about two-zero mikes, out."

* * *

While waiting for the team to arrive, Jack did a limited search of the cabinets noting food and water were available. The small refrigerator hummed and contained food and vodka. He viewed the ample furniture in the house to be reasonably comfortable.

Captain Miller arrived with the rest of the team and quickly set up security inside near the windows. There was silence as each man knew his job There was no need for talk. It became a waiting game now, waiting for Ibn Abbas or Iranian intelligence to show.

Jack looked around and realized he needed to decide which room would work best for Ibn Abbas's interview efforts. Since the house was dark, Jack sat and waited for the light to break over the horizon to shed some light on the interior.

The house was slowly lit up through the windows as the sun broke the horizon in the east. Looking around, Jack decided a small room off the kitchen would work best. The room contained a table and several chairs. It appeared someone had tried to create a small meeting room or office.

Outside, the town came to life. People walked along the streets; an occasional vehicle heard starting up and driving off as the driver shifted through the gears. Doors squeaked when opened. The sound of people's voices heard, and all seemed reasonable as life in the small town began another day. No one knew there were six men on a secret mission, sitting inside a house on their street who were about to determine if the free world, thousands of miles away, is to be attacked with a device of mass destruction.

The meeting between Ibn Abbas and the special operations team will be at 1500 hours. No one knew his description. Proving his identity first would be mandatory to make sure he was not an Iranian militia agent or intelligence agent.

CHAPTER FIFTEEN:
The Safe House

* * *

As Jack inspected the private office off the kitchen, he could hear parts of a conversation between Captain Miller and Taylor. Captain Miller asked, "What is the plan here, Chief. How are we going to trust Ibn Abbas or his answers?"

Taylor sat at the kitchen table sipping on lousy coffee, replied, "Boss, I am leaving this all up to Jack. I am sure he has some plan in mind; that is the reason he is here. I am just here to support whatever move he decides on."

Jack walked out of the room and sat at the table. He then rose and poured himself a cup of coffee. Taylor remarked, "You are not going to like that coffee." Smiling.

"That's ok; I need something strong and distasteful so that I can improve on my day. I heard part of your conversation, Captain, and I do have a plan."

"Can you share some of your plans with us, so I know where this is going?" Captain Miller responded.

Jack contemplated for a moment and stated, "Have you ever heard of Hanns Scharff, a German?"

"No." Captain Miller replied.

Taylor said, "Yes. I heard of him during Interview and Interrogation classes at Fort Huachuca Military Intelligence School. He amassed lots of information during World War II from the captured aircrews."

"Right." Jack acknowledged. "He was a psychological mastermind at obtaining information from airmen shot down over their targets during the war. He worked directly for the Luftwaffe and was devastating in his technique."

"What was his technique. Why was it so effective?" Captain Miller asked.

Jack replied, "One word. Rapport. The Scharff method is highly effective as it has become known. The airmen did not even realize they had imparted information of value. Every utterance contributed to a total collection of intelligence. The airmen expected Gestapo's harsh tactics, yet he did not use them.

"Instead, he engaged them in meaningful conversations about their families, where they lived, how they became to be in the war, and displayed complete empathy and understanding of their current predicament.

"In other words, he became their friend, genuinely. Unbeknownst to the airmen, his method of gathering intelligence revealed a complete picture as to who they are, how they viewed their mission, and ultimately during conversations, airmen slipped up because they were relaxed revealing classified information about their targets. It was a great psychological game he played."

Taylor responded, "That is a part of the story of him I had not heard before."

"Yea, rapport building will be the foundation of how I plan on handling Ibn Abbas. We do not know enough about what he has and what he is willing to reveal. Why he reached out to us in the manner he did makes me suspicious. I want to know more about his motivations.

"This is where your team comes in, Captain. I need each of you to show and treat him with respect. I know some preliminaries we must go through, like searching for weapons or making sure he is not wearing a bomb vest. However, your men need to do it with care and respect. He will understand why we are searching for weapons and bombs on him, but you will complicate what I must do if you throw him against the wall or to the ground. Is that understood?" Jack asked, looking at Captain Miller.

"Yes, I understand. I will brief the team accordingly," Miller replied.

Taylor said, "What do you want me to do?"

Jack explained, "I want you to act as my second. I understand you want to ask questions but don't. If you do, it creates confusion for him as to who is overseeing the interrogation. I do not need that confusion. He must view me as the one in charge. My approach will be oblique in conversation and not the typical Western process of straight into a discussion about why he is here. When it gets to the point, if I feel we need a shift of dynamics, I will turn to you telling you to ask your questions. Use that information you brought with you.

"Do not get carried away. I will interrupt you at a certain point. Just sit back and resume your secondary position. Do not be afraid to smile and make it genuine. I want you to make the tea and bring some of the cookies and fruit I see up on the shelves. Three cups for all of us in the room." Taylor nodded in agreement.

"Captain Miller, I know you will want information as soon as possible. Please do not interrupt us for an update. Be patient." Jack said.

"That will not be easy, but you're the expert. My instructions are to do what you advise." Captain Miller said.

"Taylor, I am going to talk to him about his family first, marriage, his children, if any, and where he was born and how he grew up. Make a mental note of what he says. It will be important later. Then I will talk to him about his responsibilities and obligation under Islam. I will query him about the reason he is cooperating with us. I want to know his motivation.

"Based on his motivation, it should provide clues as to why he is turning on Khan. My next step is determining where and when this weapon of mass destruction will be used in the United States. That is a general idea of the process. Remain flexible as it may not necessarily go the way I described it."

Taylor nodded his understanding and said, "I see where this is going."

Captain Miller asked, "How much time will you need? Can you do a polygraph?"

Jack explained, "All the time it takes to get the information and feel good about it. The polygraph may or may not happen. Time will be a deciding factor because we do not know what Abbas's time frame is. I will decide on a polygraph when necessary. There are variables I have to consider concerning him, and it would be a waste of time and effort if those variables are not working in our favor."

Captain Miller asked, "What variables?"

"Time, enough information to test, and his willingness to be tested. I cannot force the test on him as it might invalidate the results. I am thinking our best bet right now is straight-up talk and running him through multiple questions and seeing how both Taylor and I feel about his answers as step one. After that, maybe a polygraph if the variables are not skewed."

Jack stood moving back into the side room where the interrogation would take place with the explanations ended, leaving Taylor to reflect on the conversation as he finished his coffee. Jack watched as Captain Miller entered the other large room of the house where three men pulled security and explained their role in what is about to occur.

Jack overheard Captain Miller inform Staff Sergeant Conyers, "You will do the meet and greet on this tango. Check for weapons and if he is wearing a bomb vest. If Abbas has a vest, terminate him immediately and shove him back out the door. Take any weapons away from him and promise him he will get them back. Respect him and be careful. Jack wants you to smile and be of good cheer while dealing with him."

Conyers and Talbot look at each other and reply, "Roger that, sir."

"Sergeant Thomas, I want you in the opposite corner, ready to smoke this guy if necessary. Just do not look too ready." Bud Thomas nodded his understanding.

"We have some seven hours before the meeting. Set up a sleep time, for each of you, and stand security." Captain Miller ordered.

Taylor sat at the table, staring out the back window, and Jack leaned against the door jamb of the room, staring inside. Jack turned, looked at the Captain, and smiled confidentially.

Jack was utterly absorbed in how he would proceed with Ibn Abbas. Running multiple game plans through his head was normal and healthy as he prepared for the encounter. Jack played, what ifs repeatedly. The goal here was to verify the information as authentic and to locate the weapon and Khan. A failure in confirming the threat of mass destruction was enormous, with thousands killed in the United States or some other part of the world. The weight and pressure of the task heavy with dire consequences. Suddenly, Jack felt old. His brain hurt from overthinking the problem. He decided a little sleep was necessary. He found a corner, folding himself into a ball as he laid down.

Jack moaned in his sleep as he dreamed of past wars and consequences. He subconsciously could not shake off the hollowed breathing he heard in his dreams and thoughts.

Clearing a building in Bin Hoa, he came face to face with the enemy. In those seconds that followed, the Viet Cong raised his automatic weapon, fired at Jack, and missed him. Jack instinctively had his M-79 Grenade Launcher, leveled, with a buckshot round in the chamber, in place of high explosive grenade ammunition, giving Jack a weapon very much like a sawed-off shotgun.

Jack's shot entered just above VC's heart, blowing out his left side and part of his lungs, now turned to minced meat. In the darkness, the VC's heavy labored breathing gave away his exact location. His eyes were wide open, staring up at him, signaling Jack the VC's life was ebbing away.

Tormented, Jack still heard the shallow breathing coming from the man lying on the ground, arching his back as if reaching for air, sucking in hard, gasping his last breath, and the final death rattle of dying a slow suffocating death. Jack realized he had crossed the psychological barrier by taking a human life.

Jack remembered standing motionlessly for a few uncaring minutes, listening to the labored breathing until it stopped. Then slowly walked away.

It is that rushing of the air into his dying lungs he heard in the solitude of his dream. The haunted eyes staring back at him, imprinted on his brain. He can't forget, and now, many years later, he felt guilty for the lack of emotion he felt at that moment. His demons tore at his soul. Outwardly he moaned and twisted in the chair like a frightened rabbit. Breathing heavily, he woke with a start, looked around, trying to focus on the room. Sweat dripped off his face as he tried to focus on where he was located seeking relief from a pang of never-ending guilt.

Taylor recognized the symptoms and shook him fully awake, "It's OK, Jack." Taylor handed him a cup of coffee. "It is fourteen thirty hours, thirty minutes to go."

Jack had slept for six hours. Taylor showed him a message from DIA headquarters on the computer screen. It read, "Jack, the President of the United States, is waiting on your evaluation." Signed by his boss. *Shit, this is a pressure I do not need!*

CHAPTER SIXTEEN:
The Interview of Abbas

* * *

As the three o'clock hour approached, Jack remained deep in thought. *"How in the hell am I going to make this assessment of an enemy in this limited space of time? What keys am I looking for to confirm his information?"*

* * *

Taylor carefully watched Jack and could see the strain etched on his face. He did not pity him, but the task in front of him was daunting. Taylor, also an experienced interrogator had a clear understanding of the dynamics of what Jack needed to accomplish. Taylor, knowing the strain Jack was under, tried to quench the fires of doubt raging in Jack's thoughts and hoped his vote of confidence would give him the boost he needed; "Jack, relax, you will work it all out as best you can."

* * *

Everyone heard a knock at the front door. The team reflexively acted with raised weapons, adjusted their positions to take cover, and were ready to engage if necessary. Captain Miller nodded at Conyers, and he opened the door, stared at a man in traditional Afghanistan dress, sporting an orange-colored beard, of the Taliban. Conyers was surprised the man was short, a slight man, no more than five foot seven inches. Conyers quickly eyeballed the visitor and noted no weapons or vest visible. Conyers stepped back allowing the man to enter.

Bud stood alert in the far corner of the room, with the weapon held at the 10 o'clock position. Conyers motioned to the man to lift his arms, immediately patting him down. Conyers located a 9 mm handgun in his waistband and a small camera, removing both items. He took his small backpack away from him and looked inside to find only a Koran and a scarf. "Do you speak English?" Conyers asked.

"I am Ibn Abbas. Are you the Americans I am to speak with about Khan?" Abbas replied in perfectly accented British.

Captain Miller responded to Abbas, "I am Captain Miller of the United States Army, and we are here to assist you and to understand your message."

"Excellent," Abbas sighed and happily replied to Captain Miller, who displayed surprise on his face at how well Abbas spoke English. His level of confidence, walking into a room of his enemies, showed courage.

Captain Miller turned to Jack and Taylor, "These two men will discuss the communication you sent to our government."

Jack walked over to Abbas and extended his hand, "My name is Jack, and this is Mr. Taylor. We will be discussing your messages, and if you follow me, we will start. How much time do you have?" This introduction was a departure from how Jack typically handled using his real name. He decided to be truthful with his identification.

Ibn Abbas estimated, "If I have planned this correctly, I have about five hours before I must leave."

"That is great. I hope it will be enough time to discuss everything," Jack disclosed.

"It has to be enough time. I am sure you will return my firearm to me at the appropriate time?" Abbas asked, not mentioning the camera.

"Yes, of course," replied Captain Miller, turning to Conyers and telling him to keep the camera and weapon.

Jack looked at Taylor, "Mr. Taylor, will you kindly make some tea for us? We shall be in the side room."

The men in the room all looked at each other and smiled at Taylor, who rendered a stealthy "ubiquitous middle finger" to them as he turned to warm the kettle up for the tea.

Captain Miller ordered his men to be especially alert for any movement in or near the house to prevent a surprise visit from Iranians.

Once Jack and Abbas went into the room, Captain Miller requested, "Conyers, look through that camera to see what is on it."

"Yes, boss."

Jack and Abbas entered the room. A small kitchen table, four chairs, and a desk were the only furniture pieces in the room.

Jack said, "Have a seat at the table. If you do not object, I will be recording our meeting to eliminate my notetaking, save time, and give me an opportunity afterward to analyze everything we discussed."

"No objections. I had assumed this would be recorded as a precaution because I would do the same," replied Ibn Abbas. "What are these items lying on the table, this tube, and those wires?"

Jack explained, "These are the components to a polygraph instrument. I am not sure if I will conduct a test on this matter or not. As you are aware, the nature of this information needs confirmation, analysis. In the end, accepted as truth for us to act on it?"

Abbas was quiet for a moment and then promised, "I understand your concerns. Once I reveal the information I have, your concerns and my concerns will be one. You and the Western world are my enemies. I am sure you view me as your enemy. We may fight for what we believe in, but to destroy the entire world where no one can live in it is not rational for me or anyone else." Jack listened carefully to Abbas. His words rang real, rational, and dangerous in their meaning. His body language was alert, yet he sat in a relaxed, open posture. His facial expressions gave nothing away.

Taylor entered carrying a tray with tea and some food items setting it on the table and closed the door. Taking a seat at one end of the table, he arranged the cups and poured tea for all three of them. Jack observed Abbas watching Taylor and held his stare for a moment before dropping his gaze to the tray. Taylor picked up each cup, placing one in front of Abbas first, Jack second, and then his, leaving the food items where they lay.

Abbas was the first to speak, "I can see you are warriors. Both of you have the look of war. I sense there is death associated with both of you. That is good. It will be easy for you to understand what I am about to tell you."

Jack acknowledged, "We both have seen our share of war." And then he changed the subject, "Your English is excellent, and your British accent suggests your education may have been in Great Britain? Do you have a family, and can you tell us something about yourself?"

Abbas seemed to relax more and offered, "I was born in London. I was raised in various places throughout England. I was educated at Oxford and obtained my doctorate in mathematics in 1992. I have no family to speak of; both my parents were killed in an unfortunate traffic accident shortly after completing my education. My younger brother ran off to join the Jihad. He died during fighting in Sudan. I am alone now."

Jack was thinking, *"Good, he is confirming some information we know of him, but not all."* Jack asked, "How much world travel have you been engaged in since you left England?"

"My brother died in 1999. I had been working for an investment firm analyzing their net worth and investments. His death left me hollow and angry at Islam for seducing him to fight. I took it upon myself to become more involved in being a Muslim, studied the Koran, and read everything I could about the Hadith and Sharia Law, our law. I soon realized it is the only way to live, at least until I met Khan. I've had a few trips between Pakistan and the UK."

Abbas paused as if looking for a way to express his next thoughts. "I thought Khan was a genius. His fight for Islam was just. I was impressed with him and how he expressed the same concerns I had. We spent many long nights talking into the morning hours about why we are Muslim and what it means. We were both in Pakistan when New York and Washington DC attacks occurred. At first, there was great rejoicing. We both wanted to be part of the changes we knew were going to happen. We both wanted the Jihad."

Jack quired, "What steps did you take to join the Jihad?"

"I was not sure who to contact to join the Jihad. Khan knew, and within several days he had a meeting with members representing the Taliban. They urged him to contact members of Al-Qaeda in Peshawar, located on the road to the Khyber Pass, leading into Afghanistan. As you must know, this is a significant route I assumed we would take to get into Afghanistan.

"Since he is a nuclear physicist, he offered to help them make explosives. Due to Khan's controlling personality, he took over every aspect of this new adventure. However, I soon fell into a position with Khan as a follower. We were directed to Karachi in Pakistan to meet with several different groups within the Al-Qaeda network.

"Khan showed everyone he could be useful by demonstrating how to make bombs out of the materials left on the battlefields and the materials needed to create the explosions they wanted. He became a star, a teacher. He showed them sophisticated ways of using telephones and delayed fuses. His methods caused them to embrace him and his ideas." Abbas reported.

Jack was listening carefully to Abbas's story. *"Why did he allow himself to be put into a secondary position by Khan when they were equal before? His phrasing suggests he is telling the truth. His facial expressions and his eyes are consistent with a man intent on wanting us to believe him. No holes in his story, and his posture is relaxed. Yet, he is leaving out information about his personal life,"* Jack thought.

Abbas continued with his story without much thought, other than to keep his information relevant to the questions posed by Jack, "They made Khan into a leader, and he conducted classes for bomb makers sent to Iraq and Afghanistan. He was a schoolteacher. I confirmed the mathematical equations on blast radius and how many explosives to accomplish a specific mission, like the one the Americans interrupted in Kabul recently.

"I became comfortable in my role. I found myself playing the role of a butler to Khan. I am not sure how this happened. I observed Khan's ego set on fire as his talks turned to want to build a nuclear bomb. One day one of the students questioned him about such a device if it a was wise move. I guess the question directly confronted Khan's motives, or maybe it just insulted him, I am not sure. Khan pulled out a gun and shot the student in the face showing no remorse. It was at that time I knew I was in bed with a mad man."

Jack argued, "Abbas, why didn't you just leave and dissolve your relationship with Khan?"

Abbas explained, "You do not understand. I know too many things. There is no escape from Khan. I will meet a horrible death if he discovers what I am about to do. Allah has cut me in half. I want to continue the fight, yet at the same time, my desire to stop Khan's madness is almost too much. There is a conflict with Islam, and what I now believe is the truth."

"A Muslim with a conscience of right and wrong, Jack thought, *at least in my way of thinking. What is in it for him to get rid of Khan, or is that a motive? Why has he not mentioned his sister? Why is he hiding her?"* Jack questioned, "What will happen to you if Khan is disposed of or stopped from his plan?"

"Khan is a complete psychopath, devoid of any real emotions, and lacking empathy for anyone. I have studied Khan during our time together and decided that narcissism is a hallmark of Khan's personality. There are times his behavior does not regulate his impulses. I do not believe he recognizes the moral codes of life and decency."

"That is a pretty in-depth analysis of him," Jack said.

Abbas responded, "Khan is evil in his conception, sinister in his form, and malignant to his core. Khan is demanding, ruthless, and desires to be the spiritual leader of Islam."

Aligning yourself with that type of man seems to have put you under an enormous strain pushing you into this decision of betrayal," Jack said.

"I know his plans to attack Kabul this coming fall. I will gladly provide that information to you to help you believe me."

"How do you answer my original question of your plans if we stop Khan?"

Abbas answered, "I have decided I will stop my Jihad returning to England. Jihad is a waste of something that will never be. The world will not be one belief; this is impossible. Those that think so are misled, convinced with lies. My faith is weak for being a traitor to Khan. I may have to answer for this at some time. I have enough blood on my hands. It has to stop."

Jack confronted Abbas, "What about the statement you made, that you want to continue with the fight. That contradicts your other comment about having too much blood on your hands and going back to England?"

Jack watched Abbas studying Taylor. Jack sensed Abbas was mulling over his answer, knowing it was crucial. Jack verbally pushed Abbas, "What are you thinking?"

Abbas contemplated his answer, "I was thinking, Allah guide me with the truth, let my words stand by themselves, so I am believed by these infidels." Abbas continued, "My faith demands I continue my Jihad. I am conflicted with the true purpose of the Jihad, and I question if my faith is real or imagined. I have taken this step to speak to you because my humanity needs to cleanse me of the blood. My wish is to return to England and find another way, a more peaceful way to honor my faith. I am at a crossroads. You will believe what I have to say, or you will not. Whatever happens, I have been true to myself in what I believe is right."

Jack looked at Taylor and asked, "Do you have any questions at this time?"

Taylor replied, "Yes, just one. Where did the idea come from; how you contacted us?"

Abbas looked surprised. The question came from another direction intended to surprise him. A glance at Jack, then Abbas turned back to Taylor, "I am aware you listen to all telephone conversations through your satellites. I did not have a telephone number to call you and reasoned that if I made a call to another phone, I was controlling, hoping you would hear me."

Taylor disclosed, "That was incredibly wise of you, and you have impressed several very high-ranking people in our government with your intelligence on how you accomplished this communication. Thank you."

"You're a handsome man with a high degree of intellect. I am sure you are attracted to women. You are well-spoken; who do you love?"

Abbas replied, "I am not sure that this has to do with anything. There was once a woman in Pakistan. I cared for a great deal."

Taylor elaborated, "Do you wish to be reunited with Nour in Pakistan, and do you have plans of taking her to England?

Abbas was shocked, stuttering, "I... I... I... how do you know her name?"

Jack nodded at Taylor, who produced a folder with Nour's picture of her standing in front of a small house in Karachi. Taylor quired, "Abbas, you are a brilliant man. We are very impressed with you, and since you contacted us, we have been able to discover who you are, where you went to school, how long you lived in Pakistan, how you traveled to England and back to Pakistan. Many people have talked to us about you, especially in Pakistan. We suspected your life in Uzbekistan has not been pleasant. Why have you lied to us and not told us about your sister, Amal? Correct me if I am wrong, does her name mean Hope in Arabic?"

Abbas sat back, looking back and forth at both men. His whole posture changed, and the look of surprise on his face became one of concern. Abbas confessed, "You are very good at this, I see. I have not lied to you. My sister is a person I want to protect at all costs; no one I associate with knows of her because I do not want her used by these people. I will do anything necessary to protect her. Yes, Amal means Hope, and yes, I was in love with Nour, and I often think of her. It has been lonely." Abbas looked deflated as he sank into the chair. His posture changed from confidence to resignation, with his legs opened more and his shoulders slumped.

Jack declared, "We have your sister, or I should say, MI-5 has your sister, Amal, under constant surveillance. She is safe right now. Nour, on the other hand, is slightly exposed because she is not of concern to us. We have chosen to be completely honest with you about who and what we are and want the same respect shown to us concerning the information you have brought us today."

Abbas confirmed, "You have my respect. Your honesty and your information on my family and the woman I care about are commendable. I will tell you everything you want to know. No games, just the truth about Khan."

Both Jack and Taylor glance at each other as Jack pushed, "Does Khan have a nuclear device?"

Abbas nodded his head and growled, "Yes, he has the start of one. A week ago, he obtained a small amount of plutonium from the Islamic Republic of Iran, about the size of a small ball, and kept it in a steel box. He wants to travel to America and assemble a container to function and create a nuclear explosion. He explained the center of the United States works best because it is less guarded."

Taylor hissed, "What city is the target?"

Abbas gulped, "I am not sure. He named St Louis and a place called Kansas City."

Jack responded, "How and when is he traveling to the United States?"

Abbas verified, "He will travel by ship from Karachi to South America. The plan is to enter Mexico and then the United States. He already has departed for Karachi, but there is more."

"What?" demanded Jack.

Abbas hastened to add, "Khan sent several teams ahead of him carrying some form of the chemical or biological agent for release in the United States. He selected, or he will designate a target once he is in the United States. Also, multiple teams have constructed car bombs for use on other targets, one of which is Los Angeles."

"What are the identities of the teams?"

Abbas whimpered, "I do not know who they are. I do not know where they went. Look at my camera; I photographed all the documents that Khan compiled on his plan. You can keep the camera."

Jack left the room and returned with the camera that Conyers scrolled through. The menu and digital pictures of maps and other documents were all in foreign writing. Conyers brought Jack's attention to the written reports on the camera before he returned to the room. Looking at one record, Jack pointed it out to Abbas, "What does this say?"

"It is the agreement the Iranians and Khan came to about the delivery of the plutonium and the cost," Abbas responded.

Jack accused, "Abbas, is your information truthful?"

Abbas whined, "Yes."

Jack offered, "Will you take a polygraph examination right now to help us confirm your information?"

Abbas mumbled, "I have heard of this before; yes, I will take it."

Jack rose from his chair, walked over to the door, and opened it. Stepping out, he called, "Captain Miller, we need to talk, so I would like to have your men stay with Abbas for a couple of minutes out here."

Captain Miller looked at Conyers and Bud, "Get Abbas out here and standby."

Once Abbas exited the room, Captain Miller, Taylor, and Jack huddled around the table. Jack explained what had transpired in the interview with Abbas, "My assessment is he appears to be truthful, there were no indications of him lying. I want to conduct a polygraph first before any messages are sent, to be sure. Taylor, what was your assessment of Abbas?"

Taylor echoed, "I concur, I watched his expressions very closely, and his words were solid without skipping important parts of his story. My only concerns were him hiding his sister and his girlfriend, but I understand after his explanations. I also want a polygraph examination. It will be one more piece of information in my evaluation of trusting him."

Captain Miller confirmed, "I agree, it is the best course of action. I will hold off sending any messages until completion of the polygraph." They both departed the room, and Jack prepared for the test.

Jack reviewed the information and constructed some test questions concentrating on the relevant issues. He decided to use: Have you lied about Khan having plutonium in his possession now? Have you lied about Khan planning other types of attacks in the United States? And: Have you lied about Khan planning car bomb attacks in Los Angeles? Other appropriate questions decided on were constructed.

Jack opened the door and directed Abbas and Taylor to return to the room. He told Taylor to take a seat leading him to one corner of the room, out of Abbas's vision. Jack explained the basics of the polygraph and the physiology to Abbas, making sure he understood the concepts. "Abbas, do you have an understanding of what I have just explained to you, or do you have questions?"

Abbas responded, "No questions. I understand the physiological concept of the fight, flight, or freeze theory about lying on a question."

Jack, slightly surprised since he did not use the terms of fight, flight, or freeze in his descriptions, replied, "Excellent."

"Have you ever taken a polygraph before?"

"No, but I have read about them and the reasons for use."

"Do you have any questions about how it works?"

"No, as I understand it, it is nothing more than a recording of my physiology."

"OK, let's get started."

Jack ran through the test questions and collected four charts of Abbas's physiological responses. He analyzed the data deciding Abbas was inconclusive to "Have you lied about Khan having plutonium in his possession now?" but had a solid pass on the remaining two questions. He questioned Abbas about the one issue, "What are you thinking about when you hear the question concerning Khan having possession of the plutonium?"

"Abbas claimed, "I did not see him receive the plutonium, and I am assuming he has the material because that was the plan, and as far as I know, the plan worked."

Jack decided his explanation was enough to explain the inconclusive results. Jack redesigned the entire test to read: Are you lying about Khan's plan to receive the Iranians' plutonium? Are you lying about Khan planning any other attacks in the United States? Are you lying about Khan planning a car bomb attack in Los Angeles? Jack reviewed the questions with Abbas and initiated another collection of charts.

Jack collected three charts and numerically evaluated them. The score on the charts clearly showed Abbas passed the examination, "I am satisfied with your answers. You may undergo more testing in the future."

Jack explained the results of the test to Captain Miller, "Are you releasing Abbas so that he can continue on his journey to Uzbekistan?"

"Yes, my instructions are to allow him to leave. We placed a transmitter in the lining of his backpack so that we can track him." Captain Miller replied.

Jack smiled, "Good plan to see where he goes from here."

Jack reentered the room and told Abbas he is free to go, "Thank you for Khan's information. Go in peace. Before you go, do you know if Khan travels in disguise?

Abbas grinned, "Not here in this part of the world. He will shave his beard off once he has departed Pakistan. I do not know his arrangements. He was very cautious about discussing his travel plans."

Near the front door, Conyers handed Abbas his backpack and his unloaded weapon. The men in the room were looking out the window at the empty as night had fallen. Conyers gave the signal, all clear, as he opened the door. Abbas stepped through it, and as he entered the street, automatic weapons fire erupted, hitting Abbas. He went down immediately.

CHAPTER SEVENTEEN:
Escape from Serekhs, Turkmenistan

* * *

Everyone in the house went to the floor, seeking cover as bullets tore through the walls. Jack ran back into the small room gathering his equipment, shoving it into his rucksack and taking out his 9 mm. Crouching low, he made his way back to the team.

Conyers was close to the door reaching out to Abbas, grabbing him by his jacket's collar, dragging him back into the house. Conyers yelled, "Get over here, Doc."

Billy "Doc" Talbot moved quickly to Abbas. He started removing his jacket to check the wounds. Abbas was still alive, looking at Doc, as he began evaluating the injuries and how to treat him. Doc barked, "Captain, he is alive, looks like two rounds hit him. One in the right shoulder and the other on his right-side flank." He rolled him over, proclaiming, "Looks like straight through wounds."

Abbas grunted, "It's my fault for not being more aware. I have been a fool," Abbas cursed himself.

Talbot laid a hand on his chest to keep him from moving. "Hold on, buddy. We'll get you out okay."

"I should have remembered Khan trusts no one. He sent someone to follow me to ensure I made the payment," Abbas groaned.

"You made the payment," Talbot broke in, "didn't you?"

"Yes, of course." Abbas nodded his head. "One of them must have kept following me and watched me enter this house."

"People enter houses all the time," Talbot argued.

"They aren't greeted by Americans all the time," Abbas explained. "You are taller than most Afghanis. Even if they couldn't see your faces, that alone identifies you. Me just having dealings with you is enough to get me killed."

Captain Miller ordered, "Bud, check the back for a way to escape. Conyers watch the windows and streets. Taylor, you and Jack gather up all computers and electronics and put it in Jack's rucksack." He then pressed his button on his comm set and said, "Rocker two-two, this is Rocker six."

Rocker Six, this is Two-two, over." Lee answered.

Rocker Two-Two, we have been compromised. Tango's to the front of our position and checking now to the rear. The source is down. Need your long gun here now."

"Roger Six, moving now," Lee replied.

A series of shots exploded, hitting the interior walls of the house. Jack scrambled, collecting all the electronics from the others, moving back to a position inside of the kitchen near the rear door. Jack secured his rucksack on his back ensuring his five magazines were within easy reach for reloading.

Taylor was supporting Bud at the back door. Both tried to determine if anyone was out in the back or down what appeared to be an alley. So far, no one had returned fire at the attackers. The mission's success depended on them getting out without being discovered about who they are, an American Special Forces team in a hostile country.

Watching out the window, Miller saw two people with long guns moving in the shadows across the open road. The attackers, unsure how to cross an empty street, were hesitant about approaching the house, not sure who was inside.

Miller grunted to Taylor, "Chief, what does the back look like?"

Taylor replied, "Not sure, so far, we do not see any movement. Only one way to find out is to go out there."

Miller looked at Doc and boomed, "How is Abbas?"

Doc estimated, "I have the bleeding stopped for the moment. Give me five minutes to bandage him, and with some help, I can move him."

Jack instructed, "Captain, I will stay with Abbas and help Doc."

"OK, Conyers, set up some explosive charge on the front door. I am sure that soon, they will try to breach the entrance." Turning to Taylor and Bud, "You two get out back and prepare an exit route. Let's find some transportation." Miller exploded.

No one needed to acknowledge the plan. Everyone moved immediately to their assigned task. Jack crawled over to Doc, asking, "What do you want me to do?"

"Help me prop him up, and then we'll move him to the back door," Doc confirmed.

Moaning, Abbas lifted into a sitting position. Jack watched Doc give him a shot. Abbas seemed to relax. Jack asked, "What did you give him?"

Doc confided, "Morphine for the pain. It will make moving him easier."

Doc gathered up his medical supplies and medics bag as Jack helped move Abbas to the kitchen back door.

Conyers finished setting up a claymore that would explode once the door was pushed open. The force of the mine would tear down the door, and anyone close would be shredded. Conyers looked out the window seeing five of the attackers coming out of the shadows, starting to approach the house.

As the first attacker moved out of the shadows into the dimly lit area, his head exploded as he took a round from the unseen sniper. Lee had just moved into position on the south end of the road taking up a place that gave him a partial view of the safehouse and a better idea of the attackers. His silenced weapon did not give away his position. The attackers seemed to believe the shot came from within the house. Unsure of their advantage, they failed to advance on the house.

The Iranians immediately pulled back between the other buildings as they watched their comrade die in the street. They froze, unsure how to proceed. They needed to attack the house soon before local authorities arrived. People in homes were closing shutters and putting out interior lights; they have seen this activity in the past.

As the Iranian went down, Miller knew Lee was nearby. He was waiting on Taylor and Bud to alert him if the exit was clear. Bud appeared in the back door, "Boss, we have a clear exit; Taylor just jacked a truck for us."

Miller, into his comms, whispered, "Let's go. Rocker Two-Two, we have a ride out of here, Location?"

"Rocker six, I'm about 200 yards south of your location, near an alley entranceway," Lee confirmed.

Captain Miller acknowledged, "Roger Rocker Two-Two, standby, we will pick you up, look for a truck."

"Roger that," came Lee's reply.

Jack and Doc picked Abbas up. He is a small man, not stout, bulkier than anything. Although Jack and Doc half dragged him, he managed to walk as Abbas tried to find his footing. They escaped out the back door, turned left, and headed down the alley. Jack sees Taylor standing near a truck, but strangely, he was not moving. Doc whispered to Taylor, "Mike, are you OK?"

Taylor did not respond. Both Jack and Doc stopped. Abbas was laid down on the filthy dirt street. With weapons pushed out in front of them in a ready position, they approached the truck and Taylor. Jack split from Doc, moving to the right side of the vehicle, and Doc came to the truck's left side, straight at Taylor.

Jack had an advantageous position as he moved into the building's shadow; low light exposed Doc as he approached. Jack could see a man holding a rifle on Taylor with the muzzle pointed at his head. The man spoke in a language the three of them do not understand. "Doc, he is speaking Farsi, I think," Taylor gulped. "I don't think this is his truck; he just came up from behind me."

The man started talking again, indicating to Doc to lower his weapon. Jack watched Doc lower his gun. The man pushed Taylor out into the alleyway. Simultaneously, the man indicated he would shoot by pressing the rifle's muzzle against Taylor's head. Doc continued to lower his weapon.

The man showed Doc needed to drop the gun to the ground. Doc hesitated when the man raised his AK-47 and placed the muzzle against Taylor's head again. Doc dropped his handgun onto the hard dirt. The man then motioned for Taylor and Doc to get down on their knees. As Taylor and Doc began to lower themselves to their knees, Jack fired. Taylor and Doc heard a thud from a silenced 9 mm handgun. The man dropped straight to the ground with a clean bullet hole in his head. Jack walked out from the shadows with his weapon still trained on the man who was dead. He was not sure how he felt, sick from the adrenaline or from his emotions exploding inside him.

"Let's get Abbas into the truck. Stop standing around you two." Jack jeered.

Doc and Taylor pivoted at the same time. Doc moved toward Abbas. Jack walked back to Abbas as Taylor turned to examine the dead man at his feet. Taylor picked up the rifle searching the man for anything of interest, like documents or radios, and finding none grabbed the collar of the dead man dragging the body to the side of the alley discarding the corpse.

* * *

Miller, Bud, and Conyers moved down the alleyway at a quick pace. Taylor got behind the wheel. Miller jumped in beside him as the rest of the team scrambled into the back. Miller commanded, "Mike, pick up Lee at the end of this alley before we drive out of town."

* * *

Taylor allowed the truck to roll forward as it was sitting on an incline, and then he popped the clutch, causing the engine to turn over and start. This action engaged first gear; the truck rolled down the alley. Taylor stopped the vehicle at the intersection of the driveway and street, waiting. Looking around, thinking, *"This engine is a little loud. Where are you, Bradley?"*

Sergeant Lee stepped out of the shadow of the building adjacent to the alley. His weapon is cradled in his arms. There was a loud explosion, and Conyers exclaimed, "They found the claymore."

Sergeant Lee climbed into the back of the truck, and Taylor pulled out of the alley, turning right onto the street, and at the first street turned left on what appeared to be a road out of town.

* * *

At the request of Khan, the Iranian militia, at a distance, had been tracking Abbas. Once Abbas delivered the last payment for the plutonium, a tracker followed and watched him enter the safe house. Khan expressed concerns the money would not be provided to them by Abbas.

He had voiced his fears of trust only because he observed Abbas taking pictures of the Iranian agreement documents. Khan decided not to confront Abbas but to watch him, as his trust in Abbas diminished. The militia had taken it upon themselves to follow Abbas after delivering the money, at least, until he left the area. The tracker watched in surprise as he went to a small, unremarkable house and entered after a tall Westerner opened the door. In their minds, a Westerner was the enemy, and anyone so causally meeting one was automatically the enemy as well.

Hiding in the dark shadows, the Iranians decided to wait for the complete darkness of night. Their apparent plan was to raid the house and catch Abbas in a compromised position with the Infidels. As they prepared to attack the house, the front door opened, and Abbas stepped out.

One of the less experienced men unnecessarily opened fire on Abbas. Then all hell broke loose as they were forced to move toward the house prematurely but stopped after one of the men was shot and laid dying in the street. The group leader decided to rush the house after waiting to see if any more shots came from the home. He was uncertain which direction the gunfire came from that killed his comrade.

The Iranian force sustained more casualties when they barged through the door of the house. Through the door, the first man vaporized with most of the 720 pellets of the claymore mine shredding his body. The explosion tore the door frame completely out, killing three more men and wounding seven people in the pack during the assault. The group leader wished he was dead because there was no way he could explain how he failed on this mission.

The town heard enough gunfire and loud noises making them fully aware of a battle in their village. The sight caused their eyes to widen with disbelief at the carnage they witnessed. Several people in town heard the distant truck noise pulling away from the area but did not draw a connection to the scene in front of them.

* * *

Taylor drove the truck down the road, asking Captain Miller, "Boss, what is our direction; I am a little turned around here?"

"You are heading directly West," Miller responded while looking at his compass. "We need to go Southeast to reach the extraction point."

Jack could see lights in the distance, and then as they cleared a hill, it was Iran and the border crossing. Taylor slammed on the breaks. Miller demanded, "Turn around and let's backtrack."

As Taylor turned the truck around, he could see several vehicles leave the border area and head up the road toward them. He sped up, hanging onto a narrow rough road. Soon the rest of the team were watching vehicles approach. Bud yelled out, "Gun trucks, and they are picking up speed."

Jack observed Sergeant Lee move into position by the tailgate of the truck, looking through his scope. With the truck bouncing, it was hard to get a clear shot. Conyers yelled through the broken back window and pointed out, "Boss, looks like gun trucks from Iran are moving on us fast. I don't think they have authority here, but they most likely don't care."

Miller instructed, "Try to take out their tires as best you can. Wait to see if they fire first. If they do, you have a green light. If they don't, we will just outrun them. We need to avoid an international incident if we can. So far, no one knows who we are."

Jack heard Conyers say, "Roger, hold fire until fired upon, and then try for tires and engine block of trucks first." He then repeated the instructions to the team.

Doc worked on Abbas as Jack looked out the back of the truck at the approaching Iranians. Jack pulled his handgun, prepared to engage. Taylor pushed the large vehicle hard up the incline, looking for a road that would take them away from the border.

Jack held on tight when he heard Miller say, "Up ahead. I see a break in the road. A side road. Take it."

Taylor steered the truck toward the side road, stepping on the brakes hard, turning right. The back end slid on the dirt road and straightened itself out. Taylor expertly corrected the slide by adjusting his speed and direction and not oversteering. Jack saw the Iranians about a quarter of a mile back before the turn. He estimated the Iranians lost the catchup game as they were about half a mile behind. The headlights from the Iranians' truck swayed back and forth as they slid on the dirt road. Taylor shouted, "Are we heading in the right direction now?"

Miller verified, "We're going in the right direction. See those low-lying hills in the distance? That is our destination, just the other side of those hills." Jack was looking at the silhouetted hills against a rising moon just as several shots rang out.

The shots went wild and high. "Boss, they're shooting at us. Are we cleared to engage?" Conyers yelled.

"Yes, wait until they are closer. Try for the tires first."

Jack braced himself on the floor of the truck and prepared to fire.

Taylor drove around a curve, and the road became worse with large holes causing him to slow down, and the road curved back and forth. Doc yelled from the back of the truck, "We are bouncing like rubber balls back here. You're going to kill Abbas."

Miller yelled, "I have a plan. When I tell you, slow down, Lee and Bud will get off the truck." Miller turned to the back of the truck and yelled at Bud, "Get ready to dismount with Lee. You two set up an ambush for our friends back there as they come around the curve." Bud gave a thumbs up. Jack moved out of the way, so both men had a clear area to make the jump.

* * *

Bud leaned over and told Lee to get ready for a dismount while moving. Lee pulled his weapon up and wrapped a small blanket around it as both men edged toward the tailgate. The truck slowed down to a crawl as Miller yelled from the front, "Go!" Lee and Bud jumped and rolled onto the dirt road. Both men pick themselves up and move to several large boulders that provided cover for them. Lee immediately set up his sniper rifle as Bud pulled a scope for spotting. With the moon rising, they could see about a quarter of a mile down the road and hear the gun trucks' tortured engines coming.

* * *

Taylor pulled the truck off to the side of the road, about a half-mile from where the two men dismounted. He left the engine running, the parking brake on, and in neutral. Everyone, except Doc and Abbas, got out of the truck, spreading themselves out on either side of the road. Jack positioned himself at the edge of a large boulder. They were at a disadvantage with only handguns against gun trucks with

151

mounted machine guns. If Lee and Bud could stop the gun trucks, that reduced the Iranians' advantage.

* * *

Bud looked through his spotting scope estimating, "First truck is about 300 yards out, moving at 20 miles an hour." Lee saw the tires of the first truck through the glare of headlights in his scope and fired. The first truck lost control and swayed to the left, running into the side of the hill. He fired again and hit the second gun truck's tire, causing it to swing left and crash into the back of the first truck. Both men turned and ran down the road toward the team.

* * *

Conyers was the first to see Lee and yelled, "Bear left on the side of the road, big potholes." Just as Bud tripped and fell in one of the potholes, he twisted his ankle. Lee stopped and helped him up, giving him support as they made it to the cover of the rocks.

Lee cried, "Boss, the trucks have been disabled. One crashed into another one, but they are following on foot."

"OK, let's get out of here before they show. Everyone back in the truck; let's go. Move!"

Taylor drove off just as the Iranians come around the corner and manage to fire several shots in their direction, hitting nothing. Several miles down the road, Taylor pulled over and stopped. "Boss, we need to check our grid coordinates and make sure we are reasonably close to the extraction point."

Miller and Taylor scrutinized the map, then shot an azimuth on available land features they could see and decided they were two miles from their objective. There was no road, so they decided to drive overland until they couldn't travel anymore. Miller looked in the back of the truck and asked Doc, "How is Abbas?"

"Captain, he is out of it. Loss of blood and a bad ride. I had to give him more morphine. I think he will make it if we can get him to a hospital in time."

Miller concluded, "OK, we have a hard drive overland for a couple of miles, make him comfortable." Everyone else, hold on.

Taylor started driving off the road onto an area looking like a pasture. Keeping a straight line, they made valuable time. They approached a ravine a half-mile from their objective but was too steep to drive into and out again. They fixed a stretcher for Abbas out of some tree limbs lying on the ground and took turns carrying him across the terrain. The flat pasture between the hills cast slight moonlight across the land. Jack heard Captain Miller order his team to set up security and watched Bud assemble his comms to contact Danny Lopez at K2.

"Nighthawk Seven-Zero, this is Rocker Six, over." Captain Miller advised.

"Rocker Six, this is Nighthawk Seven-Zero; what is your SITREP?" Danny inquired.

"We need extraction at Grid 336788005 for seven plus one. We have one wounded that is stable. We have hostile forces trying to locate us after contact. Can you provide an ETA?" Captain Miller questioned.

Danny responded, "Roger, birds are airborne. Place strobes on a landing zone in 40 mikes. ETA in 50 mikes. Medical is ready. See you shortly, Nighthawk Seven-Zero out."

The team settled into an uneasy rest, with security positions alert listening for any noise. The night air cold at 0230 in the morning, and the darkness laid on them like a blanket, hiding them from their enemies. Each man pulled his NOD's down watching the terrain.

* * *

Jack laid quiet in the stillness, thinking, *"How did they know Abbas was at the safehouse? Is the information given tarnished in any way? If Abbas was part of a disinformation plan, why try to kill him? Can we find Khan in time? What the hell am I going to communicate to the President of the United States? The only thing I can say is we have a nuclear physicist on the run carrying plutonium, and he wants to make a bomb and explode it. Where? St Louis or Kansas City? And oh, by the way, he wants to release biological or chemical agents somewhere in our country, he may explode some car bombs in Los Angeles, but when? How does this make sense? And to make matters worse, we have no idea the location of Khan.*

The Blackhawk arrived on time. The entire team moved to the helicopter as it sat down in the field. Jack and Doc carried Abbas, placing him on the floor of the Blackhawk. At once, an onboard medic started looking him over and then strapped him down. They flew out of the area without further incident. They were landing at K2, where a medical team was ready. Doc and the medical team took Abbas immediately into surgery.

* * *

Miller called Jack over, "I heard what you did for Taylor in the alley. You did the right thing, and you were composed when you took the bad guy out. Stay composed because we have to report to everyone in the chain of command what we learned."

Jack had an edge on his voice, "Let's get this over. I am glad I recorded it all during the interview."

Jack had already transmitted the recordings and the polygraph charts to his boss at DIA HQ, Bolling Air Force Base, Washington DC via SIPRNET, highly classified secured telecommunications within DOD. The examination review and evaluation by the quality control supervisor and the entire conversation recordings were copied to DIA analysts on the other side of the third floor and analyzed by Paige Anderson FOB Snow Leopard.

* * *

On the screen of the video conference call sat Jack's boss, Stan Kaufman, and sitting next to him was Lieutenant General Bryan

Webster, United States Marine Corps and Director of the Defense Intelligence Agency.

LTG Webster said, "Mr. McGregor, how sure are you on the results of your test and the information this source gave you?"

Jack replied, "Sir, considering the source, the information appears to be good. To make sure, that is why I tested him. I feel very confident in the results of the test. I could not detect any errors in our verbal exchange. I discussed the conversation with Mr. Taylor, an intelligence Chief Warrant Officer, in the room with me, and we both agreed the information is worth following up.

As you know, any information is only as useful as its source and for that moment. Right now, I would like to believe it is all good. We need to take steps to stop Khan."

Watching the screen, Stan Kaufman was handed a sheet of paper by an unknown person and explained, "Jack, the QC supports your decision on the test and concurs with the results." He read from the note.

Jack agreed, "That is good to hear, boss; what is our next move?"

LTG Webster informed, "Captain Miller; I just got off the phone with J2X at the Pentagon and your boss at Fort Bragg. They agree that the magnitude of this is so great; they want you and your team to follow through with a new assignment to locate Khan and the nuke. You and your team are under my command and part of DIA. Your deployment is almost over anyway. Your rotation back to Fort Bragg delayed."

Captain Miller looked surprised by this development and acknowledged, "Yes, sir, what is our assignment?"

"You will replenish your equipment as needed, brief your entire team on this new assignment. You are to proceed directly to Panama to meet with a DCS case officer flying in from Ecuador. I have assigned a C-17 to you and your team to move from Afghanistan to Panama. We believe we have an idea about where Khan is going to try to enter the

United States. The CIA is working on some intelligence issues with the FBI and coordinating with Homeland Security and US Border Patrol. You will get a full briefing upon arrival in Panama." LTG, Webster concluded.

Captain Miller grinned, "Yes, sir, we will move out immediately."

LTG Webster continued, "Mr. Jack McGregor, you are now assigned to ODA-647 until this mission is complete. Go to Panama also. The C-17 will be at Bagram Air Base, waiting for all of you. Your abilities will be needed. Keep us informed. Your mission is simple. Locate Khan and stop him by any means necessary. All of you are cleared by the President of the United States to take that action. Questions?"

Jack broke in, "Sir, how about Abbas? I think he can help us develop more information on Khan that we have not had a chance to explore. According to the doctors at K2, he is going to live. Can we take him with us? I know that it is highly unusual, but I think it is a gamble we must take."

There was silence on both sides of the video screen as each participant mulled over Jack's idea. Taylor spoke up, "Sir, I agree with Jack. What is in Abbas's head is invaluable, and we need more time to exploit him on the long flight to Panama. What we can do is babysit him for the immediate future, talk to him, and once done, we can put him in GITMO."

"One more thing, General. We need a first-class analyst who is up to date on this operation. We have been working with Paige Anderson at Snow Leopard, and she is as good as they come. The bonus is she is fully read in on the operational tempo and collection to this point. We need her with us for real-time analysis," Jack insisted.

LTG Webster smiled, "Radical idea, gentlemen, I like it. Get it done, and I will tell the President we have a terrorist helping us track Khan. I will send a message to have Anderson meet you in Bagram for the trip to Panama. Jack, you are my commander on the ground and will report directly to me."

CHAPTER EIGHTEEN:
Panama and Jacobson

* * *

Jack stood in the room with Paige, Captain Miller, and CWO Taylor. The Commander of the 7th Special Forces Group in Panama wanted a word with them. The meeting room had a mahogany table with ten padded chairs, and it dominated the room. The refrigerator by the entrance offered an assortment of beverages, including water. The ceiling opposite the screen on the other side of the room was a large pull-down screen and projector. The office's appointments displayed power and control, and it was clear the Special Forces Group commander enjoyed his position, and he was irritated over the arrival of ODA-647.

Jack disliked diesel fuel's smells mixed with rotting vegetation in the humid climate because it gave him flashbacks to another war, Vietnam. Panama was as modern as it got in Central America. The local joke was to not eat at the Jose's Fried Chicken Café because the chickens used were really "tree chickens," also known as iguanas. Jack thought this was highly unlikely, but the idea persisted in his mind. The thought of eating a lizard disgusted him, as it did when he went through the Ranger course at Fort Benning.

The flight from Bagram, Afghanistan, had been long, with brief refueling stops in Guam and Hawaii, and productive. ODA-647, logistically, moved the remainder of the team from Kandahar to Bagram. The remainder of the team from K2 in Uzbekistan to Bagram with a wounded Ibn Abbas. Everyone in the process moved with purpose. It was left to Jack to explain to Abbas that he was now a "cooperating terrorist enemy combatant POW," whatever the hell that was supposed to be.

On the long flight, Jack, Paige, and Taylor engaged Abbas in a series of conversations seeking more information about Khan and his objectives. For the most part, it was productive. Little by little, Abbas revealed information that Paige recorded that could lead to the identification of others already in the United States. Their exact locations would be unknown until this information could be exploited better by some additional resources and coordination by the DIA, CIA, or even the FBI. Jack hoped for the discovery of Khan's location before he left any South American country. If the terrorist mastermind was moving through Central America, this team had to find him before he was able to build a nuclear device. Jack's concern was Khan had a three-day head start on them.

The team was directed to a secluded compound operated by the 7th Special Forces Group near Fort Clayton. Jack assuming more and more command and control over the operation, suggested Captain Miller waste no time replenishing their gear and ammo, get some food, a shower, then some rest. Jack insisted Abbas be placed in a separate, windowless room, with two MPs by the door.

Jack contacted the local hospital making sure a doctor came to the compound. Abbas was healing well from his wounds, and the doctor came by to inspect his bandages, replaced them with clean ones, and gave him some medication to prevent infection. The MPs took him to the shower room at Jack's request so Abbas could clean himself up and don a change of clothing. Abbas looked out of place wearing jungle fatigues and an orange beard.

While everyone attended to their own needs, Jack contacted the DCS operative, who had flown in from Ecuador. He was an Air Force Major on a rotational multi-year assignment to DIA and would be returning to Air Force intelligence upon completion of his duty. Jack agreed to meet with him at 1600 at the Group's headquarters near the compound's front gate.

* * *

Colonel Jesse Hancock walked into the room, and Taylor and Miller came to attention. Jack offered his hand and introduced himself, Paige, Captain Miller, and CWO Taylor.

Colonel Hancock was a large man, at least 6'5" with giant ape-like arms with matching hands. His craggy face accentuated his scars, and his piercing blue eyes and short-cropped hair, signaling anyone on the receiving end of his stare, he meant business.

Colonel Hancock boomed, "I sure would like to know what is going on. I received a call from the J2X at the Pentagon. He said you and your team would be arriving and to give you anything you needed without any necessary explanations. When I questioned him, he told me his orders were coming from the President of the United States."

Jack confided, "Colonel, we are hunting an extremely dangerous terrorist who is a direct threat to the United States homeland. We hope to cut him off here in Central America, if not South America, where we believe he has or is about to land in an unspecified country. Our immediate problem is locating his point of entry."

Colonel Hancock stared at Jack and then turned to Captain Miller, "Captain, what is this all about?"

"Sir, we have been ordered to answer only to the J2X or the President. I know that the answer is unsatisfactory for you with my team landing in your area of operation without sufficient warning to our mission, but those are my instructions."

"Bullshit," replied Hancock.

Captain Miller was becoming uneasy. Jack intervened, "Colonel, my apologies for this gross inconvenience and lack of information. I sure do not want a conflict with you, but I assure you our mission is extremely critical, and we will tell you what we can when we can."

"I understand you have a terrorist in one of my buildings guarded by my MPs. Right there is enough for me to demand what the hell is going on," replied Colonel Hancock.

Captain Miller ventured, "That is correct, Colonel. He is a source, and he is helping us locate his boss...the person we are concerned about."

Jack defended, "He is our problem, and we will manage him. Once the Defense Attaché has arrived and briefed us, we will be in a better position to provide explanations."

Colonel Hancock abruptly turned and walked toward the door, then came to a stop. He turned back around and scolded, "That attaché or whatever he is has been in my office for the last hour, and he is as tightlipped as the four of you. I will send him to you; this is bullshit!"

After Colonel Hancock left, Taylor muttered, "That went well. Are we under any obligation to tell him anything?"

Both Captain Miller and Jack replied together, "Hell no."

Captain Miller explained, "He's just pissed there's an op going on in his backyard, yet he has no influence over any of it and wants in on the action. It's that simple."

Jack joked, "Bullshit." All of them in the room laughed. Jack looked at Paige knowing she was deep in thought and found none of this funny.

The case officer, Major Don Jacobson, entered the room confronting the group of three men laughing. "I hope that was a good joke because what I am about to tell you is serious and a problem. Also, that Green Beret Colonel scared the shit out of me. He threatened to kick my ass if I did not tell him what was going on?"

Jack introduced himself and the other team members, "Don't worry about him. I'm Jack McGregor; this is Captain Miller and Chief Warrant Officer Taylor from ODA-647. Paige Anderson is a DIA analyst working on our team. We understand you have an update for us."

* * *

Before Jacobson dropped into an empty chair, he lightheartedly said, "Hi Paige, nice to see you again." Ignoring Jack's look, he continued, "Yes, I do. It is not good. First, let me thank you for the other information you provided with the names of the terrorists that are now operating in the United States. We forwarded all the information to the FBI and CIA, and other analysts are trying to piece it together. DIA is not sure which cities they're in, but our best guess is St. Louis, Kansas City, Los Angeles, and Las Vegas. Some indicators also suggest Seattle and San Francisco."

Taylor coaxed, "How firm is that information?"

"We are 75% sure as it stands now. What your team needs to know is Khan is the real deal. Our sources are saying he is brilliant and capable of bringing off a nuclear explosion. I believe Khan is here in Central America.

"We determined he came in on a private charter flight from Indonesia landing somewhere along the Peruvian coast then he disappeared. There is a high probability he flew to Nicaragua. We tracked a tail number off a private aircraft and discovered it belonged to the drug cartel known as Diablo. Later seen by some of our assets in Nicaragua, this aircraft observed a man escorted to a government vehicle describing him in a way we believe, it is Khan.

So far, everything you guys have sent us, or uncovered in Afghanistan and wherever else you were tracking Khan, as well as meeting with your source, has checked out."

Jack demanded, "How difficult, for us, is it getting into Nicaragua?"

"Very difficult. Everyone appears to be super alert along the borders, and we are doubtful a border crossing can be effective. All of us, CIA and DIA, are working assets in that country to find him. I need to talk to your source, Abbas, and confirm some information. Is that possible?"

"Of course, not an issue at all. Once done, I will take you to Abbas."

Miller exclaimed, "What is our purpose now? - - - I mean the mission - - - has anything changed?"

"No change in mission. The President is getting nervous that Khan made it this far. It is just too close for comfort if he has any nuclear material in his possession. We are to stop him at any cost."

Jack surmised, "Sounds like a wait and see to make sure it is him in Nicaragua, and then figure out how to get to him. We are not that far away and can be inside Nicaragua in a matter of hours. The clock is ticking. The man we want is just beyond our reach. It's like having your favorite steak placed in front of you when you are starving and then restrained from eating it."

"We need to tell Colonel Hancock," Miller piped up, "If we need to penetrate Nicaragua, we will need air assets he can provide. Also, I am down two men I had to leave in a hospital and may want to pull two of the Colonel's ODA resources to complete this mission."

The case officer replied, "Let me talk to Abbas first. Then we can think about the Colonel."

"Do you have anything more on the target cities?" asked Jack.

"Jack, I am not going to make any other estimates. We are not sure our calculations are entirely correct. You and this ODA team have managed to scare the crap out of everyone, and you have one hundred percent backing from the President on down. It is our next move that needs examination.

"Right now, every truck rental establishment in the United States is undergoing a check for Middle Eastern customers. We think Khan wants to inflict the amount of damage suspected would take a truck, not cars. We believe Khan's best way to make a small and dirty bomb is to use a 50-gallon barrel of some kind, so we check with users and manufacturers of those barrels. Unfortunately, there are thousands of users. The problem now for the President is talking to the Nicaraguan Government, which will alert Khan. Or we could bomb the crap out of the country in hopes of killing one Pakistani."

Taylor, deep in thought, on various scenarios, "Boss, I think we should tell the Colonel sooner rather than later. He is pissed off now, and if we wait until the last minute, he will chew your ass so bad it will drop out onto the floor."

"Chief, I agree," replied Jack, turning to Miller, "How about you two go see the Colonel allowing Paige, Jacobson, and me to talk to Abbas. Let's lay our cards on the table. Our mission will be served better by doing that with the Colonel, especially now with not knowing for sure if Khan is still in Nicaragua."

Jack looked at Miller then back to Jacobson for a response. He suspected Jacobson had not told them the worst of the news and had decided to withhold information if they were going to speak to the Colonel. When no one objected or offered a better way to move to the next step of locating Khan, Jack guessed, "OK, that sounds like the way to go under these circumstances. See what resources he has that will make your job easier. Paige, Jacobson, and I will go see Abbas."

Miller agreed, "Good decision. Chief, let's go."

"We will meet back up with you in twenty minutes at the team house," Jack declared.

* * *

As Paige and Jack walked towards the team house, he whispered to her, "How do you know Jacobson?" Paige gave Jack a sideways look with one of her slight smiles but said nothing. Jack knew not to pursue the answer now as all three of them walked straight toward the two rather large MPs standing at the door. "Any issues or problems of any kind with the prisoner or wandering Colonels?" Jack asked.

"Nothing with the prisoner. Colonel Hancock came by about five minutes ago and wanted to go into the room. We stopped him, and that was unpleasant. He ordered me to stand aside. I refused. He threatened me, and I told him I had specific direct orders from the President of the United States, and the only way I was moving is if he shot me. We had a couple of moments of staring at each other, and he walked off."

Excellent, Jack thought, a young man using his head. "Smart response, Sergeant. How did you manage to get those orders?"

"I got them from you when you and the Green Berets were talking about your next move. I could overhear everything you said. So, I used a little initiative. It worked."

Jack smiled and said, "Well done." He opened the door and walked in with Paige and Jacobson to talk to Abbas, who was sitting on the bed looking forlorn.

"Don, this is Dr. Abbas, the right-hand man to Dr. Khan."

Jack watched as Jacobson touched his heart with his right hand and said, "Peace be unto you."

Abbas appropriately replied, "And peace be upon you."

Jack knew that roughly eighty percent of Muslims worldwide do not speak Arabic. However, a high percentage speak English, so Jacobson speaking English, right off, was no surprise, but understanding the customs did surprise him since he thought Jacobson was a Latin American expert.

Sensing Jack's bewilderment, Jacobson said, "I lived in the Middle East for eighteen years before I came to this part of the world. I hope your wounds are healing, and you will feel better as time goes on."

Responding to Jacobson's inquiry, "I am better, and these men provided excellent doctors and care for me in the true way of one human for another. My treatment has caused me to rethink what I thought I knew of all Americans. We are enemies, and yet you extend your hand."

"I have traveled far to ask you some questions about Khan. Will you provide me the time I need to satisfy my queries?" Jacobson replied.

"Yes, I will talk to you in truth."

Jack, Paige, and Jacobson pulled up chairs. Abbas sat on the bed. Jack watched Jacobson pull out several sheets of paper from his briefcase depicting pictures of different men. He handed them to Abbas. "Can you identify the men in the pictures?"

Laying the pictures on the table, he studied them and said, "The first one is Jabir, a Kuwaiti. He works for Al-Qaeda, and he is a money handler.

This one is Zayad from Iraq, and there is a relationship to Abu Musab Al Zarqawi." Pointing at another picture, "This one is Abdullah Ismael. He is a chemical engineer and makes chemical weapons.

The last one I have met, he is Sulayman. He makes bombs and plans operations. Khan and I met him in Pakistan when we first started our Jihad. Sulayman spent a lot of time with Khan, always talking to him, explaining plans for this and that."

Jack watched the exchange with quiet anticipation. These guys were well-known terrorists, but for Abbas to have had contact with them seemed a little more upscale as to whom Abbas really may be. His internal alarm system was starting to fire off. Had he missed something concerning Abbas and Khan?

Jacobson seemed satisfied with the answers. Alarm bells again were sounding in Jack's head. "How do you know the first two guys in the picture?" Jack inquired.

Abbas now focused on Jack, "The first two I have seen before but have not personally met. They attended some meetings with Khan in Uzbekistan. The Kuwaiti carried all the money needed for Khan to buy his nuclear material."

"Do you know if the method of attack is biological or chemical?"

"Chemical. Khan wanted biological, but the best the Russians could do was give Khan some chemical weapons, mostly containers with gas. He wanted to release them in the most crowded American cities."

Paige interrupted, "Mr. Abbas, how sure are you that Khan's purpose is just to use a chemical, and do you know the type of chemical?"

Abbas studied Paige for a moment and finally explained, "Khan and I discussed this part of the operation he referred to the gas called Sarin. He also told me that biological was out of the question due to obtaining a virulent strain. I assumed it was a dead issue and not to be discussed again."

A cold chill ran down Jack's spine as he thought of the crowded cities, malls, subways, airports, and half a dozen other venues that Americans flock to every weekend, like zoos. The casualties would be tremendous. The connection between the people in the pictures and Khan started to reveal a deadly plan. Multiple attacks, nuclear, chemical, and tactical explosives at the same time in different parts of the country, and worse, no one knew the locations for sure. No wonder this mission ended up at the highest levels of the Government, and everyone was scared!

* * *

Captain Miller and CWO Taylor departed the Colonel's office as Jack ended his conversation with Abbas. Miller left Colonel Hancock stunned, sitting at his desk after relating his team's exploits and the information gathered so far. Miller secured two more men from 7th SF Group to place on ODA-647 for the two, left wounded in the hospital, making his team twelve again. The two chosen had just rotated back from deployments in Afghanistan and Iraq. All logistical support would be available. Colonel Hancock called the S-4 officer, giving a direct order that if anyone from ODA-647 approached the S-4 and asked for anything, they get priority and delivered at once.

Jack met Miller as he came through the door. "How did it go?"

"Everything is fine; He even apologized for being such an ass."

"Good, we just finished with Abbas, and he confirmed some troubling information whether the planned attacks are biological or chemical. We think chemical, as well as a nuke. Paige is suspicious that biologicals were discussed but not included in their plan. The attacks are part of the overall operational effort and nuclear strikes and car or truck bombs.

"The plan has started to take shape. I'm not sure why I thought the attacks would be just one or the other. It looks like it will be all three at the same time. That tells me we have some hard choices to make. Which attack takes priority? Truck bombs are bad, but they don't reach the casualty level of chemical and nuclear. The nuclear attack will take more effort. The chemical attack may already have all the components in place. Do you see our problem?"

Miller responded, "Yes, I see it, and it terrifies me. Which one do we go after, and what will be the repercussions of taking one operation out? Will it cause the other operations to speed up or falter?"

"Which operation will be the deadliest? Which one will cause the most casualties? We are going to need help with this. It is growing beyond our capabilities to stop Khan," feared Jack.

Jacobson listened to the exchange, added, "Abbas confirmed what we think we know. He also confirmed that there are enough terrorists in the country to conduct *all three operations*. What appears to be the last piece of this operation is the nuclear device being built and activated. We suspect the chemical agents, whatever they are, have been acquired inside the States. The conventional explosives most certainly have been."

"Do we make a run at Khan in Nicaragua and take him out and then turn north and head for home and try to locate the chemical weapons? The other options are that we head north now and start working with the FBI and everyone else looking for chemical weapons with a watchful eye for Khan? Does anyone know the complete picture of this operation besides us?" Jack asked.

"No, but we need to brief someone quickly. Decisions need action," Jacobson pointed out.

Paige interjected, "Based on my analysis of the information in our possession, we should expect an attack in Los Angeles. Muslims view Las Vegas as a corrupt city of immense debauchery, and we should not rule it out as a target. Still, the mystery is where would a nuclear detonation be best used. I am not sure."

A phone, ringing down the hallway, penetrated everyone's thoughts. One of the team leaned out of the office and yelled, "Is there a Jacobson here? He has a phone call from Nicaragua."

CHAPTER NINETEEN:
Khan's Escape

* * *

Jack waited impatiently for Jacobson's phone call to end. He saw Captain Miller whispering to his team. The two new members from the 7th Group listened intently. A decision about going into Nicaragua was imminent, depending on whatever briefing Jacobson was getting. Jack decided, if he was going to be part of this team fully, he wanted a long gun, as well as his 9 mm. He spoke to Miller about having an M-4, the short version of an M-16, and Miller instructed his weapons NCO to issue him one.

Entering the United States as a fully operational Special Forces team to engage terrorists is a significant issue because it is the FBI's judicial territory and a possible violation of the Posse Comitatus Act. This law was enacted by President Rutherford B. Hayes on June 18, 1878, to prevent the federal government from having too much power by using the military to enforce domestic policies and laws. Jack and the team received an overview of the law by a young female Captain from the Judge Advocates Office.

It was distracting for Jack and perhaps the others on the team. She was beautiful and serious about giving her brief, creating a conflict for every man in the room. This encounter turned into every man judging a book by its cover. Her beauty was visually distracting, not unlike the way Paige first affected him. It is like meeting someone for the first time, seeing only the outward beauty, then realizing there is more to the person than what is on display. Men are not adept at listening and looking simultaneously with a beautiful distraction in front of them.

Jack noticed Paige stood off from the group by the door, observing all the men in the room, not paying attention to the young JAG officer as she delivered her brief.

Jack zeroed in on the last part of the information she provided. "The Attorney General requested the Department of Defense, under 18 USC

169

831, to assist law enforcement in blocking the release of nuclear materials inside of the United States. The President authorized this temporary change in law, paving the military's way to engage terrorists on domestic soil. It will be a rocky marriage without a doubt for all involved. The FBI was not happy campers about this change in policy and law. So now the FBI must share their responsibilities with the military in an advisory role," she finished the briefing just as Jacobson finished his phone call.

Jack, alert, as Jacobson emerged from the office and briskly walked toward him. His facial expression was concerning. He was talking to himself, never a good sign. As Jacobson arrived, Jack motioned to the team to join them.

The team quickly surrounded them, and Colonel Hancock joined the gaggle. Jack waited for the murmurs to stop, "Was that phone call helpful? Has anything happened that would assist us?"

Jacobson informed, "Worst possible set of events transpired. The Department of State called the Nicaraguan consulate to make some inquiries. It did not go well. No one used Khan's name, but the Nicaraguan government responded with denials. The consulate was queried indirectly about any foreigners arriving. They became agitated and blamed the United States for sticking their nose into their government's private business. It went downhill from there."

While Jacobson paused, Jack quired, "Who called you from Nicaragua?"

For a moment, Jacobson focused on him, "What I am about to tell you must remain in this room and go no further, clear!"

Jack noted that everyone in the group, including the Colonel, acknowledged with a nod of their head. Jacobson disclosed, "We have a highly placed spy inside the government. The Nicaraguan government worked with the drug cartel Diablo and made a prearranged pickup of a Pakistani in Peru, known as Khan. He was transported to the capital of Nicaragua and put up in a hotel. The intelligence services of that country met with Khan, who disclosed he wants to personally deliver a "special gift" to the United States."

Jack emphasized, "That confirms the nuclear material. Is he still there, and can your spy get us into the country?"

"No to both questions, the inquiry from the State Department spooked Khan and the Nicaraguans. Diablo's mini-submarine, typically used to haul drugs into the United States, took Khan aboard and departed for North America. Our spy believes the United States is his next stop."

Miller interjected, "Where does he plan on entering the United States?"

"That is the million-dollar question, Captain," Jacobson offered. "He could be put ashore along the Mexican coast and enter through Texas or along the Texas coastline. He could be put ashore along the Louisiana coast, the Mississippi coast, the Alabama coast, or even Florida. We are working on it. CIA and the FBI have been alerted. Drug Enforcement Administration and the Coast Guard joined the hunt. DEA is actively pinging all their informants for information."

Jack's brain exploded with what-if scenarios and a desire for more information. "I am going reach out to Abbas to see if I can narrow this down. Come on, Paige."

Walking briskly toward Abbas's room, he noted Taylor a pace behind him. As they approached the room, the MP quickly opened the door, startling Abbas.

"We've run out of time for games," Jack challenged Abbas. "How did Khan plan to enter the United States?"

Jack noted his slight hesitancy, "I am not sure. The only comment ever made was about riding the great serpent into the United States. I had no idea what he was talking about."

Taylor replied, "What the hell does that mean?"

Jack was as puzzled about the comment as Taylor and Paige.

* * *

Khan was not claustrophobic, but the inside of the mini-submarine was suffocating him. Helping him overcome his fear of the tight space, the rocking back and forth of the Gulf, and the constant thumping of the diesel engine was rhythmic, lulling him into a semi-consciousness state. His journey from Pakistan, intentionally left vague in case anyone tracked him. He took a small ship from Karachi, Pakistan, to a port in Indonesia, then a chartered jet to Peru. A short eighteen hours later, he found himself escaping in a mini-sub.

Placed slightly forward of the conning tower, Khan sat between two repulsive smelling Mexicans, their sweat and stench causing him to gag. One was steering the mini-sub upfront, and the other looked through a periscope calling out course directions about every 30 minutes. Both men worked off a compass in front of their positions.

Several hours into the trip across the Gulf waters, there was an explosive exchange between the two Mexicans in Spanish, and the engines ceased. The one in the conning tower looked through the periscope, bent down, and raised his finger to his lips signaling Khan to be silent. Khan heard a distant thumping noise, steady and considerable.

Initially, it sounded like the noise was louder and approaching. After a while, the noisy craft seemed to move off and disappear. The mini-sub sat for another 30 minutes, bobbing in the water, back and forth, listening. Then one of the Mexicans uttered in broken English, "Coast Guard." The other nodded his head and restarted the old diesel of the mini-sub. They sluggishly moved forward.

Khan was sweating, feeling ill, yet the whole time he was holding on to his precious cargo in a small steel container. He was determined to deliver his prize to the United States. Khan transmitted a message for his team to meet him at a designated point in the United States. To confuse any American listening stations, he used various contacts in Venezuela and Nicaragua to maintain secrecy.

The two Mexican submariners using global GPS positions to work with did not know the exact location Khan designated. Khan cleverly only divulged pieces of his planned operation to others, using false information to mislead in the event they were captured and made to talk.

Khan hoped the submariners knew what they were doing, and the mini-sub would land on the soil of the country he despised the most, besides Israel. His two-person team awaited him on a massive 45-foot trawler with powerful engines to push through the river's current. The trawler was hiding in the waters where the bayou and the ocean meet, 95 miles south of New Orleans. The waterway of the swamp was deep enough for a mini-sub to enter. A perfect area for drug smugglers, teaming with obstacles, and the ever-present wildlife of alligators and snakes made navigation difficult.

* * *

Inside of the trawler, an empty 50-gal drum sat ready for his use. Aboard the trawler were explosives and material gathered for his purpose to construct a crude nuclear device. Unknown to Khan, his team brought him a surprise to include in his bomb.

* * *

The waiting game was now over as the mini-sub plowed through the surf into the river's mouth to disgorge its one deadly passenger.

As the mini-sub drew near the side of the trawler, the conning tower hatch opened with a bang, and Khan appeared. He gratefully stepped out into the open air away from the smells of the two mariners, onto the deck, just slightly above the waterline. He was balancing himself on the slippery wet deck until the mini-sub was within inches of the trawler before accepting the rope ladder lowered to him. Unable to climb the ladder and hold onto the box containing his "gift," he handed the box to Kamal, the electrical engineer. Khan scrambled up the lowered rope ladder onto the trawler.

The mini-sub immediately pulled away. In the night air, the hatch to the conning tower closed with a loud clang and locked. Its rusting hardware sounded like a screech owl. The mini-sub quickly slipped below the surface of the ocean, and within moments, the trawler bobbed gently in the darkness.

Located on the aft was the fifty-gallon barrel Khan requested. Kamal directed Khan to his cabin in the bow of the trawler. They would leave at sunrise because navigating these waters was too dangerous at night. Kamal and Abdul decided the surprise for Khan would wait until the morning.

The following day as the sunrise illuminated the swamp blending into the adjoining ocean, Khan, freshly showered, stepped out of his cabin onto the deck to see his two companions pulling up an anchor preparing the terrorist boat for its long cruise. The enormous nearby cypress trees filled with birds and the inlet displayed an alligator lying on the small beach near them. In the morning, the wildlife's clamor was loud, and he had to raise his voice as he addressed his two-fellow Jihadis.

"Are the fuel tanks full?"

"Yes, we filled them yesterday at a marina. Our preparation to start our journey is complete."

Abdul asked Kamal, "Should we show him now?"

"Yes, of course, let's show him,"

Khan listened and watched as the two men pulled a tarp back that had been covering a yellow 50-gallon barrel and etched with the all too familiar nuclear waste hazard sign on it. Immediately Khan recognized the container. Looking at both men, he waited for an explanation.

"Our brothers, at our suggestion, obtained this barrel for your use in building your bomb. The barrel was obtained in Somalia, where the infidels bury their toxic and radioactive waste from various European countries and the United States. We thought it would be justice returning the barrel to the owners." Kamal grinned.

Khan looked at his two companions and then back at the barrel, thinking, *"I need to surround myself with more competent Jihadists."*

Khan's malignant brain drafted a plan. This barrel obviously could not be opened, nor the contents retrieved for any practical purpose. The barrel could not be tossed overboard for fear of it being discovered and jeopardizing their mission. Obtaining the barrel from Africa violated all the security protocols Khan put in place. As soon as they reached their destination, he decided to kill these two imbeciles for breaking his rules. Instead, Khan praised both, "You have done well, brothers. We shall strap both barrels together and make a bigger bomb."

Both Kamal and Abdul smiled. They had scored a significant victory in pleasing Khan; except they did not understand him. They had signed their death warrants by their decision.

Kamal went to the pilot cabin and started the engines. He expertly turned the trawler around, setting the direction for the river's mouth, also known as the Head of Passes. Abdul pulled the tarp back over the yellow barrel securing it. Khan walked through the doors into the galley to have some food and coffee he so loved.

The Wind now started the long voyage up the great serpent, the Mississippi River. The destination was 1273 miles from their current location, where another team would meet them for their mission's final leg. The building of his nuclear device would begin immediately.

CHAPTER TWENTY:
The Serpent

* * *

Jacobson provided an in-depth intelligence briefing to Operational Detachment A-647. They listened intently to the information, everyone except Jack. Distracted over Abbas's comment about Khan riding the great serpent into the United States, he studied the Gulf of Mexico's map and the United States' coastline, trying to put the puzzle together.

His concentrated thinking almost paralyzed his abilities to reason. He was overthinking the problem of the coastline as the best place to enter the country, thinking, *"I need to step back from this. My brain is locked. I need to think like Khan. What is a serpent but a snake? If threatened, it crawls, it slithers, it strikes. The answer is in front of me."*

Jack's eyes fell on the map displayed on the screen. His brain imagined shapes finally seeing the snake. He slowly stood up from the table, looking hard at the map on the large screen. Jack's actions disrupted Jacobson, who stopped talking, as the rest of the team focused on Jack. "The snake is the Mississippi River!" he exclaimed. "Look at the map. The river twists just like a snake. The entrance is along the coastline. We have heard St Louis mentioned. The river goes right past it. That is the great serpent."

Everyone in the room studied the map. Jack proclaimed, "It is so simple I almost missed it. The Mississippi River is used by commercial traffic and sightseeing boats cruising up and down the river. No one will be watching the river for Khan. Instead, we would be looking for trucks on highways — that clever bastard. Jacobson, you better notify your contacts at the FBI and CIA. I will call Coast Guard intelligence to determine which type of boats it takes to travel up the river."

Jack overheard Miller inform Colonel Hancock, "Sir, we need to get to St Louis. The C-17 is already fueled with our equipment on board. We need to go now."

Jack informed, "We are taking Abbas with us. We'll ship him to GITMO later. He may come in handy in tracking Khan. Colonel, with your permission, I would like to take those two MPs with us to guard Abbas during our travels."

"You got it; they are yours. I will coordinate with the MP Company commander," Hancock agreed.

Jack asked, "Jacobson, what are you going to do? Stay here, go back to Ecuador or join the team?"

"I am going with you, but I need to make a couple of calls. I will see you at the airbase." Jacobson answered.

Before Jack could act, he observed Taylor taking off at a fast pace, heading down the hallway toward the MPs. Following close behind, Jack heard Taylor advise the MPs, "You have been drafted by Presidential authority. You are now part of ODA-647. Your sole responsibility is to keep that terrorist in the other room under guard. Call your unit and have them deliver a change of clothes to the C-17 within the next hour. You are going with us. In the meantime, prepare Abbas for travel to the airbase."

In unison, both MPs barked, "Yes, sir."

The senior sergeant stepped into the next room to make a phone call as the other sergeant opened the door to instruct Abbas to gather his few belongings.

Jack grinned, "Presidential authority? Nice, better call the airbase and get those two on the flight manifest."

Jack left Taylor, running down the hallway to call an old friend at Coast Guard intelligence in Washington, D.C., "Bill, I have an emergency. I need to know and understand what type of boat it will take to run up the Mississippi River from Mexico's Gulf. Since this is an open line, I can't share with you why I need this information as soon as possible."

Bill consented, "Not a problem. It is easy. You need a boat with a shallow draft of five feet or less. Due to the river flow, you will need the power to push through the current. Some boats use four outboard motors, and some use inboard engines at least 300 horsepower, better if it has two engines. I like diesel for reliability and distance. You also need to understand that since all of the flooding in recent years, new levies have removed some marinas and restaurants, making travel complicated for refueling."

"What type of boat can I look for on the river?" Jack asked.

"The most popular is any size in the 35 foot to 45-foot range. Most likely, not a sailing craft. What is the destination?" Bill asked.

Jack confided, "Not entirely sure, but St Louis was mentioned several times as part of the intel we picked up. The mouth of the river on the Gulf, also known as the Head of Passes, may be the start of the boat's journey up the Mississippi River past New Orleans."

Bill replied, "I might suggest you search for trawlers or enclosed boats of some kind as you know the weather is rainy and humid."

"Thanks, Bill, talk to you soon. My best to Alice and the kids. Get your boss to call my boss at DIA and get a brief, since that river is under your jurisdiction, and the Coast Guard can be a tremendous help." Jack hung up, heading toward the meeting room.

The rest of the team moved outside with their gear throwing it into trucks and Humvees. Jack spotted the two MPs with Abbas in a Humvee and decided to ride in the vehicle immediately behind him. As he passed Abbas's Humvee, he noted the strained look on his face, and he appeared to be talking to himself. Jack climbed into the Humvee, sitting next to Paige. He gazed over at her, noting her red hair and how it added to her fire when she became upset with him. Her lack of response about how she knew Jacobson annoyed him, but he let it pass.

Thanks to Colonel Hancock, the convoy arrived at the airbase without any interruption. Passing through the gates onto the airstrip, they parked next to the open ramp of the C-17. ODA-647 picked up their weapons, gear and trudged up the ramp into the plane. The two MPs gripped the arms of Abbas, guiding him up the incline toward the front of the aircraft, placing him in a seat with an MP on either side of him.

Jack strolled over to the MPs, "Appreciate you guys joining us on such short notice. Did you receive your change of clothes as requested?"

Both MPs replied, "Yes."

"We were not formally introduced; I am Jack. What are your names?"

"I am Staff Sergeant Tom Evans," replied the senior MP.

"I am Sergeant Phil Tomkins," remarked the junior MP with a slight southern drawl.

"Great to meet you both. As you can tell, this operation is nothing normal. There will be some ups and downs as we work out searching for Abbas's boss. We need to find him and stop him no matter what else we do. If not, he will kill a great many in our country." Jack explained.

Both MPs glared at Abbas, and Evans grunted, "Don't worry about us, do what is needed. We will take care of Mr. Abbas."

Jack smiled, "This young lady is Paige, our analyst. She will speak to your prisoner throughout the flight and should have one hundred percent access to him." Both MPs acknowledged the directive just as Jacobson came running up the ramp. When he overheard Captain Miller advise the crew chief/loadmaster everyone who was going, the entire team was aboard. Jack motioned for Paige, Miller, Jacobson, Taylor, and Lopez to gather around as he explained the Coast Guard's information.

Jack described, "I did a quick search on the internet about boats. I suspect Khan chose a trawler because it is big enough, and they are popular on the river. They will be a ghost. On the deck, a large canister or barrel is easily concealed. Jack turned to Jacobson, "What have you got from the Bureau or Agency?"

Jacobson disclosed, "Interesting news. The Agency sources reported some toxic waste barrels, reportedly dumped in Somalia back in the 1990s, have surfaced. About four months ago, a barrel was observed, by a source, on a ship bound for Miami. The original information stemmed from media reporting, yet no one followed up on it until now. They are confirming this through operational means and will get back to us.

The Bureau is also checking out a boat purchase in Florida near Naples at the Kimber Marina. Some old Mexican guy bought the boat called the "Midnight Run." They recall the sale because he did not look like he knew anything about boating and asked all the wrong questions concerning a seaworthy boat. The seller sold it to him anyway because he was willing to pay the asking price of $200,000 and did not quibble over the money."

"What kind of boat is it?" Jack asked.

"A 45-foot trawler," Jacobson replied.

"Where's the boat now?"

"No one seems to know. It disappeared from the marina shortly after purchase."

"Is the Bureau doing any further checking?" Miller asked.

"Yes, they are, and they have the Coast Guard doing the same all along the Gulf Coast," Jacobson described.

Master Sergeant Danny Lopez asked, "What are we missing for information? We need to confirm the color and who is the present owner. They most likely changed names on the boat, so the old one will have to do for identification until we learn the new name. How many are on the boat besides Khan? We have gaps to fill in, or we are not locating this boat."

"Once we are on the ground in St Louis, we each have our sources and ways to obtain information. I suggest we use them," Jack directed.

The assessment of the collected intelligence demanded action. Everyone on the team knew that a guess about Khan's operational plan could mean failure of finding and disarming the nuke. They had to nail facts down. Since Khan's penetration of the United States, stringing the facts together to form a solid picture is more critical than ever.

The C-17 engines revved up, and within minutes the aircraft taxied along the airstrip. It paused for a few moments, turning, and immediately, the engines roared, pushing the big Air Force jet down the runway. As it hit 200 mph, the pilot pulled the nose up. The fat aluminum bird lifted into the sunny sky banking north, heading for St Louis, Missouri, and their deadly encounter with Khan.

* * *

Khan decided once they were on the Mississippi River, north of New Orleans, he would start assembling the bomb. He was pleased to find out during the trawler's refurbishing; someone had placed a gyroscopic stabilization torque in the trawler to counteract the boat rocking. The lack of rocking on the river would go a long way in helping him assemble the bomb. They quickly moved through the swamp entering a large lake. Cutting across the lake past New Orleans, they would soon meet the river again. So far, the trip was uneventful. Khan felt relaxed and confident, slipping the noose of any would-be trackers.

One of the last messages he received from his Iranian contacts after Abbas dropped off the money was Abbas's death. There were no details, and Abbas a closed chapter, even though he suspected him of betrayal. Nonetheless, he fed him false and misleading information.

* * *

Seven hours later, the C-17 began its descent into St Louis Lambert International Airport. Soon it was parked with other military aircraft of the Missouri Air National Guard located on the far side of the airport.

Jack led ODA-647, two MPs, and a terrorist into the Air National Guard terminal; he spotted a couple of suits and a General with scowls on their faces. Jack glanced at Miller, who also took in this welcoming committee.

Jack contacted the Director of DIA, briefing him on their travel plans. Most likely, this reception is the result of his presentation.

"Which one of you is Jack?" the General asked.

Jack began, "I am, and you are...?"

"I am General McMichael, commander of the Air National Guard, and these two gentlemen are FBI agents, Sawyer and Bolton. One hour ago, I spoke with the DIA and the President of the United States and directed to render all assistance to your team without exception. About fifteen minutes ago, the FBI showed up and asked about your authority to conduct operations in the United States. I am concerned and confused about what the hell is happening."

Jack thought to himself, *"Doesn't anyone talk to anyone and explain things?*

"Sir, we need a place to discuss this operation. The FBI may join us, or they can contact their boss in DC to obtain an explanation," Jack hissed.

One of the FBI agents spoke up, "I am Percy Bolton, Supervisory Special Agent here in St Louis. Your men are too heavily armed, and your authority is suspect to be on my turf."

Jack growled, "Agent Bolton, time is limited. We are giving the General a quick down and dirty brief and suggest you join us if you want to be part of this operation. If not, I suggest you call the Attorney General or your boss in DC to receive the classified version of this briefing. Lives are on the line, and you are eating up too much of our precious time."

Bolton responded, "I can't allow you and these heavily armed men to leave this terminal."

"Agent Bolton, you have a problem. A standoff with a Special Forces operational team acting on the President's orders is not in your best interests. You will lose this engagement," Jack protested.

Agent Bolton reached under his coat as if reaching for his firearm. Halfway through that motion, he glanced up at twelve men, their various weapons all raised in his direction. "I would not like to start this meeting off with shooting an FBI agent, but I will. We're willing to brief you or shoot you, as deemed necessary, to carry out orders from the President. Your choice," Jack reiterated.

Captain Miller echoed, "What is your answer, Bolton?"

The seconds ticked by, and Bolton noted each soldiers' eyes and Jack's, all lethal and committed. He slowly removed his hand from the inside of his jacket and agreeing, "Let's talk. I was reaching for my cell phone."

The General and the local FBI agents received a detailed briefing. Bolton left the room, called several people, and returned.

Jack asked, "What are your instructions, Agent Bolton?"

Bolton gagged, "My clear instructions are to work with you as a team. We both have certain responsibilities. I want to capture this guy alive, but I also understand the necessity of locating the bomb, or kill him to stop the threat. We are on board with the operation; in fact, a small group of suspects was located on the north side of St Louis. Based on a tip from an informant, our Hostage Rescue Team is heading there now. I will meet the HRT to learn if there is a connection to this operation."

Jack promised, "We'll talk later; you have Captain Miller's and my cell phone numbers."

After Bolton left the room, Jack grumbled, "General, this did not start as smoothly as we needed, but we appreciate your help and the two Blackhawks you put on standby for us." Jack then asked, "We need a place to hold Abbas and to give the two MP's a break. Do you have a suggestion?"

"Yes, I contacted the Air Force Security Police Detachment and special agents from the Air Force Office of Special Investigations to assist in housing your terrorist. They are on their way over. Also, we have a small dining facility on the tarmac for flight crews. I ordered them to open up and feed your team."

Captain Miller admitted, "Thanks, sir, that is one big assist for us. None of us have eaten in almost two days."

General McMichael ordered, "Captain, take your men to the dining facility, turn left as you exit this building, about 300 meters from here," Turning to the MPs, "Sergeant, take your prisoner to the dining facility. I will have the SPs meet you there."

Both MPs replied, "Yes, sir," grabbing Abbas's secure arms walking him out the building with the rest of the team.

Alone now with Jacobson and the General, Jack confided, "The intel omitted from the FBI concerns a separate barrel of toxic radioactive waste smuggled into the country through Florida. We are not sure if it is part of the bomb or part of a separate attack. The CIA is working on that information, and we did not want to provide unconfirmed information."

Jacobson announced, "Jack, it looks like you called it right. I just received a message from my contacts at DEA. Moments ago, intel from one of their informants concerning a mini-sub transporting a foreigner to a New Orleans waterway, it is the Mississippi River."

General McMichael concluded, "Now, the immediate issue is locating and identifying the trawler on the river. I assume if we can find this boat, you'll want the Black Hawks available to intercept the trawler. I hope you realize if that bomb detonates on the river, the contamination will last hundreds of years on everything down the river and within several miles of the blast area."

"Yes, we have discussed that possibility, and that is the reason we need this Special Forces team to board the boat and kill or capture Khan before the bomb explodes. I am sure the FBI's Hostage Rescue Team can do that, but politics interfere with their decisions. We do not have that problem."

Jacobson's phone disturbed the conversation, incessantly ringing before he could remove it from his pocket. "Hello.... Yes, we need whatever information you have …. Where...How many? OK…. How reliable is your source? OK…. got it…Thanks!"

Jack exclaimed, "Well?"

"The FBI picked up some information about a trawler refitted in Mississippi. They located the marina in Biloxi, speaking to the owner who confirmed two friendly "brown guys" spent the last year and a half working on a trawler. He has no idea where they are from and just referred to them as "brown guys" being friendly sharing a beer with the yard workers. He did not think they were Muslim because he heard Muslims do not drink alcohol."

"That is incorrect. Given the opportunity, they'll drink. We used to pay off our spies in Iraq and Afghanistan with scotch and Irish whiskey, and sometimes with Viagra," Jack revealed.

Jacobson continued, "Jack, you will have to tell me the Viagra story sometime. Anyway, these men seemed to have enough money and did most of the work themselves, one being an electrical engineer and the other a mechanical engineer — two things he recalled.

When the boat arrived, there was no name on the boat's aft section, which was curious since all crafts are named. The trawler refitted was called *The Wind*. The new name inscribed on the aft of the vessel, and he thought that odd. *The Wind* is the type of expression that would appear on a sailboat. He recalled the delivery of a large box.

One evening before closing, he made his security rounds, seeing the box opened and a tarp thrown on it. During the interview, he revealed he was curious and peeked under the tarp seeing a yellow barrel. The owner never said a word to anyone about it because he did not want anyone to know he is nosy."

"Bingo," said Jack.

CHAPTER TWENTY-ONE:
Misleading Intelligence

* * *

The trawler slowly made its way up the Lower Mississippi River, hiding along the shoreline during the day and traveling by night, while another part of Khan's plan went into action in Los Angeles.

* * *

The small box truck driver pulled to a stop underneath I-405, where it crossed I-105 near Los Angeles International Airport. The paneled vehicle was filled with 3 tons of explosives. The barrels of jelled JP-4 fuel filled the truck. It would stick onto surfaces, especially skin burning like napalm. Due to the weight, the truck's axle was slowly collapsing, giving the vehicle the appearance of a breakdown alongside the interstate. This scene was played out daily throughout the country, a truck breaking down during rush hour traffic.

The driver, a young Middle Eastern man, clean-shaven slightly dark-skinned to the casual observer, would take him for a Mexican. He jumped out of the truck slamming the door, playing the part of a man irritated at his misfortune of breaking down during delivery. He pulled some red reflective triangles out, setting them up to the truck's rear to prevent anyone from driving into the vehicle.

Drivers involved in bumper-to-bumper traffic near the exits to LAX only glanced casually at the truck. The commuters ignored the driver's actions.

The truck driver returned to the cab, opened the door, and reached into a small box, turning it on by flipping a switch. He stared for a moment, waiting while a green light lit up, indicating the receiver was now set to receive a phone-activated signal. Then, setting the box back down on the floorboard, he slammed the door. Everything was ready.

The driver held a cell phone, pretending he was calling someone. When he noticed no one paid attention to him, he jumped the guard rail, scrambled up a small hill over another guard rail to a surface street, and then jumped into a waiting car.

The car was about four blocks away from the truck when the driver shouted *Allah Akbar* dialing a number sending a signal to the tiny receiver lying on the truck's floorboard.

The explosion was incredible. There was a moment of a flash that drivers nearby witnessed before being evaporated. They never heard the explosion. All six lanes of traffic on I-405 and I-105 for a quarter of a mile disappeared as the two interstates melted into one asphalt heap. Past the quarter-mile of the blast area, windshields collapsed onto the occupants, side windows blew out, and tires on cars and trucks exploded from the pressure of the blast crashing into each other. Los Angeles came to an abrupt stop. Jihad had arrived in greater Los Angeles with a bang.

* * *

Jack ordered Jacobson to call DIA to provide drone support to fly along the Mississippi River to spot the trawler just as Captain Miller ran into the room, shouting, "Jack, turn on the TV and find a news channel."

"What's going on?" Jack demanded. The room was cavernous, like a warehouse. By the time Miller arrived at their table, Jack had the TV on and searched for a news channel.

Miller, his eyes stark, stated the obvious. "Los Angeles just took a big hit."

Jacobson grabbed the phone, called DIA, demanding information. Jack found a news station on cable. He stared, horrified, into the blackened crater where two interstates had intersected. Cars, trucks, and bodies lay scattered over the lanes and sidings like some kid who picked up his toys and threw them everywhere. Fires raged were several big rigs and tankers broken apart and thrown together. Some fuel trucks exploded high into the sky with truck parts flying in every direction, taking down one helicopter shooting the scene.

Other helicopters hovered higher over the devastation gaining altitude to avoid vehicles exploding from the heat. The television showed emergency vehicles clustered at one end of the crater, along the debris field's edges, unable to find a way forward.

"My God. Is this Los Angeles or Kabul?" Jack cried.

The announcer on TV reported, "The blast area ... appears to be half a mile wide. The death toll is unknown, but by the vehicles and the roadway's looks, it is safe to say the death toll will be in the hundreds. It is rush hour in Los Angeles, and here interstates I-105 and I-405 cross forming the main corridor to get into LAX.

"Officials are not saying what caused the explosion, but local Channel 2 reported they received a phone call claiming responsibility from a previously unknown terrorist group. The group's name has not been released, and the station is assisting law enforcement by providing the recorded message." The announcer explained.

"Jack," Jacobson interrupted. "DIA, CIA, ATF, Homeland Security, and FBI are going balls to the wall on this attack. 'The Wind of Islam.' is the name of the group. It was on a recorded message the media received. No one has heard of this group, but you may note the name of the trawler we are looking for is '*The Wind.*'

Jack groaned, "Captain, we need some predator drones in the air pretty quickly. We were discussing drones when you entered. If you make a demand for drones through your channels and we do the same, maybe we can convince someone to make it happen. There may be an issue getting them if all the resources move to Los Angeles."

Miller tore his eyes away from the devastation on the screen. "I agree; I will make some calls to Fort Bragg."

Jack nodded grimly. "Jacobson, call DIA. I'm going to talk to Abbas again. Captain Miller, I need Taylor or Lopez with me."

"No problem," Miller croaked, his eyes riveted to the screen again. "They'll meet you at the holding area."

* * *

Khan worked on his nuclear bomb, attaching components, wires and checking electrical currents inside the barrel to ensure perfect insulation between the circuitry and the housing. The trawler pulled into a small alcove along the river overhung with trees hiding the vessel from searchers by air or water. The anchor set and the boat floated gently on the water, hardly rocking due to the gyroscope stabilization torque installed.

Kamal approached him from the front of the boat. "Khan, the attacks have begun. The truck bomb meant to serve as a diversion in Los Angeles exploded, and news reports show everyone's resources focused on Los Angeles."

"Excellent," Khan yelled, turning back to his task. Kamal walked away without another word.

The bomb was now in its fifth day of construction. Soon it would be time to insert the fissionable material into the containment unit. The material was two half-spheres of purest plutonium. Only his iron will keep his nerves and excitement in check, his hands steady. The heat and humidity of the day were almost at the maximum for the day. He needed to take a break in the coolness of his cabin before continuing with his deadly task. In the next two days, another attack on an American city would draw the infidels away from the river and into more considerable confusion. He smiled at what was going to happen next. His plan was brilliant. It could not fail.

* * *

Jack, Lopez, and Taylor sat in a windowless room with Abbas. Jack bent slightly toward Abbas, who sat on a bed. Lopez, intimidating as ever, positioned himself against the table, as Taylor sat in the other chair watching intently. Jack asked, "I do not believe right now you have told me the entire truth of Khan's plan. A bomb just exploded in

Los Angeles, and you falsely lead us to believe the attacks will be at the same time. What is happening with Khan's plan?"

Abbas revealed, "It is my understanding he wanted to use his plan to attack multiple targets as Al-Qaeda does at the same time. He had a backup plan to attack cities individually if he thought his efforts would be compromised, to create confusion with a diversion to his real purpose. Khan must feel threatened in some way. He wants a diversion, maybe more than one, to draw your attention away from him and his primary target. That is the only reason for Khan to change from what I thought was going to happen."

Lopez, his face stern and his eyes hard, asked, "Have you heard of the group calling themselves *The Wind of Islam*?"

Abbas was scared of Lopez for a reason he was having a hard time recognizing. "Yes, that was Khan's original name for this operation when he devised his plan. He never committed to the name, and I never thought any more about it," Abbas answered.

Jack asked, "What are you withholding about Khan's plan? I have seen you talking to yourself on the trip from Panama on several occasions, and that only spells trouble when men speak to themselves."

Abbas replied, "Nothing, I have told you all I know. My talking is nothing more than prayers."

Taylor insisted, "Jack, I think it is time for another polygraph examination so we can delve into this better. Suddenly I feel like we are operating on incomplete information."

As Taylor proposed another test, Jack watched Abbas and noted a change in body posture, looking down and crossing his arms and legs. It was clear to Jack that Abbas did not want to take another test, which was reason enough to give him one. Jack explained, "I am going to give you another test, different from the one you have already taken. I will be back with you shortly." The three men stood up and left the room, leaving Abbas to contemplate his next move. Jack ordered the MPs by the door, "Watch him. Stay in the room with him."

Taylor headed down the hall to arrange for a proper room for the test. Jack and Lopez headed back to the team's operational room. Once outside of Abbas's hearing, "What do you think we need to ask Abbas?" Jack asked.

Lopez replied, "We need to dissect what Abbas knows or thinks he knows of Khan's plan. Is the plan being played out as expected? Is there another plan? Besides nuclear, is Khan going to use chemical and biological? What are other cities involved and targeted? That is just off the top of my head."

Jack's thinking was the same. "All valid questions. He originally told us that one of the weapons was chemical. When I tested him earlier on that issue, he passed the test. He led us to believe the biological agents were too hard to transport and that part of the plan was canceled. We have no intel saying that biologicals are even in play." Jack grunted.

Lopez growled, "Yea, we were so wrapped up on the nuclear device trying to confirm if that was the weapon of choice. Maybe we overlooked chemical and biological. The making of a car or truck bomb was a sure bet since it is easiest to manufacture."

"You're right. I'm going to put together two examinations. One will verify Abbas's answers from the earlier test and tell us everything about Khan's plan. The other will be a searching peak of tension test if he fails the first one. The SPOT will be administered immediately after the first test and will be your signal; he failed the initial test. If he passes the first test, I'll hold back the SPOT and talk to him some more to refine the intel," Jack explained to Lopez.

An hour later, Jack was in the room and all the polygraph equipment set up, questions prepared, and watched Abbas sitting opposite him. The audio was installed in the outer office, so Lopez and Taylor could listen to the examination. Paige joined Lopez and Taylor to listen to Jack's analysis of Abbas. Just before joining Abbas, Jack learned Scott Air Force Base in Illinois launched Predator drones along the Mississippi River on the President's orders.

Jack lectured, "Abbas, we will go over the details of this polygraph examination, much like the one you took before. The questions are different because I need to test your honesty and all aspects of your information.

"In our hurry to verify he had a nuclear device as the primary weapon of choice, we took your word for it that chemical weapons may be in play, and biological weapons were not. For the record, the only thing I will confirm now is a nuclear device on a trawler on the Mississippi River. The truck bomb in Los Angeles exploded several hours ago, and they have mass casualties of over 400 Americans and counting."

Abbas replied weakly, "But I told you everything."

"We'll find out shortly, is there anything you would like to tell me before we get started?" Jack coaxed.

"No," Abbas declared.

Jack went through the preliminaries and explanations Abbas heard before reinforcing Abbas's psychological position about the truth. Jack decided he would use a Modified General Question Technique test reviewing the relevant questions: Are you intentionally withholding information from us about Khan's plan? Are you lying to protect Khan's plan? Are you deliberately misleading US intelligence about Khan's plan? Abbas answered "No" to each question.

A review of the rest of the test questions and then Jack collected four charts. He decided Abbas had failed the entire test. Jack deliberately moved at once into the second examination. He could have stopped and interrogated but knew this might harm the SPOT results and render it useless.

The SPOT examination was entirely different. It is akin to a Guilty Knowledge Test, but not the same. There were no comparison questions introduced, just specific issues of interest. Those questions consisted of: Is Khan using other weapons as part of his plan? Is that weapon chemical? Is that weapon biological? Is that weapon nuclear?

Is that weapon explosives? Is that weapon something you have intentionally withheld from me? Jack ran through the questions four times and evaluated the charts.

The peak of tension consistently showed responses on two answers, another weapon used and the biological question. Abbas did not respond to nuclear and explosives questions because psychologically, he already provided that information knowing it to be true.

Jack, at once, went into interrogation mode. His deep thoughts about bashing in Abbas's face were hard to control while he struggled with his anger. He knew Abbas was lying, and Jack was having a tough time controlling his emotions, knowing lives were on the line. Jack took a moment to compose himself, using silence as a weapon while staring at Abbas.

Finally, against the elicitation rules, he broke his silence, "Abbas, you lied to me. You've broken our trust and bond. You're now part of the problem, and you have those people's blood in Los Angeles on your hands. You are a fraud, a deceiver to your faith. Your word cannot be trusted, and your punishment will be just when you go to hell." *A little over the top, Jack admonished himself.*

Jack's two-hundred-pound frame of hard muscle and his menacing green eyes bore into the very being of the terrorist. Abbas stared at Jack, wide-eyed. "No, No, No, I have not lied. I am telling the truth; Allah is my witness."

Jack waited for the effect of his words to register on Abbas. "This test shows you have lied about the biological attacks."

"I – I wasn't sure! I told the truth about everything else. The biological attack was a plan that was never approved, and it was too difficult to make it happen," Khan confessed.

"You think that is what he said. In other words, you do not know for sure. Our discussions were clear on that point." Jack repeated.

"Khan made plans and told me the plans were no good because the biological agent could not be carried safely to the enemy."

"What was the plan?" Jack asked.

"To release a strain of weaponized Ebola, he would get from the Russians."

"We are talking in circles, Abbas. There was a plan, then no plan, and you were sure, now you are not sure, and there was a plan with the Russians with Ebola. You're playing games. If you were so sure about this information and plan, you would not have reacted so strongly on the test to biological weapons questions. Tell me the truth now. If not, I will call MI-5 myself and have your sister held in jail for the rest of her life."

"Please, no, not my sister. She has nothing to do with this. The original plan was to have a weaponized version of Ebola brought to the United States and released. The problem was how to release it. Khan said it was too complicated. Just days before I met you, I overheard Khan tell a courier to proceed with an operation he called, 'The Wind,' and after hearing your questions about a terrorist group called The Wind of Islam, I thought that was the same thing.

"I remembered Khan telling me once his idea as to how to infect many infidels with a disease. The carrier of the disease would take the biological agent into his body, and it was to be the type of illness that quickly spreads on contact. He described spreading a virus like the wind. I'd dismissed the idea because he said it wouldn't work. I put it out of my mind until you caused me to remember."

Jack pushed, "How would you do this? It would have to have a long enough time in a body to incubate with travel times before being contagious. What timelines are we talking about?"

Abbas bowed his head, rubbing his temples and holding his hands tightly together as if forcing himself to push the truth out of his body, "I recall a time frame of ten days Khan suggested."

"Why ten days? How is the Ebola weaponized?"

"The time frame of incubation *was* the weaponized part of the plan by altering the protein cells. As a result, the carrier would be contagious and able to travel from one coast to another, with frequent stops in major cities long enough to contaminate infidels," was Abbas's chilling answer.

CHAPTER TWENTY-TWO:
Ebola

* * *

Jack was on a highly classified computer, writing an urgent message to his boss at DIA regarding Abbas's new information. No one had any ideas about where a person carrying Ebola may come from and which coast, he would land on first, the East or the West. Jack finished the brief report, picked up the phone, and called the Director of DIA, bypassing his boss, who would chew his ass for this breach of the chain of command. Jack did not care under the circumstances.

"General, I just sent you a short report on a polygraph with new information I obtained from Abbas. There is a big problem outlined in the report regarding an unknown person entering the US infected with a weaponized virus of Ebola. Khan also directed this attack."

The General's voice was rough with fatigue and exhaustion. "Why in the hell are we just now finding this out?" he demanded.

"We concentrated on the nuclear device. No one has ever put a single plan together combining nuclear, biological, and conventional explosives before. I know it's unprecedented," Jack replied.

"You work on the nuclear issues, and I will get onto the biological issues with CIA, FBI, and Homeland Security. Find that damn bomb! Out here."

Jack held the dead phone, staring at Miller and Jacobson just as Taylor and Lopez arrived. Taylor asked, "Any word from the drones yet? I feel the need to be flying up and down the Mississippi River myself. This sitting here is nerve-racking. It has been seven days of absolutely nothing."

* * *

The past seven days, *The Wind* successfully hid from the drones traveling only at night. They made better time than expected, with the extended fuel tanks allowing *The Wind* to stop only once for fuel. They approached Grafton, Illinois, just north of St Louis for the last fuel stop. The next step would be to turn directly north into the Illinois River, traveling east toward Chicago at Granville, Illinois. Their target for the explosion was a mere 127 miles from Granville.

* * *

Standing among the dead bodies of the raid in north St Louis, Supervisory Special Agent Bolton of the FBI analyzed the aftermath of the Hostage Rescue Team's attack. A young person of Arab descent was wounded, captured, and transported to a hospital leaving behind four others who died during the assault. It was a damn mess! What had caught his interest were the many maps and photographs lying on the table and floor. The forensic IT team scooped up the computers rushing to download the information back at their labs.

Bolton looked at his partner, picking up various photographs and maps. The photos disturbed him; it showed power plants as possible targets. "Is there any indication about the location of those power plants?" Bolton asked.

"Not by the photographs, no names, and I don't recognize them," his partner grumbled.

"Let's look at those maps to see if we can piece this together quickly and make sense of what we have," Bolton's phone rang. "Yea, Bolton here," he answered.

After a few minutes, Bolton closed his phone. "The other Arab died on the way to the hospital. It is up to us and the IT guys to figure this out."

His partner was carefully studying each map noting a small "x" located by Seneca, Illinois. "Boss, take a look at this," indicating the "x" and the city. "Looks like there is something there that interested them."

In the far corner of the room, another agent inspected documents, exclaiming, "Receipts for gas in a place called Seneca."

Bolton pulled out his phone, called the office analyst relaying the information at the crime scene, asking, "Have the IT people broke open those computers yet?"

The voice on the other end replied, "No, but as you were talking about Seneca and the photographs, I pulled up some information about a nuclear power plant located eleven miles southeast of Ottawa, Illinois. Seneca Unit One and Seneca Unit Two. I am looking this up and will get back to you."

Bolton fought to keep the panic out of his voice, "Pick up every scrap of paper in here. Damn the crime scene protocol. These guys are dead. Move people."

Lights and sirens blazed a path through St Louis to the FBI office. Three sedans raced against the clock to unravel the puzzle of the maps and photographs in their possession.

* * *

Khan sat below deck in the comfort of his air-conditioned cabin as the trawler refueled. They soon would have to leave because there was no room in the plans for a delay. The chances of being detected were high. The team he expected had not arrived to meet the trawler. Unbeknownst to Khan, they were all dead.

Kamal entered the cooled cabin asking, "No one is here, and we're refueled. What should we do?"

Khan, deep in thought, was momentarily silent as Kamal waited patiently for an answer. Khan groaned, "Leave - We shall travel during the daylight hours at best speed. The bomb is almost ready."

Khan feared the worst. His team discovered, and if valid, the chances of exposure to his plan created tensions he least expected. He hoped his misleading information deceived his hunters. For the first time, Khan was nervous. The trawler's diesel engines came to life moving off from the docks on its deadly mission.

* * *

Jack's phone rang, and before the second ring, he was speaking with Bolton. "What do you have?" he asked.

Jack listened as Bolton described the events, the documentary evidence collected at the scene, and the seizure of the computers. "The target is a nuclear plant on the Illinois River just outside of Chicago?"

Jacobson and Taylor pulled out maps of Illinois tracing the river. Jack assumed, "Seneca is the location, got it; we are deploying there now." Jack turned to his men, "Maps and photographs support the town of Seneca as a target for Khan because it has two nuclear power plants," Jack fumed. He looked at Miller, "Everyone, it is time to saddle up. Get those Black Hawks ready. Jacobson, get those drones re-tasked to the Illinois River."

Everyone grabbed weapons, rucksacks and climbed into waiting Humvee's. The tarmac was minutes away, and when they arrived, the Black Hawks already had their engines warmed up for immediate takeoff. Jack and ODA-647 loaded into the Black Hawks, which moved immediately.

Jacobson dialed a number at DIA headquarters picked up at once by the Director of DIA, who announced, "We found the Ebola-infected guy on a flight to Hawaii from the Philippines. It looks like the Russians screwed Khan because they used non-weaponized Ebola that incubated for two to three days. The flight attendants noticed the carrier bleeding from his eyeballs and called in an emergency as they descended into Honolulu. Everyone on the flight was in a total panic."

The Director asked, "What've you got?"

CHAPTER TWENTY-THREE:
The Nuclear Facility

* * *

Lieutenant General Bryan Webster, Director of the DIA, received a full; but quick briefing from Jacobson, then made a call, "Mr. President, we believe we have the bomb and target located. Our team is acting on the information now. The FBI wants to help but operationally is a little slow. The data exploited at one field office; however, another field office wants to assume command and control since the target is in their area of responsibility.

"The disagreement needs resolution at once. In the interim, the Special Forces team and DIA are moving forward. I am going to activate another Special Forces Detachment out of Fort Campbell to reinforce my original unit."

President Mike Turnbull, a seasoned politician and no-nonsense decision-maker, "Son of a bitch," he responded. The Director heard the President address someone else in the room, "Get that damn FBI Director on the phone now. I want to talk to him." Turning back to the Director of DIA, "General, keep me informed of every detail and how your team handles this problem. Activate any resource needed and bypass the Joint Chiefs and Secretary of Defense. Come directly to me. I will let them know. Call back when you have an update."

"Yes, Mr. President, out here." Picking up another phone, he directly called his boss, the Chief of the Vice Joint Chiefs of Staff at the Pentagon, explaining the President's instructions. Webster did not make three stars without avoiding landmines, and this was one of them, placing him outside his chain of command, an unforgivable landmine to step on in the military. The President meant well, but Webster sidestepped the predicament quickly.

The next call went to the 160th Special Operations Aviation Regiment commander, often referred to as the "Night Stalkers," at Fort Campbell, Kentucky. The Night Stalkers are part of the special operations cadre that could airlift another Special Forces team from Fort Campbell to Illinois on short notice.

"Colonel Pitts, I am giving you an *alert* notice per Presidential order *to send* four of your aircraft with a Special Forces team to Seneca, Illinois, and connect with Captain Miller ODA-647. Captain Miller will be senior and direct ground operations for all teams. There is one civilian from DIA with ODA-647, my commander on the ground, and answers directly to me. The alert is a Bright Broken Arrow Level One operation approved by the President; do you acknowledge the order?" he asked.

"Order has been authenticated and acknowledged. ODA-890 is the standby team activated for this op. Birds are warming up now. Trojan six-six is the call sign for ODA-890."

"Call me if there are any issues. Also, alert the Fort Campbell community for a mass casualty event. Out here," said Webster.

General Webster turned to his aide and ordered, "Contact Captain Miller and give him the ODA-890 call sign to let him know they are on the way to augment his mission; he maintains command of both teams. Also, get me a direct line to the mayor of Seneca, Illinois."

"Yes, sir," Captain Coughlin replied. He picked up the phone to the communications director found buried in the Pentagon's bowels with the best and most sophisticated telecommunications gear and computers in the world.

"Sir, this is Captain Coughlin, aide de camp to General Webster. We have a developing situation of an attack on the homeland, Bright Broken Arrow Level One. DIA has a team we need to reach, already in the air and heading to the attack location. We need to apprise them of the incoming Special Forces team, ODA-890. Our point of contact is Special Agent Jack McGregor or Captain Miller. General Webster needs to speak to them now."

"Roger that Captain … standby," came the reply.

* * *

Jack and his Green Beret team endured a turbulent ride through an advancing storm system on the helicopter racing to Seneca as the crew chief waved his hand, motioning Jack to pick up the headphones. Jack quickly picked the headset off the hook on the ceiling. "Jack here." He recognized General Webster's voice.

"Mr. McGregor, please answer correctly. Your call sign is LDO one, mine is Eagle one, and Captain Miller is Rocker one, are we clear?" asked the General.

It was not a question; it was more of a statement from Webster. He was in operational mode. Straight talk the only conversation. However, he noted his call sign of "LDO" was given with a sense of humor, meaning Lie Detector Operator, a term thrown around by polygraph examiners within the community of that specialty. "Roger Eagle one, this is LDO one."

"You need to coordinate with Rocker one to let him know that ODA-890 from Fort Campbell is inbound meeting you in Seneca. Miller will keep command of the operation. The FBI may join later, but they seem to be slow getting out the gate. I just checked with the Predator Operation Center and have nothing on the trawler. Are we sure about this intel?" Webster asked.

"Eagle one, we will be landing in about 30 mikes to the north of the river and power plant structures. We will advance on the facility from that direction. I will brief Rocker one. The intel is as good as we have. I want confirmation on the trawler on the river." Jack's thoughts raced. He remembered one of their problems, no bomb tech. "Also, we need a bomb tech. We are moving so fast on this anyone will do, any suggestions?" Jack asked.

The Director already ahead of Jack's request, with a bomb tech for conventional explosives from Fort Campbell EOD assigned to ODA-890. A traditional bomb tech is necessary to stop the explosion from going off and would prevent the nuclear explosion, Jack thought. "LDO one, there is a bomb tech with ODA-890. I will contact you once you land with an update, Eagle one out."

Jack made a talking sign with his hands to the crew chief yelling at him over the engines he needed to connect to Captain Miller on the other chopper. Within moments he heard Miller's voice.

"Rocker one, your new designation from Eagle one, Webster, I am LDO one." He then briefed Miller and brought him up to date with the augmentation of ODA-890 and the bomb tech.

The two Black Hawks continued to follow I-55, the most direct route to their destination, as lightning flashed in the distance. When they approached an intersecting road near Dwight, route 47 marked their departure from I-55. Both helicopters banked hard left-turning north and then adjusted their direction to the northwest directly to Seneca.

* * *

Paige stood by the doorway to the terminal hanger watching Jack and ODA-647 climb into the Blackhawks. She was worried, and her heart troubled her about how she felt. She had fallen in love with Jack, a feeling she had not entertained for many years after a failed marriage. Paige also recognized Jack's issues relating to his past, and she wanted to know about it, but he constantly changed the subject, so she had not pressed him. There would be a day she would push him. Now, she had to do her job.

She knew better than to ask to join this operation telling Jack she could be more useful talking to Abbas. If anything developed, she could relay the information. Jack agreed, knowing how much she wanted to be part of the action. Paige wanted to talk to Abbas before it got too late into the day. She did her best analysis in the morning with a cup of coffee. She gathered up a tray with that thought in mind, placing two mugs, a thermos of coffee, and some breakfast rolls on it before walking to the holding area to talk to Abbas.

Two Air Force Security Police sergeants stood by the door, holding up their hands, stopping her. The senior SP asked, "Who are you? We cannot let unauthorized persons in the room."

Paige, irritated, said, "I'm the DIA analyst on this team. I need to talk to Abbas."

Before they could argue further, one of the Army MPs arrived. Taking in the situation, immediately directed, "Sergeant, Ms. Anderson is allowed to see Abbas anytime she wants to. Let her in!"

The SP looked back and forth between Paige and the Army MP, then turned opening the holding area door. Paige turned to the young MP who had the smooth southern drawl, and smiling, gushed, "Thank you."

Paige found Abbas sitting at a single table in the room. Quickly he rose as she entered, sniffing appreciatively. "I love coffee. I need some sitting here thinking over my circumstances."

"Along with the coffee, I brought you breakfast rolls and jam. I was hoping to talk to you if you do not mind the company of a woman," playing to the Islamic view of women.

"I'm grateful, your company is most welcome. I have been deep in thought about Islam, and I need a break from my contemplations. I have entertained the thoughts about becoming a Christian. The idea is new and very foreign to me. I need something to believe in."

"I can help you with becoming a Christian when you are ready," Paige said, as she poured coffee from the mess hall thermos into the two mugs, pushing the plated rolls and jam to him, along with a butter knife, sat back, and watched as he picked up the steaming cup. Fatigue lined his face making him seem older than when he first arrived. The morning sun shone through the barred windows bringing with its light warmth and shadows. She sipped her coffee and patiently waited as she saw Jack do so many times with someone he was interrogating. She let the silence in the room guide her.

Abbas arranged his bed pillow, sitting back on the soft bed against the hard wall, sipping his coffee. Then, changing the subject, he said, "Have your soldiers left to kill Khan?"

"They left to locate him and his bomb. Based on some information, they may know where he is going. I do not know the plans or the location of their mission," Paige lied when, in fact, she knew every part of the plan and location.

* * *

Abbas could not determine her sincerity. He often had a hard time discerning if a woman was lying or not, and a Western woman, well, that was impossible, especially one in intelligence. Abbas enjoyed her company and the coffee anyway. He decided he would use her as a sounding wall to his thoughts about Islam. "How much do you understand about my religion?" he asked.

"Are you going to try to convert me?" she replied, smiling.

The smile was disarming from a beautiful woman, and the question direct, creating confusion for Abbas. *Is she playing with me?* He decided she was not. "No, I find it hard to convert people to our way of thinking and understanding. It is like you are on the dark side of the moon, and we are on the light side of the moon. So, the two shall not meet."

She chuckled, "You have our positions exactly opposite of where I think they are. I see you in the darkness of the moon, not us."

"That does explain many things. First, we believe Mohammed, Peace be Upon Him, and the Koran that establishes Islam, then there is Sharia Law as the law for our guidance in Islam. Are you a Christian?"

Abbas listened carefully to her reply, "Yes, I am Christian. Our law is derived from our Constitution and the Ten Commandments. Islam fits more easily into a political movement that wants to control everyone, a totalitarian government, much like socialism. Islam means submission, as I understand it. This submission is supposed to be total in every aspect of one's life. A Muslim is essentially a slave by submission to Allah. Your religion lacks respect for other beliefs. It also imprisons you."

Abbas watched her as she sat back, tasting her coffee, looking over the edge of the cup at him, ready for his response.

"Yes, you seem to have the definitions somewhat correct. Islam is a religion, but not in the western meaning of faith. We are monotheists, and you are polytheists. According to our belief, Allah was before Mohammed ever set foot on earth, even though he claimed to be the first real Muslim because he bowed to Allah as commanded. At the same time, there is a contradiction in our dogma. Just because one is Muslim does not necessarily mean they support Islam, as they should. I suspect this is true of all religions and people who believe in their faith.

"The Koran also states Moses was a Muslim, and what about Abraham, the alleged father of all religions, Jews, Christians, and Muslims. They are supposed to be Muslim but are corrupted due to sin. Therefore, Mohammed is the first to submit to Allah. My problem is we are not allowed to question any of this belief, and I have a curious mind. How could Abraham be Muslim when he existed over three thousand years before Mohammed? There is a knowledge gap that I cannot reconcile."

"That is remarkably interesting. It's the first time I have heard an honest response about that area of belief of Islam." Paige said.

"Also, there was the first prophet, the first man named Adam. I am thinking about how all of this conflates with Judaism and Christianity and the Bible stories. I find it confusing that Islam claims all these beliefs and stories are about Islam, I think not. I question all of it. Respect is a two-way street, and I fear we have not earned your respect.

Abbas continued his argument, "You believe we are extremists. On the contrary, we are nothing more than merely pious in our beliefs in my world. We are rational, not extreme."

"What about the tactic I have read about called 'Muruna' used by those that are spreading Islam throughout the world?" said Paige.

"The Muslim Brotherhood is using this tactic, I think it is called Muruna, where Muslims can violate Sharia Law. This tactic tries to make Americans believe Muslims are like us, and we both know we do not believe in the same concepts of life," argued Paige.

"Yes, yes, that is a tactic I am aware of in our fight. Islam has 1400 or 1500 hundred years of tradition. Yet, we are stagnant in our beliefs because the Koran is the literal word of Allah. We depend too much on historical information to maintain our current position on Islam. Instead, we should learn from our history and advance ourselves.

"I am not sure of anything anymore. The tactic is simple, expand the Muslim presence through birth rate, immigration, and refusal to assimilate, just like we did in Europe. The tactic also includes trying to control key leadership positions and using what I would describe as lawfare invoking lawsuits to stop discussions. Part of our efforts is to infiltrate Middle Eastern studies in universities to influence those ideas and control the narrative. There are many other efforts to denounce Western societies and traditions so we can establish Sharia.

I ask myself, what has Islam contributed to the world? This question circulates in my mind like a whirlwind, never settling down to see what the answer is.

Abbas asked, "Have you ever read the Koran?"

"Yes, what I see in you is your pride has created a cage for you. You assume all is right when intellectually you know it is not, and your pride keeps you locked up." Paige answered.

Not directly answering her, Abbas said, "You are very astute, madam. To understand what you are reading, you first must understand the concept of abrogation. The easiest way I can explain the verses in the Koran are deemed peaceful in tone and spirit but overridden later with verses that are not peaceful. Those verses stand as the literal word of Allah. Every word is from Allah and cannot be changed or questioned.

"Mohammed established, through Allah's word, the treatment of Christians and Jews will be fair and even as friends. But later in another Surah, Allah has deemed those Christians and Jews as enemies, unbelievers to be treated harshly and with death. That stands as our guide for almost 1500 years and never will change until Islam dominates the world.

"The last Surah stands as the abrogation, never to be changed, and Islam will always be enemies with non-believers until you convert to Islam and obey."

"I see how that would influence the reader of the Koran if that rule were understood while reading it," said Paige.

"Pious Muslims understand this rule, but most Westerners do not. As a result, some claim Islam is a religion of peace when it is not, it is only at peace with itself and not the rest of the world. We are at war with the unbelievers until all convert to Islam. Islamic Law recognizes a separation and two worlds," said Abbas.

"One is "Dar al-Islam, the house of peace or some call it the house of submission in the Islamic world and society already under Sharia Law. The other is Dar al-Harb, the house of war, or the war domain, and some call it the house of the sword. That is the infidel's world, and Islam believes there will be a constant war until all infidels convert or are dead.

"Islam intends to rule the entire world, without exception, and all non-believers should fear the sword and what it brings, death or conversion to what we believe. Anyone that believes differently is a fool."

"That is remarkably interesting. How does that cause you to question Islam? It seems that you or any Muslim puts themselves at risk for even questioning your religion or laws. Is this why you suggested Christianity as a possible move for you?"

"Correct. While deciding to turn my back on Islam, I have been in an incubation period like the caterpillar before becoming a free-flying butterfly. I have taken steps to ensure my betrayal is irreversible by disclosing Khan's plan and simply making you aware through Islam's debate and questions. If I meet the conditions of apostasy, sound mind, an adult, and of my own free will, then my blood will be shed with impunity. Making such a public statement condemns me. My fate sealed in my decision; I am the butterfly. I have indeed thought about becoming a Christian. I do not know how."

"Abbas, I cannot disagree with your thoughts about being a Christian. Becoming a Christian is straightforward, and I will assist you when you ask me. In the meantime, I will pray for you."

Abbas, nodding his head, lamented, "I am listening to my soul speak. I hear voices advising me to stop Jihad because it is senseless. We produce nothing except death and destruction when it is over. We end up standing on the rotting corpses of humanity, and for what? We are commanded to spread a belief that we are superior in every way over the world. That is what I question in my mind. That is why I betrayed Khan; a man stuck in the past. He is so intelligent his mind has slid into insanity."

"Khan is in a cage, also entrapped with pride and revenge. He will soon be trapped in another kind of cage if we can find him." She said softly.

"Throughout Islam, whoever controls the sword controls the earth. That is why the sword is the symbol we all believe in and found on our flags. The best move the Western countries ever made was to break up the Caliphate into many pieces or countries after the first great war. But unfortunately, it slowed the progress of Islam to a crawl and did not stop some aspirations. So, ISIS and al Qaeda are trying to stitch it all back together. The world needs to listen and beware." Abbas finished his comments.

* * *

As Paige listened carefully to Abbas, an idea formed about pressing Abbas for more information concerning Khan's plan. She once observed Jack's polygraph test. He managed to cut through the lies by revealing what he knew and understood about Muslims lying under certain conditions.

Jack had confronted a captured terrorist in Kandahar by opening his interrogation by telling the terrorist he was very aware of the manual of Sharia Law, allowing Muslims to achieve objectives in war by misleading with information and lying. In other words, it was obligatory to lie in these circumstances. Thus, Jack cut right to the center of the resistance eventually obtaining the truth he was after from the terrorist.

"Is there anything you have kept hidden about Khan's plans?" asked Paige. "If a nuclear weapon goes off, and you have not shared everything, the blood of all of humanity will be on your soul. I know this to be true by every fiber in me." Paige sat very still, letting her words percolate as she appealed to his humanity.

Abbas responded, "I am guessing now about his real target. I say this truthfully; I do not know for sure. I have overheard him many times state he would put out false leads to confuse the Americans. He would create many incidents; no one would know his true intentions. He may have given me false information helping his plan. I believe I am right in saying this now. He plans to destroy you financially, as he considers this the Achilles Heel of your country."

Paige picked up her cup and sipped slowly. *Where is he going with this? The nuclear plant is not the target? Is it to draw everyone away from his real goal? Smart because this is what we would expect, a nuclear dirty bomb strike on a nuclear plant.* "What do you think is his real target, Abbas?"

"I heard Khan speaking about certain buildings outside of Chicago; he referred to them as "sites" that collected information for all finances in the United States. I did not emphasize his conversations, as he spoke of them differently as in passing, until I compared other information about nuclear plants. He deceived me, as he must have known I was listening. It all makes sense now, in hindsight. I have no idea where these buildings or facilities are located."

"Thank you for this conversation. I have learned something about you. I feel I can trust you. That is more important to me than anything else. Let me know if you feel the need to continue your decision process about being a Christian. Just let me know when you are ready. In the meantime, I need to report what you have revealed in our conversation." Paige picked up the tray of coffee cups and butter knife, leaving the rolls behind.

She exited the room, setting the tray down next to the wall, breaking into a fast run back to the operations center. Her shoe leather slapped the hard concrete echoing down the hallway as she thought, *this information must be correct. It made sense and was expressed believably.*

CHAPTER TWENTY-FOUR:
Betrayal

* * *

The Wind eased into the docking area near the gas pumps and would be the trawler's last refueling. The sign on the dock read Pamala's Pumps and Food, Ottawa, IL, Population 5,023. Thus, the trawler and its deadly cargo were eleven miles from one of two remaining targets.

Khan was in a state of despair and dangerous to be around. His Jihadis scheduled to meet him three days ago, and he assumed the worst. This mission has to be completed solely by him and his two imbeciles. His only hope was the backup plan he put into place a year earlier. The trawler eased into the dock, bumped slightly against the wooden structure bringing him out of his thoughts. He heard footsteps on the deck above and conversation about the fuel, the price, and the type available. He ignored it as he put his mind back to work, trying to resolve his problem.

As daylight faded with the sunset, the air-cooled in the late summer and the humidity became stagnant. Kamal and Abdul both were looking around, trying to judge activity at the docks. They were searching for anyone who looked like law enforcement. Abdul took the diesel hose offered by the attendant at the pumps and handed it down to Kamal to start fuel flow.

Abdul continued looking around, suspicious of everyone and anything that moved. He noted a white van was slowly pulling into the parking lot, followed by a small blue sedan. He reached into his belt and felt for his gun as two men got out of the van and started to walk toward him.

As the men approached the trawler, Abdul pulled his Glock 9mm, keeping it next to his leg. He did not recognize these men but did suspect they were Middle Eastern because of their complexion and indifferent manner. He hesitated in bringing his weapon up when one of the men proclaimed, "Peace be unto you brother, we come in friendship. We are looking for Khan. He is expecting us."

Abdul studied the men carefully before speaking, "Peace be with you also. We do not know Khan."

The man that spoke first replied, "I understand your concern and caution. We know Khan is on this boat. The FBI killed the team in St Louis. The team managed to get a message to us to finish the mission. We are the backup team Khan put in place in Chicago. Please tell him we have arrived."

Kamal listened to the conversation while he pumped the fuel into the tanks. He finished, handing the hose back to Abdul and insisted, "Wait. I shall return."

Kamal knocked on the door to the cabin and heard, "Enter, what do you want?"

"Khan, two men are here claiming to be a backup team from Chicago. The team that did not show up are dead at the hands of the infidels. They claimed you are the one that placed them in Chicago."

Khan smiled. The first time Kamal had seen him smile.

"Show them to my cabin and wait outside," Khan commanded.

Kamal led the two strangers to Khan's cabin and then went back up to the deck. Smiling, Khan praised, "Ali Saed El-Hoorie and Ibrahim Al-Yacoub, welcome to my humble office."

Ibrahim marveled, "We thought this day would never come. When we received the message from our brothers before they died bravely, we thought the mission was over."

"The mission is not over. I have a few more adjustments to the device and then final activation at the target. This mission will move forward; nothing can stop us now. There is a change in the plan since I suspected capture of the other team when they failed to meet us."

Ali Saed asked, "What change? Does it have to do with the van we were instructed by the other team to bring with us? Khalid, the one that called us before he died, told us to make sure we understood this requirement."

"Yes, the van is important to move the barrel and device to the van so that we can set the bomb next to the target. The boat will be a decoy for anyone searching for us. I am extremely disappointed in Kamal and Abdul. They will be part of our decoy along with the other barrel they obtained," Khan's eyes hardened at the thought of the two imbeciles. The idea that someone would even think they could enhance his plan was so demeaning to his ego; his first instinct was to murder the offenders. "Also, there are plans I will include you in, just the two of you, no one else. There are spies among us."

Ibrahim noted the change in Khan. How distant and hard his eyes became as he explained the change in plans. Ibrahim was sternly warned about Khan and was more afraid of failing him than setting off a nuclear device that would kill a hundred thousand infidels.

After arranging an overnight slip under a false assumption, the boat members would be spending a leisurely night before continuing their fishing trip up the Illinois River. Kamal pulled away from the pumps. The dock fuel station owners and the restaurant were thrilled, so many people would patronize their establishment as it meant added income for the struggling restaurant.

* * *

The restaurant closed at nine. The team of five men and the men on the boat all consumed their last meals. One of the waitresses left about 15 minutes before closing. Khan and his men did not notice her going. As she drove home to her children, she felt a strange apprehension about the men showing up; all Middle Eastern descent caused her internal alarms to kick off. By ten o'clock, the restaurant owners and employees departed for their home's unsuspecting of the trawler and its contents.

* * *

By eleven o'clock, the five-person team moved the barrel off the trawler's deck at Khan's direction. The barrel had to be in an upright position and could not be bounced against the trawler's side or jarred in placement on the dock. The men strained in the humid night to meet his demands and put it into the van over the rear axles to make sure it could support the weight and give Khan room between the barrel and the seats to finish setting the timing devices. They needed to be out of the area before the business opened in the morning.

Khan made two decisions. The first one was to brief Kamal and Abdul about their roles as decoys with the trawler pushing up the river to Seneca. Unknown to them, Khan had placed a timing device in the explosives around their barrel they had thrust into his operation. A simple phone call would activate the timer, exploding on-demand by Khan.

He did not bother to address this since he wanted to kill both men for their disobedience and create a diversion. Both men believed they would abandon the trawler and escape the blast by the nuclear plant. The evil diversion would take place at six o'clock in the evening. The detonation Khan had in mind would be at five o'clock, catching both men by surprise. Problem solved.

The second decision was a core part of his plan. Khan, Ali-Saed, and Ibrahim sat in the coolness of his cabin, and Khan asked, "Did you acquire the rooms at the hotel near Seneca as I requested?"

Ali-Saed replied, "Yes, we have three rooms reserved at the Starlight Motel on Route 6. One room for you, one room for us, and one room for the four martyrs."

"Excellent. I want the other white van in place by four-thirty and ready to crash the gate at the plant once the diversion explosion pulls the guards away. Based on the pictures you took of the plant, the area to attack has gray cylinders, twenty-five feet high and twelve feet in circumference. These cylinders will be atop and part of a concrete pad.

There will be between twenty-four and thirty-seven cylinders on the pad.

"Exploding the device on the pad is mandatory. Inside of the cylinders is highly radioactive water. The explosion *will* create a cloud of deadly particles blasted high into the air. The weather systems will spread the particles with the wind and will contaminate and kill thousands of infidels."

Ibrahim liked the plan and knew parts of it previously. The detail he was most concerned with was gaining entry to the nuclear power plant grounds. Their recon of the area showed a large guard force and barriers, making penetration exceedingly tricky. The plant revealed doubled gates with what appeared to be a pit that could swallow a semi-truck and obstacles which looked like they arose from the ground. That nuclear plant would not be penetrated by a reinforced van no matter what plans were in place.

Both men knew Khan was not a tactician. His plan was a risk neither man was entirely willing to accept, but they would not openly challenge Khan's ideas as it would mean their deaths. Instead, they separately made their plans secretly. They had no intention of dying along with everyone else. Ibrahim confided, "Your plan is foolproof. We will be carrying it out correctly, Master."

* * *

The van was reinforced with heavy metal as a battering ram meant to break the gates. The vehicle made more substantial with the bomb containment barrel centered between the two axles and the weight aiding it as it crushes the barrier.

Khan made sure the bomb, packed with carefully shaped explosives in two layers around two plutonium half-spheres, met his specifications during construction. The shaped explosives in the outer shell would force the plutonium half spheres together, creating a supercritical mass. The nuclear chain reaction would instantaneously convert the bomb into the equivalent of five tons of TNT, which triggers X-rays that cause the rest of the nuclear weapon to detonate.

Khan aligned the detonator and explosive lens and attached the firing set. He had installed the command trigger circuit, arming device, and thermal battery in the last few hours. Once Khan inserted electric blasting caps, he sat back, trembling. He changed the command trigger circuit to activate off a telephone. They would be miles away from the blast. However, more work on the trigger device is necessary to ensure it functioned properly, thought Khan. His last act will be to weld the top of the barrel and lid together. The nuke was not yet ready for use. But the diversion bomb was all set to go in the other white van already at the motel. The yellow barrel was sitting on the trawler deck, lined with explosives around the exterior and would destroy the boat along with Kamal and Abdul.

CHAPTER TWENTY-FIVE:
Billy Thompson

* * *

Jack McGregor and Special Forces ODA-647 landed a quarter of a mile north of the river and the facility. The nuclear plant's security force just received a warning notification, "Alpha Alert Seven, the alert no one ever wanted to hear. *Attack of the facility is imminent – This is Not a Drill.*"

Jack sprinted toward the gate as he observed men running and armored vehicles moved into position. They assumed the attack would come from the north side of the plant, not the river. *What information are we missing, if any?* As he approached, he watched one of the guards pull up his scoped weapon, knowing, at once, he was the target and halted at 100 meters out from the gate.

He yelled, "Jack McGregor from the Defense Intelligence Agency and ODA-647. We are the team that initiated this alert. Lower your weapon; we are here on Presidential orders."

Jack caught sight of Captain Miller sprinting hard to catch up. He stopped next to Jack yelling at a man standing by an armored vehicle, "Billy, is that you? Billy Thompson from 10th Group, 2005, Baghdad?"

Jack watched the man cautiously step forward, stood for a moment, trying to locate Miller. He replied, "Damn, Joe, what the hell are you guys doing running up on us like that? We are about ready to smoke you. We're thinking … Never mind. Both of you slowly walk to the gate."

Jack allowed Miller to take the lead. Both men slowly walk with their weapons pointing down. The men behind the fence never lowered their guns, signaling Jack and Miller that Billy was not joking.

Jack did a visual survey as they approach the gate, recalling what he read concerning the established multiple defenses at the nuclear facility; he knows they come in several assorted flavors. Entrance into any plant by a vehicle would have to pass through a security checkpoint. The entire outer perimeter had substantial barricades with supermassive, reinforced concrete blocks, about 4 x 4 x 10 ft. They were designed to keep out *tanks*. Additionally, gates are booby-trapped with drop pits that can swallow an 18-wheeler or sheer a commercial truck in half. The entire complex is also under 24/7 surveillance. Just approaching the gate might not get the bomb close enough to do the needed damage, thought Jack.

Billy asked, "Joe, I recognize you, but not that other fella. Is he a spook, said he was with DIA?"

Jack held back from making any comments deciding it was best if Miller handled the negotiations at this point. Miller grunted, "Damn Billy, you are still the same, suspicious of everyone and everything. Jack is on our team assigned to DIA. We are tracking a terrorist who has a large group helping him. We believe he is about to deliver a nuclear device or dirty bomb to your doorstep."

The rest of the ODA sees what is happening and holds their positions so as not to provoke an unnecessary firefight. Taylor, listening carefully to the comms, to both Jack and Miller.

Billy was slowly mulling over and absorbing this information. He turned his head, looked at his team, and asked, "Is that your team out there by those Black Hawks?"

Jack, getting impatient, stepped into the conversation, "Billy, we do not have much time if our intel is correct. We need to give your team a briefing and coordinate our efforts. There is another ODA team inbound who should be arriving within the hour. Let's talk about this threat."

"I thought that is what we are doing, young man, discussing the threat. No one has given us any information about a terrorist. The only intel provided to anyone here is an imminent attack, then you all show up."

"We are not attacking you or this facility. We are trying to prevent it from becoming a pile of ashes," defensively Jack retorted.

Miller fumed, "Billy, I know this is coming quickly. I am sure you do not think we are the bad guys. Call someone in your chain of command to get a brief if you want, but we have to act soon."

"Joe, even I know the FBI is in charge of stuff like this. Where are they?" Billy suspiciously asked.

"The FBI is having coordination problems with their HRT. Their people have not deployed as far as we know. President Turnbull directed us to handle this situation because we are the only ones with the updated 'intel and immediately available. Would you like to talk to the President and ask him if we're OK?" Miller inquired.

Billy chuckled, "Damn straight, I would. If he says you guys are on a real mission, that is golden in my book, get him on the phone."

Jack looked to Miller, "He is calling your bluff. Better get some comms working."

"Bud, call General Webster and connect him to me," Miller yelled into his comms. While they waited, Miller questioned Billy, "Why are you so defensive? You know me. You know what we are and how we work. What has changed you?"

"What has changed is I am standing on top of a nuclear reactor, and if harmed or damaged because I fail at doing my job, I will be responsible for thousands of deaths; American deaths. I will not allow that to happen. No one, including you, my friend, will create a scenario that causes me or my team to fail.

"I see the world differently than you do, Joe. I cannot tell the difference between our friends and our enemies. There is nothing conventional, no flags or uniforms to help tell the difference. It is confusing. I stand by my statement, and I stand my ground. Until I know for sure who and what I am dealing with, no one tells me what to do regarding my job."

Jack asked, "I understand your responsibilities, and I see your point of view. Do you see ours? Jack is trying hard to respect Billy for his stance, but his stress-related PTSD is slipping into anger and impatience mode. He did not like authority, and Billy's position smelled like authority, working against Jack's timeline for action.

Within moments, the DIA Director is on the comms, "What's the problem, Captain?"

"We hit a slight snag. The security cadre at this nuclear facility seems to think we are the threat and will not allow us access to the plant. The chief of security will not talk to us about our mission. The supervisor, a retired SF guy I know, will only cooperate if the President directly informs him. He wants to hear the President on the phone."

"Damn it; I cannot just call the President on every decision; let me talk to Jack."

"Jack here, Miller is right in what he describes to you. We are running out of time. The supervisor refuses to allow an armed team on the plant because, as he specifically states, he is standing on a nuclear reactor, and his job is protection. He wants to hear the President's orders."

"Stand by and let me get him on the phone," General Webster grumbles.

Moments later, a slightly angry President Turnbull booms, "Jack, hand your comms to the supervisor there and let me talk to him."

Jack approached the gate smiling, "Billy, the President of the United States, would like to have a word."

Jack listened to the one-sided conversation as Billy explained his position, "Yes, Mr. President ... I understand ... of course I am ... I do recognize your authority ... yes, sir, I will comply ... yes, sir ..., no sir ... he wants to talk to you again," handing the comms back to Jack.

"Yes, Mr. President, ..." Jack replied.

"I do believe that he will cooperate now. Give me a situation report as soon as you can."

The comms went dead. Due to the comms' setup, everyone on the line, including Webster, just heard the best ass-chewing a President can give. Billy stood there with his butt chewed so thoroughly it fell off onto the ground. "Billy, what say we bring you up to date on what we're facing," Jack jeered, feeling a sort of satisfaction that POTUS zinged Billy. He heard one of Billy's men tell him that their chain of command just received a phone call from the President directing them to cooperate. Verification is now complete.

"Let's talk. I did not like that at all, but I guess I asked for it." Billy turned to his men and told everyone to stand down.

Jack motioned for ODA-647 to approach the facility, and as they moved forward, some of the team branched off, setting up another security line.

* * *

As the sun reached into the morning sky, Khan and his team drove away from the restaurant. They had a relatively short ride of twenty miles to Seneca and the motel. Since the rooms had already been reserved by the team a day earlier, there would be no check-in issues.

The white van pulled into the back, parked on the motel's north side, hidden away from the main road. The team covered the van's windows from the inside. Then, after being up all night, the Jihadists went to their rooms to rest.

The motel, nondescript with faded paint and a sign outside with partially working neon lights, was a great pick. They would not draw attention as they rested. Before securing the van, they placed placards on each side of the unmarked van that read, "Abraham's Janitorial Service, Call Us at 312-883-6520". The license plates were also changed to reflect a commercial business vehicle. Another white van sat in the parking lot with identical signage on it.

Khan was not worried about the trawler's explosives impacting their location. The bomb was enough to destroy the trawler and the two idiots. Kamal and Abdul did not understand that the barrel contents were not radioactive, only medical garbage of little concern. This barrel was an unexpected gift for Khan's plan. He was going to make full use of it. The rest of his plan still needed to be shown to his team, but only in parts.

They would be disappointed with the power plant, which is not the actual target. Khan decided it would be difficult to penetrate the facility to create extensive damage from an explosion. He deceived the team members appointed as martyrs allowing them to believe the nuclear plant was the intended target — martyrdom by betrayal senseless.

The other white van driven by a single Jihadist was delivered to the motel two days before the operational team had arrived. The mission and plan were slowly coming together. Inside the other van sat a barrel holding explosives but no nuclear material. This van was to be driven by the martyrs to the nuclear plant.

Another decoy, another misleading attack, as Khan and his remaining four Jihadists drove the other white van containing the actual atomic device to the Chicago outskirts. His target was the heart of the secret financial computer systems that stored Wall Street, the Chicago Exchange, and the Federal Monetary System. The destruction of this site would cause the collapse of the financial system in the Great Satan. On top of economic devastation, the psychological edge of a nuclear explosion in the heartland would indeed create havoc.

In his room, Khan turned on the TV and watched the breaking news of another misleading attack he planned, drawing authorities away from Chicago. The newscaster exclaimed, "In the latest attacks against the United States by terrorists, Sarin gas is suspected in the most recent attacks at multiple casinos in Las Vegas.

"Reports coming in from law enforcement describe several Middle Eastern men, observed by patrons in the casinos, running through the area with spray containers. Security personnel quickly reacted by shooting two of the three men. However, enough gas has been released to cause an unknown number of causalities. More news to follow as we get it from official sources. Reporting to you live from Las Vegas, this is Jennifer Schultz for TV15."

Khan smiled and laid back on his bed.

CHAPTER TWENTY-SIX:
Spies

* * *

Less than four miles east of O'Hare International Airport, on State Route 19, is the tiny enclave of Oakfield Park. A business and industrial area is primarily known for its many buildings housing various enterprises and small businesses.

None of the buildings exceeded five stories, except one. That building had six levels of nondescript offices containing computers with blinking lights emanating from panels. Rows and rows of machines always at work, collecting information, and storing in various data banks housed in the basement underneath the parking garage.

Khalid Abu Farouq, his two wives, and two sons worked at this building as the janitorial team keeping all the dust and dirt from accumulating on the computers that function twenty-four seven. They had worked for two years quietly managing to collect information on the building: its structure, how many rooms, and how many computers. Several doors were locked in the parking garage next to the main building preventing access to the janitorial team.

They befriended the guards who roamed the facility and protected the entrance. They cleaned every room in the building many times. The only area they had not been able to access were the rooms underneath the parking garage. Only a few can gain access to that area, and they had failed at trying to offer their services to clean that section of the *cool site.*

Two weeks earlier, Khalid received notification Khan was coming for the mission they had been working toward for the past two years. Their time in Satan's lair was almost up. Soon they could return to Syria. Khalid's family would be meeting Khan to present him with the building's blueprints and, most importantly, the parking garage. Khalid had no idea as to what Khan's ultimate plan is, except to destroy the building. He wrongly assumed it was with a conventional car bomb.

* * *

The Wind moved slowly from the slip back into the current of the river, eastbound. Abdul and Kamal received their final instructions, believing they were the trigger to destroy a nuclear power plant. They had no idea they would be nothing more than a tactical diversion, a feint, to Khan's operation's real purpose. They soon would be a bloody mist, never knowing the betrayal.

The trawler stayed close to the shoreline and moving leisurely at two knots so as not to draw attention. They looked like they were trolling for fish.

* * *

High above in the early morning skies, a Predator drone slowly searched the river for a trawler. The drone operator, sitting at his flight control desk, watching the screen while sipping coffee, noted a trawler was moving slowly along the river. He reached over and pushed the toggle stick, increasing his zoom by moving the camera to focus directly above the trawler.

The image enlarged on the screen as he pushed the camera slightly back and forth, searching for a name on the boat. Also, he tried to determine who was in the wheelhouse, then turning to his assistant, he suggested, "Check this out. It may be the trawler we have been searching for."

"Look at the mid-deck; there is a canvass cloth slightly collapsed over what appears to be a barrel. Look, I see one person in the wheelhouse, at least a shadow of a person," the assistant claimed.

"Roger that. Let's see if we can get a view of a name," The operator lowered the nose of the Predator, shifted it for a better angle of view, circling at 15,000 feet.

"Got it, the name is *The Wind*," he exclaimed. The operator instructed his assistant to contact Eagle One, confirming their find and location of the trawler at grid coordinate 223456, about one mile east of Ottawa, Illinois, moving slowly.

* * *

Special Forces Operational Detachment Alpha – 890 with 12 team members and one bomb tech from the local Explosive Ordnance Detachment at Fort Campbell landed near ODA-647's perimeter. The team commanding officer, Captain Michael Marlow, walked up to Chief Warrant Officer Taylor taking a knee next to him. "Chief, I am Captain Marlow. Can you show me Captain Miller, or do you want to brief me?" he asked.

"Sir, the boss is briefing the security detail at the facility. I am to hold until he gives us a signal to come forward. I suggest your team blend in for the moment with my guys. I can give you a quick update until you can discuss this mission with the Captain. We are chasing a terrorist with a nuclear bomb and believe this may be his target. We had a little issue with the facility's security team, but that's all corrected now. We are acting under Presidential orders to locate, capture, or kill the bad guys and disarm the nuclear bomb," he replied, smiling at the blank look on the team commander's face.

Taylor stood up as Jack came running toward the group. "I am Jack with DIA," he informed Marlow. "Chief, hold what you have, Marlow; you are to come with me. It looks like they spotted the trawler a few miles from here on the river. Predator found them, but the Predator is not armed, according to the report we just received on the landline."

Without another word, Jack turned and ran back toward the facility gate, Marlow right behind him. As they approached, the men gathered at the facility. Miller turned around and said, "Mike, how the hell are you? Homecoming has never been better." Miller nodded at the other man next to him, "You remember Billy Thompson from Baghdad and 10th Group?"

Marlow teased, "What in the hell is going on, Joe? Your Chief just scared the hell out of me about a terrorist running around with a nuke. Hi Billy, nice to see you again."

"The Chief has it right," Jack ventured. "We are chasing a guy named Khan, who is a nuclear physicist and appears to have a nuke he wants to deliver to us at this place. We need to stop him!"

"We just received word the trawler we have been searching for is on the river about five miles or better from us. We think the nuclear device is aboard, and the trawler is moving slow." Miller reported. "I will have to brief you as we reposition ourselves to intercept the trawler. It looks like it will come near the back of the facility."

A phone rang, and everyone looked around. Jack realized it was his phone on the second ring and dragged it out of his back pocket. "Yes, … OK …Paige, again, slow down. Are you sure? What does your gut tell you…? OK … Reach out to the FBI and ask them if they know the location of those types of sites. Call me back when you have some answers." He hung up and looked at Miller and Marlow.

"This place may not be the primary target." Jack thought, *Is the nuke on the trawler or not? It is not time to have doubts*. He kept his thoughts to himself.

Jack's head was reeling. "We're like dogs chasing our tail. Las Vegas is under attack with Sarin gas. Abbas imparted some information suggesting this facility may be a diversion, and the actual target is some financial sites near Chicago. Of course, no one knows where specifically."

Miller retorted, "We need to check out the trawler no matter what if nothing more than to confirm your suspicions."

Jack verified, "I agree. Billy and his crew can hold this down. You and Marlow's team head for the river and set up an ambush for the trawler. I will brief DIA and Webster; maybe they know something about these so-called sites near Chicago."

Miller turned to Billy and ordered, "Hold this position. We are going after the trawler." All three men turned and ran towards the teams waiting near the Black Hawks.

CHAPTER TWENTY-SEVEN:
The Deception

* * *

"What can I do for you both before you leave this life to be with Allah?" asked Khan.

Young impressionable martyrs viewed their pending sacrifice to honor Allah, the Jihad, and all of Islam. Both men, terrified of their imminent death, hid their fear. The younger one pleaded, "Please tell my mother I have rendered a great service to Allah."

The other man, staring out the window of the motel room, stated calmly, "May Allah be pleased with my sacrifice in my Jihad. Tell my father I have done what he requested."

"Your father and mother will know about your heroic deaths and the meaning of your great sacrifice." Khan continued his lie, "You will deliver the nuclear bomb to the plant, and upon entrance, trigger the device. I will remove the shield from the container before you get into the van, exposing you to enough radiation that will kill you slowly within seven days — tremendous pain results from that type of exposure. By exploding the device, your death will be fast and painless, finding yourself, seconds later, with the promised 72 virgins. *Allah Akbar! Allah Akbar! Allah Akbar!* Khan belched, with the others joining in.

"In two hours, drive the van to the facility's front gate following your normal routine, providing cleaning service for the past eighteen months. The arrival time is critical for the mission. As the trawler explodes to provide a diversion, you must prepare to crush any barriers to reach the containers."

Both men nod in agreement, then turn, leaving the room to prepare for their deaths.

* * *

Jack finished talking with Webster. The General was not happy. He expected results and Jack's analysis of the ongoing situation to be correct and on track. Unfortunately, Jack did not have all the puzzle pieces and could not verify the right target for Webster. Jack was upset with himself, believing he missed something in his interrogation with Abbas. The operation was flipped on its head by Paige's latest information. Turning to the EOD technician sitting nearby. Jack asked, "What is your name?"

"Sergeant Judd Bennett, or just Judd," he replied.

"How do you disarm a nuclear device," Jack queried.

"You don't. The easiest way is to disarm the conventional explosives' trigger, stopping the weapon from going off. Suppose the explosives detonate when the trigger is activated. In that case, they force two pieces of plutonium into a perfect sphere causing neutrons to penetrate the nuclear material, creating a chain reaction and implosion. Then it is bye-bye in a flash!"

"Let's get down to the river to support the ambush. Judd, you'll have to get aboard that trawler and disarm the device. We have no idea who is on the boat, nor how they will respond when they trip the ambush." Both men stood picking up their weapons. Jack turned to the pilots, "Since we have four Army choppers, one of you can inform the two Air Force birds to return to St Louis. There is no reason to expose additional personnel to a nuclear explosion."

Chief Warrant Officer Five Chris Knight offered, "I'll handle that. Is there anything we can do at this point? I believe our presence is needed. Besides, I am not sure how far the blast radius may be and what is considered a safe distance. My mission is to support you guys on the ground, and that is impossible if I'm ten or fifteen miles away."

"Thanks, Chief. I guess we're all in on this one. I can't think of anything else you can do."

Trotting, Jack and Judd took off to the river's edge. When Jack arrived, he spotted Miller and Marlow. Miller was talking to Sergeant

Lee, his sniper, "... so you can get a clean shot of the wheelhouse. Do not wait on an order. If you have a clean shot, take it. We'll have men in the water who will swim to the trawler. The initiation of the ambush will happen in one of several ways: you're shooting at the wheelhouse, the discovery of men in the water, or if we open up from the river bank."

"Jack, what was the General's reaction to our plan?" Miller asked.

"He was pissed, and he ended the call with a question, 'Can you stop the nuke from going off?' I assured him we could."

Miller looked at Bennett, asking, "Can you swim?"

"Yes, sir, not an issue. Just get me on the boat without getting me shot."

Miller turned to Marlow, "Can you put two of your men with the EOD sergeant and make sure he gets aboard the trawler?"

"Will do." Signaling two men who are in a crouch position in the reeds, "You two make sure this young Sergeant gets aboard to defuse that bomb."

Two Black Hawk helicopters went screaming overhead in a southerly direction. Reading their expressions, Jack did not wait for questions and informed Miller and Marlow, "I gave the order for both to return to St Louis."

"What kind of ambush are we setting up?" Jack asked.

"We are going to try an "L" shaped ambush. I have five men extended into the river: waist-deep. They will crouch low, submerged up to their necks.

"The rest will be spread out among the reeds and river. Sergeant Lee is situated about halfway up in that oak tree. Under the circumstances, the structure of the ambush is the best we can do. Our primary goal is to get on the boat," Miller explained.

"OK. I'm going to center myself on the riverbank above the reeds in a prone position. About there," Jack gestures to a jumble of logs and rocks at the curve of the river.

All the men took their positions and lay low in the reeds. It became tranquil and still as the sun climbs higher into the sky. Jack noticed the sun was obscured partly by the clouds, working to the team's advantage by creating shadows on the water and along the bank, keeping the men masked. In the distance, getting louder, a diesel engine chugged slowly. All eyes were on the river. The ambush position was a mile from the facility.

* * *

The two martyrs left the room and walked down the stairs, noting two vans bearing the cleaning service's name. Khan stood next to the one van containing the non-nuclear explosives, allowing the martyrs to believe it was the nuke. "The protective shield has been removed. Once inside the truck, do not leave for any reason."

Both men quickly entered the vehicle; in their minds, they were now dead. They did not look back at their cargo. The passenger picked up the toggle switch with the button holding it in his hand. The wire snaked underneath the seat and to the van's back to a hole drilled in the barrel. The driver started up the van, slowly pulling away. As they rounded the corner of the motel, a woman waved at them from the front door of the office. They did not return her gesture and turned onto the road heading west. Their pending death and trip to hell would happen in ten miles.

Khan instructed Ali Saeed and Ibrahim to ride with him in the other van. The other two Jihadists would drive the blue sedan providing security to Khan on the journey to Chicago.

* * *

Several calls trying to locate FBI Special Agent in Charge Percy Bolton were unsuccessful. All Paige could do was leave messages. While she waited for a return call, she drafted a report on what she believed to be accurate from Abbas's discussion. Included what she felt were possibilities and short link analysis of her conversations with him. Nothing in the link analysis connected as quickly as she hoped it would. The thought entered her head, *"What if I got this all wrong? Jack and the entire team will die; thousands of people killed? Damn it!"*

Before the first ring of the phone could complete its cycle, she exclaimed, "This is Paige."

"Bolton here. I heard you were trying to locate me. What's up?"

Paige described the interview of Abbas, explaining her thoughts and what she believed were possibilities. "The truth of this is in the possibilities of Abbas's explanation and cannot be discarded. I believe the real targets are the server sites. Have you any knowledge of these buildings? Are these sites real? Is stored information about our country's financial data located in these buildings?"

"They are real, and it will take me about 30 minutes to fix their location. First, I need to make a couple of calls to verify the locations. I'll call you back."

Paige's attention was drawn to the helicopters outside of the hanger. Thinking Jack had returned, she ran to the door. The Black Hawks rolled up to their previous positions. She watched the chief crew jump from the side door and threw blocks under the wheels as the engine noise dropped, the rotors slowed and stopped. No one else exited the helicopters. She ran to the crew chief.

"What happened?" she demanded.

"I don't know. We were told to leave in a hurry," replied the crew chief.

The pilot dismounted his seat and heard part of the conversation, chiming in, "Your team is still at the nuclear plant. They were setting up an ambush for the trawler. Four Army birds came in with another team and are also on the ground. That's all I know."

Paige returned to the hanger and waited by the phone. The wait was nerve-racking. She was stuck with no place to go. Her thoughts turned to Jack and how she felt. Her emotions roiled with worry, and tears dampened her eyes. Jack could be injured or killed. At that moment, her true feelings for Jack surfaced, and she knew she was really in love.

Paige's inner thoughts were disturbed by the ringing phone, and she grabbed it before the second ring. "Yes…this is Anderson."

"Bolton here. The information is correct. There are specific buildings near O'Hare Airport that contain financial computers." He rattled off the address. I have to say the FBI analyst still believes the nuclear plant is the target based on the computers we seized, the maps, and other documents. There are no indications otherwise."

"It's a diversion. I've talked to Abbas for days as we traveled together from Afghanistan to Panama and here in St Louis. After a while, you get to know a person and sense when he is truthful. I'm telling you the plant is not the target for the nuclear device."

"I'm sure you are adept at being an analyst for DIA, but I have to go with our people on their evaluation. We dispatched our Hostage Rescue Team to Seneca to help the SF guys. They are in the air and should be there any minute. You have a great theory, but that is all it is. If there is nothing else, I need to go."

"No, nothing else. Are you at least sending anyone to check out the address?" Paige asked.

Bolton's irritation was obstructive. "No, we are not. As far as I'm concerned, this is a dead issue. Bye."

Paige looked at the silent phone caught in a conundrum. She immediately dialed Jack's number, but it went to voice mail. "Damn it, Jack," muttering under her breath. She tried two more times with the same results. This time left a message, "Jack, I'm heading for O'Hare Airport in Chicago. The address where I believe the nuke will explode is 9786 University Drive, Oakfield Park, Illinois. They call it a cool site, a storage area with servers and computers keeping all country's financial data. Abbas believes it is the main target for the nuke. I'll call again once I'm there."

Paige exited the hanger and walked toward several buildings that looked like offices. Finding the one she wanted, she knocked on the door and heard, "Enter."

"General McMichael, I'm Paige Anderson, DIA analyst on the team with Jack McGregor."

"Yes, I'm aware of who you are; what can I do for you."

"I need to borrow three items from you. An airplane to take me to O'Hare Airport, and two M-4 automatic rifles for the MPs traveling with me guarding Abbas. Jack requested we meet him and the rest of the team there."

"OK, but why the M-4's and will I get them back?"

"I just spoke with the FBI. There is a good chance we can intercept Khan near O'Hare and I need Abbas to identify him. There may be other terrorists with him. Jack requested all military be fully armed."

"OK, I will call the flight operations center and ready my Gulf Stream for you. Say in about one hour with fueling requirements and getting a pilot here."

"Thank you, I appreciate all your help, sir. We'll pass that on to the President."

Paige left the office, heading back to the hanger without one ounce of remorse that she lied to the General. She was angry that no one believed her.

Paige found the two MPs guarding Abbas's room. "We are going on a trip to Chicago. Let me in so I can talk to Abbas."

As the door opened, Abbas looked up, and Paige uttered, "We're taking a little trip to Chicago to test the information you provided earlier. Be ready to leave in about forty minutes." She quickly turned, leaving the room, making sure the two MPs heard her instructions to Abbas. "Meet me at the hanger entrance with Abbas in forty minutes."

While waiting, she gathered her belongings off the operations table in her trade's hanger and essential tools, her computer.

At four-thirty in the late afternoon, Paige, Abbas, and two MPs stood at the hangar door, observing a sleek Gulf Stream with Air Force markings roll up to a parking position. General McMichael walked up with two Security Policeman, each carrying an M-4. "You will have to sign for these," he ordered, addressing the MPs.

Without a word, the MPs signed the documents taking possession of the M-4's and a bandolier of ammunition, each containing twenty magazines for their newly assigned weapons. Both expertly adjusted the slings and placed them on their shoulders, barrels down for the plane ride. Abbas looked up at the sky, taking it all in, and felt a chill run down his spine. His warning of death was close at hand.

Paige turned to the General and hinted, "We need one more item. A vehicle on the other end, maybe an SUV."

"No problem, young lady, you will also have a vehicle. I will make arrangements while we're in flight. We'll discuss this while we are airborne." General McDaniel sternly said.

Paige suddenly felt a pang of fear in the pit of her stomach. Her lie, had it been discovered?

CHAPTER TWENTY-EIGHT:
The Ambush

* * *

Jack looked down the river for the trawler. Before laying down in a prone position behind some boulders and dead trees, he'd turned off his phone. Silence gripped the area as everyone strained to see the trawler. The sun was moving and setting to the west, just enough to make the vision of the trawler difficult as it moved east. The only breaks were from the clouds as the sun played hide and seek in the heavens.

Jack looked over his shoulder. A white van moved down the road towards the front of the facility. He turned his attention back to the sound of the trawler.

* * *

The security force led by Billy Thompson spread out to predesignated areas scanning for anything unusual. The white van approaching was not uncommon and expected at this time of day. The van would be allowed into the sally port area as part of the regular security practices it has gone through for several years.

The van slowly pulled up to the outer gates and sat waiting as the gates opened. The two martyrs waited patiently. Psychologically, they had already given up and accepted death. They looked straight ahead as they typically did when entering the sally port. Once they cleared the security review, the inner gates would open. Once inside, it allowed them to enter the inner compound and recalling Khan's instructions to make a run at the gray cylinders located to their right on concrete pads, just before the main building before detonation or to explode the bomb if they were about to be caught, before reaching the cylinders.

Thompson positioned himself near the front entrance of the main building. His men spread out across the wide-open area, some behind cement structures and some in the open. All watched, but none suspected the white van.

* * *

Sergeant Lee hiding in the big oak tree was the first to spot the trawler and whispered in his comms, "Target acquired... standby..."

The tension mounted as the trawler slowly bobbed in the water, pushing forward. Three swimmers from the reeds slowly moved forward as the boat neared their position. As they touched the side and grabbed a handhold of the railing, Sergeant Lee said, "Execute...execute..." and fired one shot from his weapon, striking the head of whoever was in the wheelhouse.

The suppressor on his weapon subdued the blast of the gun. The boat momentarily shuddered and turned out to the middle of the river and then back to the shoreline. The three men on the side of the trawler climbed aboard. One of the SF troopers went for the wheelhouse, and steadied the wheel, and cut back the engine to stop. The soldier in the middle of the other two headed straight for the barrel found mid-deck. As the boat stopped, other SF team members swam to the trawler climbing aboard.

Below deck, Kamal felt the boat stop and heard boots hitting the exterior deck. He picked up his AK-47 and rushed to the upper deck, firing as he opened the door, cutting down two soldiers. Three soldiers returned fire, peppering Kamal's chest with well-aimed shots as his bloody corpse hit the wooden deck.

The bomb tech opened the barrel, noting nothing inside except medical garbage. He pulled the rest of the canvass back, exposing multiple layers of plastic explosives around the outside of the barrel. Judd bent down and went to work at once, inspecting the various connected wires, and then he noticed the small mobile phone attached. The phone lit up as the incoming call was received, and the trawler disappeared in a blinding flash.

The explosion was big and loud. The concussion knocked Sergeant Lee out of the tree and left Jack unconscious. Marlow and his team disappeared in the blast. Miller lifted out of the water, thrown onto the riverbanks with two broken legs and a broken arm. Taylor and Lopez were in the leg portion of the "L" shaped formation just far enough away to be knocked unconscious, bleeding from their ears and eyes and left floating in the water.

Chief Warrant Officer Talbot, the team medic /physician's assistant, had his left eardrum blown out and was bleeding down the side of his face. He dragged himself out of the river moving directly to Miller, lying on the ground, unconscious with obviously broken legs, and rendered medical attention.

* * *

Thompson and his men heard the explosion and immediately went to the ground. The two guards in the sally port looked around in the direction of the blast as the two martyrs quickly shot both men dead.

The driver hit the gas on the van ramming the gate, breaking it open but not far enough for the vehicle to move through. It backed up and ran into the portal again, full force. Thompson and his men opened fire when they saw the two security guards fall, and the van rammed the gate, immediately killing the driver.

The passenger's reflexes had been to recline in the seat. He had the trigger to the bomb. Realizing he could not get the weapon to the facility's interior, he let go of the button on the dead man's switch. The bomb exploded, turning vehicle parts into shrapnel, hitting the exposed guards, killing them instantly. A front axle to the van flew across the open area, striking Thompson midsection and cutting him in half.

The sally port disappeared. One of the gates tore loose and flew across the open field, hitting a Black Hawk in the rotor housing unit and crushing the engine. The crews fell from the concussion of the blast onto the asphalt. They looked on with horror as a large black mushroom-like cloud rose two hundred feet above the main gate.

The FBI helicopter carrying the HRT was close enough to catch the concussion from the river's first blast. The pilot corrected his flight heading and turned toward the facility when the second blast hit the chopper, sending it out of control, spinning madly into a line of trees on the far side of the access road. The helicopter exploded, taking out the entire FBI team.

The Army pilots and crew chiefs raced toward the facility. They could not see anyone moving and, not sure of what type of explosive they were dealing with, halted their advance. CW5 Knight ordered, "Back to your birds, grab your medical kits and head for the river to check on the SF guys, move it now!" Knight drew his weapon and ran toward the river with the other three pilots while the crew chiefs retrieved the medical bags.

* * *

The Gulf Stream climbed steeply out of St Louis and banked hard to the East for Chicago, about one hour away. Both MPs and Abbas sat at the rear of the cabin. Paige and the General sat near the door to the cockpit staring at each other. "What is going on? Why the lie?" asked General McMichael.

Paige adjusted herself. In the next several minutes, the lie she used to obtain the plane was about to be exposed. "I have information that no one seems willing to accept as a true possibility about Khan's real target. The FBI wouldn't believe what I had to say; I couldn't get Jack or the team on the cell. Finally, Abbas is telling me the truth. Someone has to try and stop Khan, and we are it."

"I do not like being lied to for any reason. For all I know, you are going on a shopping trip in Chicago, that is why I'm on board. I can recognize a lie. Telling me the truth would have been a better decision on your part. I'm a reasonable man. I'm willing to listen. By the time we reach O'Hare, you had better convince me that this trip is vital, or I will order this jet turned around. Are we clear?"

"Yes, sir."

Before Paige could begin her explanation about what Abbas said to her, the cockpit door opened. The co-pilot said, "General, you are needed on the radio right away."

"Ms. Anderson, I'm not finished. Hold that thought. I'll be right back."

CHAPTER TWENTY-NINE:
Failure and Death

* * *

Knight and his fellow pilots and crew chiefs entered the battleground of hell. Human body parts lay over a wide area. Knight refocused and saw one of the medics working on another soldier. He raced to them, announcing his presence, and offering assistance.

Talbot shook his head. "My eardrums... blown, I can't hear you. Put pressure on the wound of this soldier," as blood ran out of both ears and down his cheeks.

Knight dropped to his knees and applied the necessary pressure as his men fanned out to others lying on the ground writhing in pain. Knight noted the rank of the soldier, Captain, his face bloody and unrecognizable. He read the name tag on the uniform, Miller.

"Where is Captain Marlow?" he screamed at Talbot.

"No idea, he was further down the river from our position," Talbot yelled.

Knight turned to his crew chief with the medical bag and barked, "Stay here with him, place your hands here, and put pressure on this wound. Give me your bag."

Knight took off, looking at each soldier he came across, checking for signs of life. Almost everyone was unconscious or seemed so, maybe even dead. He reached the end of the area but could not find Marlow. He went back up the riverbank and joined several other people treating the fallen.

* * *

Sergeant Lee picked himself up off the ground. Still stunned by the concussion and fall from fifteen feet up in the tree, he unsteadily made his way toward the carnage. Jack was lying on his side by some boulders, not moving. Everyone was pulling together to help each other; he turned his attention to Jack.

A close examination of Jack revealed blood coming from his left ear. The explosion appeared to have punctured his eardrum. Jack was coming around and struggled, managed to sit up with the help of Lee.

* * *

Jack's head was spinning, and his hearing was affected. He saw Lee's mouth moving but heard no sound except a rushing noise. Slowly his ability to recognize speech started to seep into his brain. Lee sounded far away. The pain on the left side of his face forced him to reach up slowly and placed his hand on his cheek and jaw to feel if his sore face got ripped away. He withdrew a bloody hand.

Lee screamed at him, "You're OK, the blood is from your ear. A busted eardrum. Do you have any more pain in your body?" Jack shook his head. "OK, I am going to check on the rest of the team. Stay here; it's over."

Jack slowly looked around, trying to gather his thoughts. He could see Talbot working on someone. He could see Taylor and what appeared to be Lopez lying on the riverbank in the other direction. There were others, but his eyes had a tough time focusing and identifying the soldiers. He slowly rose and fell back down, his legs wobbly. Again, he tried and, even though not steady on his feet, started to walk to Taylor.

As he got near Taylor, Jack shouted, "Can you hear me?"

There was no response, and his breathing was labored but regular in rhythm, and nothing was torn open or bleeding on his body. Jack bent down and started checking him but found nothing. Finally, he looked at another soldier nearby and realized it was Lopez. He went to him and repeated the exact search he had conducted on Taylor, yelling, "Danny, can you hear me?" Jack noted Danny stirring, starting to move, and then his eyes blinked open and closed again. "Danny, this is Jack. Can you hear me?"

Suddenly Danny sat up, "Shit, that was one hell of an explosion. Was it nuclear?

"I do not think so. There is nothing but boat debris floating on the river, and all other nearby structures, trees, and plants remain standing. Most importantly, we are still here and not fried. I would say no to a nuclear blast. How are you feeling?" Jack asked.

"Like a bad night with Tequila, maybe worse." Looking at Taylor, "How is he? Is he alive?"

"Yes, he is alive but is unconscious, like you were. Just waiting for medical help before I do anything to him, like trying to wake him up. I saw Talbot working on someone; let me see if I can get him over here."

Jack left Danny sitting next to Taylor and stumbled toward who he believed to be Talbot. His eyes were watery and still trying to adjust. In the distance, he could hear sirens and knew help was on the way. He saw the soldier's legs and an arm splinted with various wood pieces picked up off the ground as he arrived. A closer examination of the wood disclosed parts of the trawler. The soldier applying pressure was one of the crew chiefs of the Black Hawk. He heard Talbot yell at the soldier, "Release your pressure now," as Talbot applied bandages and started to wrap the wound.

Jack bent over and helped Talbot. That is when he recognized Miller. Jack could see Talbot had been bleeding out both of his ears and understood the yelling. Jack yelled, "Will Joe make it?" Talbot looked up and nodded his head.

Talbot screamed again at the soldier and ordered him to aid others. Jack yelled at Talbot that he needed him to come to where Taylor and Danny were lying to examine them. Talbot nodded, picking up his medical bag.

They both walked back to Taylor; Talbot yelled, "My hearing," pointing at his ears... "shot, I can barely make out what anyone is saying." Jack responded by showing him his left ear and yelled, "Same here."

Talbot started working on Taylor, parting his hair looking for open injuries. He then pulled his stethoscope and started to put it in his ears, stopping, realizing that it would be useless. He instead placed his hand over Taylor's heart and along his neck to feel for a pulse. He then went to Lopez and yelled, "Danny, how do you feel?"

"Like crap, my head hurts. I am having trouble focusing my eyes," Danny yelled back.

Jack was down on his knees next to Danny when Talbot rendered his assessment. "Looks like traumatic brain injury right now. We need to get everyone to a hospital for CAT scans and a more thorough examination than I can give here."

Jack yelled, "I am going to ask those pilots to transport these men to the nearest trauma center if we can identify one," and Jack left, heading toward the senior pilot, Knight.

Jack explained to Knight what Talbot had said, "We need to start getting the men to the helicopters." Knight replied, "I can do you one better. See that open area about a quarter of a mile upriver. I can set one bird down at a time and load from there. Get everyone moved to that clearing. I will get the other pilots ready. The explosion damaged one of our aircraft; we're down to three birds."

"Do you have enough fuel to make multiple runs to a hospital?" Jack asked.

"Yes, we refueled about fifty miles from here at a small airport; we're good."

"OK, got it, I will start organizing whoever can move people. Do you have any stretchers on your Black Hawks? Jack asked.

"Yes." He turned to the nearby crew member and ordered him to sprint for the helicopters and retrieve all the stretchers and bring them down to the wounded.

Jack soon realized that most of ODA-890 were dead in the explosion, including Marlow. Two of his men were left alive but seriously injured. ODA-647 was in somewhat better shape, but not by much; everyone sustained a wound. So far, Miller and Taylor seemed to be in the worst condition. They, and two from the other team, were put on stretchers and taken first to the extraction LZ. Sirens announced the arrival of help as one Black Hawk after the other touched down, picking up the survivors.

* * *

Knight located twenty-three level-one trauma centers in or near Chicago and other parts of Illinois. The communications director for these facilities had him spread out the wounded to the nearest three centers so the medical system would not be overburdened. Knight headed straight for the nearest one in Chicago, calling ahead, telling ground operations, who they were, and the type of injuries to expect.

* * *

Jack was the last to be evacuated since he determined he had the least of the injuries suffered. He was on the return flight with Knight, making fast travel at 800 feet, asking for immediate clearance of the airways to the trauma center through the FAA and air traffic controllers at Midway Airport. Jack's flashbacks to Vietnam made him sick; this was too much like being back in that war.

* * *

Khan's vehicle left Seneca on Route 6, heading for I-80 East maintaining legal speed. Once on I-80, they would travel about fifteen miles and pick up I-55 North to Chicago. Pulling onto Route 6, Khan noted the time on his watch. The martyrs would be in place now. He picked up the cell phone and pulled up a number, waited for two breaths, and sent the signal.

Just as Khan and his fellow Jihadists reached the I-80 turn-off, they heard an explosion in the distance. A second, much louder, explosion followed several minutes later, denting the air.

Khan and his henchmen turned onto I-80 and headed toward Chicago, the recipient of his "gift" for the country he despised more than Israel. Khan more comfortable now about completing his plan. The plan worked in ways he least expected and much better than he hoped. Allah was indeed on his side. "We need to find a place that sells electrical wire. I need a specific one to finish the trigger device," he ordered the driver.

* * *

The General returned from the cockpit, peering down at Paige, a brutal look in his eyes. Then, as he took his seat on the Gulf Stream across from Paige, he glanced at Abbas. Paige instinctively braced herself for a challenging conversation and criticism from the General. "Paige, I am sorry for doubting your instincts, and I now understand why you lied. I just received a message about two explosions at and near the nuclear power plant. There are mass causalities.

"Preliminary reports show the entire security unit at the facility is dead. The destroyed Special Forces teams with some survivors still alive have been evacuated to three different level-one trauma centers in and around Chicago. I suspect you are close to Jack since you are both from DIA. I'm sorry to report I have no direct information on him."

Paige, stunned, sat in silence. Not expecting to hear this from the General, she started to feel sick to her stomach. She tried to organize her feelings and put her emotions in check. The only thing she could ask was, "Nuclear or conventional explosions?"

"Preliminary information indicates conventional; however, the Nuclear Emergency Support Teams or NEST have "sniffer" aircraft flying into the area to see if they can detect any signs of a nuclear explosion or leaks from the facility. So, we should know something within the hour."

Paige slumped in her seat, her emotions raw and tearing at her, her thinking crushed. She tried desperately to force her brain back into the mission. Khan had to be found, and soon.

"General, are we still going to O'Hare?"

"Yes, we should be landing in twenty-five minutes."

CHAPTER THIRTY:
Its Chicago!

* * *

Jack patiently sat in the treatment room. His left ear ached from the perforated eardrum. The rushing noise decreased, and some of his hearing returned. The doctor walked in with a nurse asking, "Were you with the blown-up Army guys?"

"What did you say?"

Raising his voice, he repeated, "Were you in that explosion?"

"Yes, the left side of my face hurts, and my hearing is screwed up."

"OK, sit still, the nurse will clean you up, and I will examine your ear. You are one of the lucky ones."

The nurse quickly started cleaning the blood off his face and swabbed out his ear. She did a preliminary check around his head, searching for additional injuries. She took his temperature, blood pressure, and heart rate, recording the results onto a clipboard.

"I'm Doctor Kennedy. I am also a combat veteran of Iraq and have witnessed these types of injuries before. It is my understanding of this injury caused by an IED or something along those lines."

"Correct doc."

"Can you tell me anything else about the explosion?"

"No, I was knocked unconscious in the initial blast and came to with my face hurting. I thought the side of my face shredded because of the blood."

Dr. Kennedy glanced at the nurse and ordered, "When we finish here, schedule him for a CAT scan." He explained the nature of this type of wound, "A ballistic injury like this one is caused by overpressure waves, or sonic shock waves, and the closer to the explosion, the more traumatic the injury. Since the ears and the lungs, and the gastrointestinal tract, are hollow organs, the GI tract may present issues in twenty-four hours. We're going to take some pictures of your head and GI tract."

"How are the others? Any word on soldiers by the names of Taylor, Lopez, Talbot, Miller, or Lee?"

"Those are not name's I know. There are three level-one hospitals involved, and they could be at the other facilities."

"Can my eardrum be repaired?" Jack asked.

"Yes, it will need an operation. We can graft a piece of muscle tissue over the perforated eardrum. It will grow and adhere to the wound giving your hearing back to a degree. Do not expect it to be a hundred percent again. Expect you will have hearing aids sometime in your life."

The examination over, the doctor pushed a wax pellet into Jack's ear to make him more comfortable and reduce noise levels like the rushing sound while he waited for the CAT scans to take place. Jack's body ached all over. The tension and adrenalin were receding and left him in a sore muscle state, much like working out for ten hours with weights. The nurse arrived with a wheelchair to escort Jack to radiology. Jack did not fight it and climbed in for the ride down the hallway and to Radiology. The technician positioned him on the table and ran the images of his head and mid-section, and he returned to the treatment room.

The nurse whispered, "After reading the images, the doctor will be in to discuss the results of the test." Jack barely heard her.

As he sat deep in thought, blaming himself for not being as bright as Khan, Sergeant Lee strolled in and asked, "Jack, how are you doing?"

"Wow, good to see you. As far as I know, I am going to be alright. I hurt, but I will live. How are you? How are the rest of the team, do you know?"

"I'm fine. Just sore from being knocked out of the tree. I did not lose consciousness like everyone else.

"Taylor and Danny are at another hospital, along with Miller. I cannot find Talbot, Bud, or Conyers. The two new team members from the 7th Group are alive but banged up good. They are upstairs in ICU. The two survivors from ODA-890 are in bad shape and are also in ICU. They were close to the trawler. Everyone on the trawler is gone, evaporated in the explosion. That bomb tech was on the trawler."

There was a moment of silence. Jack blamed himself, asking himself how he misread the tea leaves or misunderstood Abbas, or did he.

Experiencing survivors' guilt and not sure anymore, Jack felt the cell phone in his shirt pocket, pulling it out. He recalled turning it off and switched it on to call Paige.

Jack watched Lee; fatigue etched across his face, sit down in a chair. Jack wondered what he was thinking and if Lee blamed him for the missions' losses. The phone came alive with musical tones, and the screen lit up, indicating he missed several missed calls and messages. Jack ran down the list, searching for the ones that seemed important, noting that Paige had called multiple times, leaving a message on the last call. He listened to her messages.

"Crap, the missing piece of the puzzle. Khan is after something else. A computer center, if destroyed, could cripple our economy. According to Paige, it's in Chicago somewhere. She is going there with Abbas and the two MPs," he explained to Lee.

Jack tried to call Paige. Her phone went to voice mail. He left a quick message that he was alive and needed to talk to her. Jack waited for a return call.

Dr. Kennedy returned and looked at Lee, explaining to Jack, "The CT scan does not show any other apparent damage, but some of that may materialize in the next day or so. Therefore, I am going to admit you for observation and check the schedule for an operation date to repair your ear."

"Not now, doc. We need to move out our mission is not complete.

"I am waiting on a phone call. I have to decide which direction we need to go to finish the mission. Sergeant Lee and I will complete this mission together."

"I have heard such words before. I can't order you to a bed and a room, but I will tell you it is critical you stay here so we can make sure there is no brain trauma from the blast. Sergeant Lee, can you talk some sense into him?"

"Hell no. I am going with Jack wherever it is we're going."

"Doc, give me whatever meds it takes to sustain me for a week, and after we complete this mission, I will return for treatment, promise."

Dr. Kennedy recognized the spirit of the soldier in both men and could not fight against it. He supplied some antihistamine medication for Jack's ear along with muscle relaxers and Naprosyn for pain, then discharged both over his objections.

CHAPTER THIRTY-ONE:
Jack, Paige, Abbas, and Bradley Lee

* * *

The Gulf Stream touched down lightly on runway 29L at O'Hare International Airport, then quickly taxied to a set of hangers on the far side of the complex reserved for military aircraft. Paige turned her cell phone on and received immediate tones as messages were downloaded. One was from Jack. She could not activate the phone fast enough to listen to the voice mail and almost dropped it.

"Jack's alive," she yelled into the phone as the General looked on. "I have to call him right away."

The phone rang once, and in the middle of the second ring, Jack answered, asking, "Hello, how is your day going?" Hearing his voice, Paige almost collapsed into hysterical laughter from relief.

"What happened? Are you OK?"

"It's a little complicated. We were about to ambush the trawler when the damn thing exploded. I was knocked out, and while I was out, a second bomb detonated at the main gate of the nuclear plant. We lost big on this operation, and I'm to blame. I failed to recognize Khan's plan."

"Thank God you are alive; I was sick with worry. Where are you now?"

In Chicago, at a level-one trauma center. The doctor checked me out.

"I am banged up a little. Sergeant Lee is with me.

"The rest of the team is in ICU at different hospitals. Are you at O'Hare? I need to get to you and learn what you have discovered."

"Yes, and Abbas is with me along with the two MPs. General McDaniel is here. He did not appreciate how I enlisted one of his jets.

254

Any chance you can get here? We are on the military side of O'Hare," Paige replied.

"Yes, I have an idea and hope to see you shortly. Stay in touch and do not do anything until we arrive and talk." The cell went dead.

Jack explained Paige's side of the conversation and suggested, "Let's find CW5 Knight and see if we can get a ride to O'Hare."

Jack found Knight and his crew sitting in the cafeteria drinking coffee, discussing the events of the last six hours. "Chief, we need a ride to O'Hare to the military terminal. We have unfinished business with some terrorists."

Knight smiled, "Your timing is right, our nearest refueling spot is O'Hare, and I just received orders to fly there. My other two crews already started their flight to O'Hare."

Jack grinned, "You now have two passengers; when are you leaving?"

"Now," as Knight put his coffee cup on the table.

Sergeant Lee insisted, "Give me a minute. I need to retrieve something. Meet you at the helipad."

Jack waited on the helicopter watching as the crew chief, pilot, and co-pilot ran through a series of pre-flight information, turning on the turbines, causing the rotors to start spinning the blades. The crew chief jumped off the helicopter and pulled the wooden chocks away from the wheels just as Sergeant Bradley Lee sprinted toward the bird with his sniper rifle. Both Jack and Lee strapped themselves in for the ride as the chopper picked up rotor speed, lifting off the helipad. Dropping its nose and gaining altitude, the helicopter turned west toward O'Hare.

The ride lasted twenty minutes. Jack saw O'Hare with planes landing and taking off in the distance. Knight banked the Black Hawk right and headed for the north side of O'Hare, dropping in altitude as he neared the tarmac. Everyone jarred as it plopped down on the concrete, then rolled forward toward the hangars and the Gulf Stream, where several people stood around watching. Before the helicopter can shut off its engines, Jack leaped out and ran toward Paige, embracing her with a kiss.

The chopper engine stopped, and Knight disembarked and walked over. "I guess this is so long for now. I am refueling and heading back to Fort Campbell. It is good to know you and your team."

Jack responded, "Thanks for everything, Chief. Have a safe flight home." Knight turned, walked to the operations center to begin his refueling, and filed a flight plan.

Inside the hangar, Jack, Paige, Lee, and the General huddled to discuss newly developed information and how best to proceed. The General ordered several of his men to have the terminal canteen provide food and drinks. Abbas and his two escorts were kept several tables away. It was noisy enough to keep Abbas from overhearing their conversation.

Paige informed Jack of her conversation with Abbas and, at the same time, apologized to the General for lying. She explained how Abbas convinced her of his truthfulness and why she did not doubt him. Jack listened carefully for any way to discredit the information and decided Paige's analysis was correct.

Jack declared, "Paige, I do not want you involved in any tactical operations we put together; I do not want you hurt."

"You are not my husband, you are not my supervisor, and you are not going to tell me what I can or can't do. Abbas and I need to go along. He is the only one that knows Khan and can identify him. It is my belief Khan thinks Abbas is dead. Surely, word has gotten to him about your escape from the Iranians and the shooting of Abbas. I would wager Khan believes he is dead."

The men sat silently at the table, looking at Jack. "I guess you are going with us," he apologized. "We will get you a handgun. Try not to get shot. Let's look at the logistics on how we are going to accomplish our mission."

The greater Chicago area, specifically Oakfield Park, was displayed on a map lying on the table. After calculating the team's upcoming actions, Jack decided to include the two MPs and Abbas to join them at the table for a discussion.

General McDaniel objected, "I do not like the idea of having Abbas's involvement in a tactical discussion."

Jack explained, "Sir, this entire operation, from the start, has been unusual. We have managed to get in front of Khan; he always seems to be a mile down the road when we figure it out. Abbas is necessary, and I want to watch his reaction to our discussion around this table and evaluate him, which is a continuous process. What's left of our team is right here. The FBI refused to believe Paige's analysis when she informed them about her discussion. At this time, I have no idea if they would even assist us with our mission. We are it, and we are going to stop Khan!"

General McDaniel reluctantly agreed. Bold plans and actions typically saved the day, and they were talking about a nuke and a maniac.

The first part of the plan, agreed by all, was surveillance of the intended target. Sergeant Lee interjected, turning to Jack, "Let me have one of the MPs, and we can set up surveillance. We need a radio and a vehicle. The target is about four miles from here, and the sooner we set upon it, the better."

"Sergeant Evans, you're senior here for your part in this. Can one of you watch Abbas and one join Sergeant Lee?" Jack asked.

"Not a problem. So far, Abbas has been cooperating and is no problem for either one of us. Sergeant Tomkins can go with Sergeant Lee. I will handle Abbas."

General McDaniel ordered an unmarked Air Force pickup truck to be brought to the hanger and then gave Sergeant Lee's keys. "I want this back, undamaged Sergeant."

"Yes, sir." Lee and Tompkins picked up their weapons, making for the truck.

Jack yelled at Lee, "Call us when you are in position."

Lee raised his hand without turning around to acknowledge he heard Jack.

"General, it is close to twenty hundred hours. We must decide how our team is going to approach the building. To bolster our forces, I would like to pull in any military folks in the area— no telling what we are up against with Khan. The bomb is the biggest issue. My main objective of any encounter with Khan is getting to that damn bomb. I am not sure how far to go with informing anyone of anything, except to let them know there is a good chance of being turned into a bloody molecule by a nuke."

"We may be in luck. O'Hare is home to the 15th Special Operations Squadron. They have Para-Rescue Men or PJ's and combat control technicians who are the most experienced combat force in the Air Force. Let me see if I can pull some strings quickly."

Paige turned to Jack and asked, "Who are you talking about?"

"This is a lucky break for us. These airmen are the best in Air Force Special Operations and have been at the heart of many battles in Iraq and Afghanistan."

A brief time later, the General showed up with four men from the 15th SOS and apologized, "Sorry, this is the best I could do on short notice. All of these men have combat experience."

"Any help at this point is appreciated. Have these men been briefed at all?"

"Not really; I'm leaving that up to you."

Introductions made all around, and Jack explained, "We have a big problem. Paige and I are from DIA, and the little guy next to the MP is a terrorist by the name of Abbas. He is not a good guy, but he is helping.

The terrorist, Khan, is our objective. We all have a common interest in working together. Khan is holding a nuclear device and is determined to detonate it in the Chicago area.

We have tracked him from Uzbekistan to South America, to Central America, and then here. Somehow, he has managed to stay ahead of us. Those attacks going on now in Los Angeles, Las Vegas, Hawaii, and a short time ago in Seneca are due to Khan."

Jack observed the reaction of the men as the information started to sink in, "Our most immediate problem is twofold. One, we need to locate Khan. We believe we know where he is going. I have a two-person advance team on the location watching for him. Two, we must kill Khan and stop the nuke from exploding. We should not expect any help.

"The destruction of two special operations teams, along with an FBI HRT in Seneca, has been knocked out by terrorists. All the assets have diverted to where attacks have already taken place. For whatever their reasons, the FBI does not appear to think we are working on the correct information and are currently investigating Seneca's two explosions. We are alone in this mission."

The senior sergeant from the 15th SOS asked, "What can we do to help?"

"Right now, I need experienced fighters. I need weapons and communications. I was hoping you could go to our two-man team site and set up on the building and prepare to engage Khan. It would be nice for someone to be a bomb tech."

"No bomb tech here, but we can fulfill the rest of your needs. We'll be ready in fifteen minutes."

"One last thing," Jack demanded, "Paige needs a handgun and holster with mags."

"We'll bring her one. See you in fifteen."

Jack turned to the General, "Sir, we need transportation."

"Already requested." As three large SUVs pulled into the hangar.

* * *

"Jack, I need to talk to you in private," Paige asked.

"OK, what's up?"

Both moved out of hearing distance from the group as Paige explained, "Abbas said something rather interesting to me. He is deciding if he wants to denounce Islam and become a Christian and asked for my help. Do you think this is a ploy to gain my empathy and make himself believable about the information he gave to me?"

"That is an interesting question. My impression is Abbas is not the type to manipulate. He may have been lax on key points of information with Khan, but I see how Khan may have manipulated information flow to hide his true targets. Let's assume for the moment he is sincere."

"OK, I just do not want to be the person that creates another failure in this operation," she said.

"That is my burden, and I take full responsibility for what happens with Abbas and Khan's insanity."

CHAPTER THIRTY-TWO:
The Wait

* * *

Sergeant First Class Lee and Sergeant Tomkins hid their vehicle behind a dumpster two blocks away from the building they were to surveil. In the darkness, both men crept toward their objective, hiding their weapons as best they could. Sergeant Lee watched, stopped as he searched the area to find how he could gain an advantage. He noted the front to the structure, and an attached garage appeared to have three levels, with a shared frontal exposure to their location.

"There is a similar garage structure of another building directly across from our objective, Sergeant Tomkins, the elevated position and clear area, gives us a great field of fire. We'll set up on the top floor."

Sergeant Tomkins reached the third floor of the open parking garage first and immediately started sweeping the area for any threat. Checking behind a small structure on the far side of the garage's upper level, he saw no threats and gave Lee an all-clear signal.

Lee directed, "You take a position about two hundred feet to my left. I will remain here to give me a clear view and shot to the entrances across the street. If I fire on anyone, do not fire yourself. Keep your position concealed. If they think there is only one person up here, we'll keep you as a surprise in the event they decide to come after me."

"Got it. I understand. I'm going to check in with Jack to let him know our location and plan." The area was noticeably quiet, like many industrial parks at night. A few lights on in the buildings, several cars in the garage, and a security officer stood outside smoking a cigarette. Tomkins called in his report and explained his observations of the area.

* * *

Jack listened to Tomkins's report. He informed him they had picked up four more fighters from the Air Force special operations, and they would arrive soon.

"They are in place, and all is quiet for the moment," Jack explained to everyone waiting. One of the Air Force operators handed a shoulder holster, a Barretta 9mm pistol with four 15 round magazines, to Paige. She expertly handled the weapon, first pulling the slide back, clearing the gun, then inserting a clip, and allowing the slide to slam forward, chambering a round. She made some quick adjustments on the shoulder holster, then put it on and holstered the weapon.

"You've handled weapons before?" one of the airmen asked.

"Boys, I grew up on a ranch in Montana. Guns are nothing new to me. I can shoot with the best of you," she smiled. Jack thought that the smile was so disarming, but her words had steel in them.

Jack briefed all on the exact location of Lee and Tomkins. "Let's go get Khan. General, once we are in place, I will call, and you can advise the Chicago Police about us, as we agreed, our location and mission. Please request they stay out of the area so as not to spook Khan. If you decide to brief General Webster, tell him I am sure of this information."

Everyone climbed into the three SUVs. Jack, Paige, Abbas, and Sergeant Evans in one, and the Air Force operators split into two teams to take the other two SUVs. Jack already decided driving up to the second level with Lee and Tomkins on the third level would be his best location for command and control of the operation.

* * *

Khan's caravan pulled into a motel along I-294, just south of O'Hare Airport. One of his Jihadist handled the reservations checking his men into three rooms. They requested rooms facing the motel's back and parked their vehicles out of sight of the main road.

Khan provided a phone number instructing Ibrahim to call Khalid to demand a meeting before entering the office complex with all the servers. The time has come to make Khan's dream come true.

Khalid, his two sons, and his two wives arrived at the motel for the meeting. Khan gave a quick brief telling Khalid his mission was to destroy America. He intentionally omitted the part that his weapon of choice was a nuke allowing them to believe it was a truck bomb.

"Khalid, I need to access the restricted servers underneath the garage's first floor. What is the best direction to get there?" Khan said.

"Once you enter the garage through the secured gate, turn right, and look for an up and down ramp to the lower and upper levels. Take the down ramp to the bottom and park near the elevators on the garage's east side. The parking position will allow you to be close to the servers and an escape route with the elevators."

"Excellent, you have done well, and Allah will protect you and your family. Here are your weapons."

Ibrahim gave Khalid an AK-47 and a handgun. He handed his sons two AK-47's and gave one pistol to each of his wives. Each weapon had several magazines for a brief firefight.

"We will enter the garage at two o'clock this morning, just as you finish your cleaning services. You will kill all the guards allowing us entry to the front of the building and the garage, no exceptions," ordered Khan.

* * *

Khalid listened intently, acknowledging his family's mission. His excitement to finally kill infidels almost overwhelmed him. He only saw success in the efforts he and his family were going to initiate. Upon returning to Syria, he would be a hero to the Jihad and share beautiful stories about his accomplishments.

It was now seven in the evening. Khalid and his family typically showed up at the office building by eight-thirty to begin cleaning the facility, "We have to maintain our cover and arrive on time," he told Khan.

* * *

"Go, and may Allah smile on your success."

Khan and his team watched Khalid and his family depart the parking lot of the motel, "By the full morning, they all will be with Allah," Khan idly mused. His hate for America was all consuming. When his wife and children died in an explosion he believes was by the American military, he only thought for years has been collecting on a blood debt.

* * *

Ibrahim silently worried that all of them would be with Allah. He did not trust Khan to initiate the explosion or make the secured escape he promised them. Achieving enough distance from a nuclear bomb would be a challenge in the time allotted before Khan detonated the device. No infidel knew of their plan or target due to the multiple attacks Khan arranged. Khan's operational diversions made sense Ibrahim as it allowed him to arrive in Chicago undetected, or so he thought, drawing all the military authorities away from Chicago.

Khan ordered, "Give them fifteen minutes to leave. I'm going to the van to figure out why the cell phone is not connecting. I may have to use a different trigger device. Prepare for the final part of this operation. Check the maps and escape route to the north to make sure we do not get lost."

CHAPTER THIRTY-THREE:
The Target

* * *

In the distance, lightning, and thunder slowly marched toward the computer complex. The humidity increased as the storm drew near. Crickets and frogs from a nearby decorative pond added a chorus to the moonless night.

Jack positioned his vehicle on the second level of the garage, below Lee's position on the third level. He ordered the four operators from the 15th SOS to split into two locations, one in another garage with an open view of the target building, the other in an alley where their SUV sat behind a dumpster. Both places provided a clear picture of the target. Now they waited.

Jack reaffirmed the pending field of battle. He sat across from the target building, staring into a lobby and an open garage complex to his left. In between the target and his position was a large grassy area along a black asphalt street with different turnoffs into adjacent garages. A typical industrial collection of brick buildings does not exceed five stories, except the target has six levels.

Jack watched through binoculars as a white van pulled up to the front of the target building and heard Lee's assessment on his comms, "I see three men and what appear to be two women. They're getting out of the van; what I believe are buckets, mops, and brooms. They look like the janitorial staff. I didn't see any weapons."

"Roger that," Jack replied. He switched comms to the other teams and relaying Lee's information.

Team one asked, "Are they good guys or bad guys?"

"Unknown at this point. Let's assume everyone's a bad guy until we know for sure," Jack confirmed.

Jack simplified the comms issue by running an extra set of communications gear up to the third level so communications were instantaneous with Lee, perched with his snipers' rifle. Now everyone was on the same set of comms. "See anything we can use to confirm our target?" he asked.

"Nothing yet, Jack, only the janitors."

Jack ran back down to the second level, where Abbas, Paige, and Evans waited in the SUV.

As Jack climbed into the vehicle, "Abbas, how do you think Khan will arrive. ---? Car, truck, or van?" Jack asked.

The General objected to Jack's decision to bring Abbas on this operation. Jack's reasoning centered around Abbas's knowledge of the bomb and how to disarm it since he was intimately familiar with Khan's devices' construction. He managed to convince the General it was a good idea and hoped his decision to be the right one. Besides Jack was the only one trained to understand deceptive body language and verbal misdirection.

"It is hard to say, if he has the bomb in a truck or van, I'm sure he will be in that vehicle. He is such a controlling person; he would never trust anyone else to fire the device or have command over it."

"One more time Abbas, why are you helping us? Why do you believe Khan will be at this target?"

I'm helping you because I have lost my faith in Islam," Abbas jabbered. His eyes bleak, he huddled between Paige and Sergeant Evans, looking smaller, "It is a corrupt religion with backward thinking. Once I am discovered, I will surely die for being an apostate."

Abbas suddenly pointed his finger at Jack as his dark eyes turned fierce. "You must understand. Khan is a precise and controlling man. Because your country supports Israel, he hates this country. Despite any proof, Khan blamed the United States for the explosion in Pakistan that killed his wife and children. He decided it was the Americans. He will be here because he cannot control or help himself, and he is willing to die to make this explosion happen. You must not let him succeed!"

Paige changing the subject, "Abbas, give us a description of Khan again."

"He is Pakistani. He is five feet eight or nine inches tall with black hair. No scars. If he shaved his beard off, which I believe was his intent, he would leave a mustache. He was fond of his mustache, and I'm sure he would have kept it."

"Does he have any injuries, something in his walk, his arms or hands?" she pressed.

"Yes, when he was a child, he suffered a broken leg and still walks with a slight limp. He told me once he fell down a flight of stairs, and the leg did not heal correctly. I think it was his left leg. Do not let that old injury fool you. I have watched him play soccer, and he can run very well.

"There are two other items," Abbas added. "The bomb will have a green wire representing Islam as a direct connection to the trigger. Khan always used green wire to trigger whatever bomb he makes. I'm sure this one will be no different. I'm aware that Khan has direct contact with leaders of ISIS, and it's my belief they're formulating plans to move many of their men through the Mexico-US border in the chaos that will follow a nuclear explosion. Stopping Khan will hurt their plans."

* * *

Lightning streaked across the black sky. A massive peel of thunder followed, catching everyone by surprise at the closeness of the storm. The rain started. On the roof, Lee and Tomkins had no cover. Both men covered their weapons and hunkered down to wait out the rain. Lee pulled out his binoculars and continued to scan the area.

Lee, a man not typically given to anxiety, found he was feeling nervous. Tomkins scanned the area without binoculars. The rain came down harder, pounding them, creating pools of water in their shirt collars irritatingly running down their necks and backs.

* * *

Jack heard the rain hitting the side of the building. It was well after midnight, and he wondered if he made the correct call. Lighting flashed, and rolling thunder made communication difficult. Jack sat up in the driver's seat and stared hard. Was that a flash inside of the building or a reflection of lightning off the glass? Again, he saw it. "Team one, can you see anything going on inside of the building? I think I see some flashes."

"Team one, negative. Just lightning and thunder."

"Roger, break-break, team two, can you see anything going on in the building?"

"That is a negative, nothing."

Jack asked Lee. "Did you see anything like a flash inside of the building?"

"Yes, two flashes. I'm looking again; nothing is moving. I think those were muzzle flashes."

"Jack, I see another white van followed by a blue or black car driving up the road," Lee reported. "They're slowing and heading right toward the target building."

The unmistakable sound of a gunshot reached the garage. Lee spoke again. "Jack, I have eyes on a male carrying a long gun running from the garage to the main building. I think we have the right place."

Jack ordered, "Lee, hold your position." Team One and Two advance on the building. "Watch for a second white van now moving toward the target building from the east."

Inside the SUV, Jack turned to Paige and Sergeant Evans, "We're moving to the building and garage. Abbas, I warn you, one outburst to warn Khan, and I will kill you without hesitation." Jack instructed,

"Sergeant Evans remove his handcuffs. I do not want an unintended casualty."

Paige stepped out of the SUV first. She kept her Beretta pointed at Abbas, "If Jack misses you, I will not."

Abbas nodded his head and jumped out of the SUV. Evans grabbed Abbas by the back of the collar and moved him in Jack's direction as they headed down the stairs to the first level.

Both SOS operators' teams moved to cut off the approaching vehicles, weapons at the ready and braced against their shoulders. Jack and his team were quickly bringing up the rear.

The grass was wet from the rain, making everyone's footing a little off balance. Abbas lost his footing and went to one knee, only to be jerked up by Evans. Lightning and thunder pounded the sky with visual and auditory distractions, providing them cover. Streetlights blurred, making a ghostly landscape. They stopped in the middle of the large grassy area, short of the roadway. All of them knelt in the wet grass and watched the vehicle's headlights piercing the darkness like laser beams cutting through a solid object drive up to the garage. Another flash of lightning tore across the sky.

Team One focused on approaching vehicles. It was clear neither the people in the van nor the car saw the operators advancing on them under cover of darkness and rain. The van stopped briefly at the gate to the garage pushing through the aluminum arm, bending it into a worthless U-shaped piece of scrap. The car quickly followed.

Team Two moved toward the front door of the lobby and saw several people inside. Two of them had weapons in their hands. Jack directed Team Two to engage the office lobby people as he redirected his attention toward the white van.

"Lee, take any shot that is appropriate; you have a green light on all targets," Jack growled. "I need to get to that van." It was the best place for the nuke, Jack thought, and Khan was doubtlessly inside. The van had not proceeded to the down ramp to the lower level.

Team One neared the garage, observing a man in uniform, unmoving on the ground. Copious amounts of blood pooled on the pavement around the head wound as rivers of rain ran around his body. Two men with AK-47's exited the blue sedan taking positions near the van. Team One crouched behind the wall to the garage, and the leader whispered into his comms, "One in position. Two tangos with automatic weapons guarding the van. Van is stationary."

Jack's team was too exposed and needed to get near the wall for cover. Jack replied, "Wait for us; we are right behind you."

* * *

Lee had a clear view of the people in the lobby and took the first shot. The thunderstorm muffled the shot.

Glass in the lobby window broke as one of the women dropped to the floor with a bullet through her frontal lobe. At first, the second woman did not see her drop nor hear the glass break. As she turned around, she gasped and fell to the floor in a heap, flattening herself, crawling toward her. Lee waited for her to expose herself again. "One tango down in the lobby," Lee said into his comms.

Jack looked over the wall and watched the two men with automatic weapons guarding the van. Jack knew he was right. He turned to Abbas, "The van must contain the nuke."

"Yes," Abbas hissed. "Khan must be putting the finishing touches on the device to detonate it. We must not wait."

"Kill those two if they see me," Jack directed the operators. "I'm going to try and close the distance to the van first. Paige, you guys, wait here."

CHAPTER THIRTY-FOUR:
Firefight Over the Nuke

* * *

Khan bent over the barrel containing the dirty bomb, placing the green wire onto the trigger. Due to the bad reception in the area resulting from the storm, the cell phone trigger was not going to work, so he switched to a time-delayed trigger. Khan would get away from the center of the explosion in one hour. He set the time for the blast at zero four-thirty. Khan was almost laughing at the thought of the explosion and the glint in his eyes gave his emotions away.

"Ibrahim send the other two men outside to secure the building. Once they're gone, we'll take their car and drive north. If the infidels show up before the explosion, they'll think the building's main lobby is the target where we are operating our mission and ignore the garage. Hide the body of that guard."

* * *

Jack crouched behind the two cars as he edged up to the van. The two terrorists looked around the garage, starting to make an additional sweep of the area when another man stepped out of the white van. Jack heard him say something in Arabic and watched him point to the lobby. Both men walked in that direction toward a door leading to the office lobby. Jack watched them leave and blessed his good luck.

Not wanting to alert Khan if he was indeed in the van, Jack pulled his knife. It was a dagger he picked up off the battlefield in Vietnam many years ago and always carried it with him. Laying his M-4 on the cement floor, he prepared to rush the terrorist standing outside of the van.

The SOS operators could see Jack. One of the airmen picked up a small rock, threw it into the far end of a dark garage, causing the terrorist to turn and peer into the darkness with his AK-47 pointing away from Jack. Thunder rolled loudly and repeatedly as Jack made his move. Quickly covering the fifty feet or so, Jack was on top of the terrorist. He brought the dagger down hard in one swift motion, knocking the weapon to the cement floor of the garage. His other arm slipped over his shoulder, and his hand went directly beneath the terrorist's neck and chin, yanking back his head.

Jack plunged the dagger into the space between the neck and shoulder, severing the man's carotid artery and clamping his mouth shut. He held the terrorist as blood spurted out of the wound onto Jack's face and arm as the man fought against his death. Jack felt the body start to go through spasms as the man succumbed to his wounds. Once Jack decided he was dead, he unceremoniously dropped the body to the floor like a bag of garbage.

The two operators appeared from behind the wall and swept the area with their weapons. Another terrorist stepped out of the passenger side of the van.

The terrorist and the two operators engaged each other at the same time. Automatic weapons in an enclosed garage are deafening. Jack took cover immediately behind the van as rounds skipped off the pavement, striking the wall.

Jack saw the other two terrorists run from the lobby and started to take cover along the outer wall when one of their heads exploded in a bloody mess from Lee's sniper rifle. Looking around, Jack could see one of the airmen lying on the garage floor. The other operator grabbed the wounded man's collar and tried to drag him to cover when he was hit in the leg and went down.

Jack scrambled back to retrieve his M-4 as the staccato firing from the lobby area continued with rounds ricocheting in numerous directions.

Entering the garage from the lobby, two more terrorists advanced on Jack's position, firing in a coordinated fashion, each allowing the other to reload magazines. It was immediately clear they had training. The noise was deafening, crushing their hearing.

Paige, Evans, and Abbas continued to hide behind the outer wall as stray rounds from the Khalid family danced around their position. Evans, an experienced combat veteran, positioned himself between the edge of the wall, and Paige and Abbas then waited for the opportunity to rise to engage the terrorists.

In the distance, Jack could hear Team Two operators engaging whoever was in the lobby as AK-47 and M-4 fire mixed in the back and forth of a fierce firefight.

* * *

Lee decided he was now out of position to effectively identify targets for his snipers' rifle and signaled Tomkins they were leaving the garage. "Let's go; we have to get into this fight to stop Khan. We need to be closer," yelled Lee. Both men sprinted down the three floors and exited the garage running hard across the target building's open field. The rain beat down on them mercilessly.

* * *

Inside the van, Khan set the green wire in place, adjusted the trigger mechanism, and rechecked the detonation time as zero four-thirty. The firefight raging allowed him to slip out of the driver's door opposite the action and run into the darkness. His only problem was transportation.

Khan ran hard, jumping over the wall at the end of the garage, and hid while he figured out which way to escape. He had just over one hour to put distance between him and the van.

* * *

Jack, busy with the firefight, did not see Khan disappear into the darkness. Instead, he rose above the car door and saw through the window, two terrorists from the lobby advancing and posing an immediate threat and blocking him from getting to the van.

Jack moved to the wall and edged along the area between the cars and the wall when he saw Lee and Tomkins run across the open grassy area. He rose enough to wave at Lee. A burst of automatic fire skipped on the cars and wall penetrating the car hood around Jack. Lee saw the wave and adjusted his direction, arriving at the low wall behind the two terrorists.

* * *

Both soldiers raised together, parted left and right as they went over the wall blazing away on semi-automatic to control their fire rate. The terrorists, caught off guard, were first confused about the attack and where it came from, the front of their advance or the flank.

The older terrorist was the first to figure it out. He turned and fired. Two rounds tore into Tomkins' shoulder and left arm. Tomkins kept firing as he went down, hitting the old man in the knee, his hand, and the left side of his torso. Lee zeroed in on the younger terrorist, who kept advancing on Jack.

Lee closed the distance quickly, leveled his snipers' rifle at him, and blew a hole through his chest. The bullet tore through his body, taking out part of his heart and lung, expanding and hitting him in the spine, breaking his back before exiting. He lay on the pavement gasping for air. Lee watched the old man try to crawl to the other terrorist but not making it before the boy started coughing up frothy blood and died.

Tomkins got up off the cold parking garage cement and walked over to the terrorist. He did what his training taught him kicking the weapons away from the man on the floor, searching him for firearms with his unwounded right hand. Lee assisted him in placing plastic restraints around his wrists. Lee yelled, "Stay with this guy. I'm going to check out the lobby."

* * *

Jack, seeing the attackers stopped, jumped up and ran toward the van, opening the back doors. He could see a fifty-gallon barrel sitting in the middle of the cargo area. A lid lay slightly skewed on top of the barrel. It looked like Khan tried to weld the top onto the barrel. Breaking the cover from the weld, he looked inside the barrel, seeing wires and what appeared to be C-4 explosives surrounding other components and a digital clock counting down — the time set for zero four-thirty. "Shit!" he exclaimed out loud. He did not see the green wire. "Paige, get Abbas up here now."

Jack found a flashlight because the light in the van was low. Bending over into the barrel, he started his search for the green wire as Abbas, Paige, and Evans climbed into the van.

"The green wire and the trigger, where is it?" he asked Abbas.

"It will be located under the trigger. Look along the edge of the explosives until you locate the wire and trace it back to the trigger. Also, follow any wires from the timer backward. You will locate the trigger."

Jack's large hands created difficulties penetrating the mess of wires and components, scared he would pull on something that would activate the detonation. His hands were wet from the rain, adding to his difficulties. He was jittery and had to pull himself back from his search to calm down. He stared, not moving, and the sweat was rolling into his eyes, burning as he tried to focus. His PTSD was interrupting his thought process. He was getting angry at himself for his lack of control of flashbacks.

Jack could hear from the far side of the garage and lobby area the exchange of gunfire. He knew nothing was secure.

* * *

Lee advanced on the lobby entrance and carefully pushed open the door. He could see his handiwork lying on the floor of the lobby, a woman in a hajib with a bullet hole in her forehead, her hand tightly around a pistol. Looking for additional terrorists, Lee eased into the hall. The ongoing gunfire masked his approach. He let his rifle drop to his side in the sling, and he pulled his handgun, a Springfield Forty-Five. Slowly he eased around each corner as he made his way toward the terrorists.

A young man crouched behind the lobby wall, an AK-47 in his hands, fired at the two SOS operators outside through the broken window. Lee looked around; seeing no one else, he crept up to the terrorist. Hearing a noise, the terrorist turned, and the bullet from Lee's gun entered his right eye into his brain before he could register the flash of the muzzle. The terrorist dropped dead to the ground.

Lee sensed motion behind him and turned to see another woman in a hajib running out the lobby door into the garage. Lee yelled at the two operators outside, "This is Lee. The lobby is partially secure. Get in here and do a sweep."

Both operators entered with weapons up and ready. Seeing Lee, they split left and right and started their sweep. Lee barked, "I'm going after the one that went into the garage."

The woman in the hajib was a hardcore terrorist. She wanted to kill infidels, especially since one had just killed her son. Entering the garage, she approached her husband lying on the pavement tied up with a soldier guarding him. Tomkins did not see her coming.

As Lee entered the garage, he could see the woman sneaking up behind Tompkins. She had a weapon aimed at him, closing the distance. Tomkins was busy trying to stop the bleeding from his shoulder.

There was no time. Lee yelled at Tomkins, "Get down!"

The woman veered right at hearing his warning. Lee fired and missed.

* * *

"She ran toward the van. Paige," hearing Lee, she stepped out of the van and saw the woman running toward her screaming, "You killed my son and my husband." She raised her handgun and fired at Tomkins as she ran past, striking him in the leg.

Paige stepped around the van, directly in the path of the running woman. She raised her weapon and waited for her to close the distance. Paige watched her run another twenty-five feet before stopping and fired her gun directly at Paige. Paige was struck on her right side but did not fall. Instead, she calmly corrected her sight picture, squeezed a round off, hitting the woman in the mouth, partially severing her spine. The woman in the hajib did not fall immediately but slowly sank to her knees. Paige could see blood as it dribbled out of her mouth as she walked toward the terrorist, shooting her in the chest.

Paige stopped, dropped to her knees as Lee arrived, catching her from falling too hard. He laid her down and started working to stop the flow of blood.

* * *

Jack concentrated on the bomb. Lee entered the van and groaned, "Paige and Tomkins are wounded. It looks like all the bad guys are down."

Jack faltered, "How bad is Paige?"

"I think she'll make it. It looks like an in and out wound to her right side."

"Go take care of the wounded. Abbas, stay with me. Evans, go help, Lee."

"Anyone see Khan?" Jack asked.

"When the firefight was going on, I saw him running away to the far side of the garage, jumping over the wall," Abbas reported.

"OK, first things first, let's take care of this bomb. We need to stop this clock."

Jack and Abbas continued to work on the nuke.

"The clock continued to tick away. Twenty minutes to go and no green wire. "Abbas, are you sure there is a green wire?"

"Yes, that is his signature. A bomb this important would have it."

"I'm going to start pulling detonator caps away from the C-4. That should help, I think. I'm shooting in the blind here." Jack pulled out the caps; the clock kept ticking down. Removing the caps revealed more wires. Toward the bottom of the barrel were two spherical objects, the plutonium sphere split in half. Lying to the right side of the plutonium sphere was a green wire. Gently, Jack pulled the other electrical cords out of the way. Even though he was halfway in the barrel, he could barely reach the green wire.

"Abbas, hand me the wire cutters and a screwdriver. Do I cut the wire or unscrew the connectors?"

"I do not know," Abbas replied with fear in his voice.

Jack studied the structure of the trigger device. The ends of the green wire were underneath screw heads. If the trigger device experienced any disruption, it could cause the bomb to explode. He recalled that comment in a class he went to at an EOD presentation. *The wire needs a clean break with no chance of the wires touching again.* He had five minutes.

Jack took the wire cutters and placed them over the green wire. He said a silent prayer, and suddenly, he felt calm. He cut the electrical cord. The clock kept ticking down. *Now what*, he thought.

"Why is the clock still ticking? I cut the green wire," he fumed at Abbas.

"Look for a red wire that is going to the clock from the explosives. There will be two red wires. One is for the clock, and the other is for the trigger device." Abbas gulped.

Jack pushed himself up, so he was looking directly at the clock. The digital red numbers were ticking down, blinking each number downwards to destruction. Two minutes to go. He found the two red wires and traced one red wire to the clock from the trigger. The other red wire to the explosives. "Now what?"

"Cut both wires together at the same time," Abbas whispered. His eyes closed, and he prayed.

One minute until detonation. Jack carefully pulled both wires together and placed the cutters onto the electrical cables. He cut. The clock stopped at 20 seconds. Jack sank to the floor of the van, soaked in sweat.

Jack saw Lee looking into the van. Lee stared at Abbas as if he'd never seen him before. "We're still here," Jack coughed. "Now, I think we need to find that bastard, Khan."

Speechless and drained of all emotion, both Abbas and Lee nodded in agreement. Khan was on the run.

* * *

In those few moments, before the bomb was stopped, Abbas made his final private decision. He decided to become a Christian and stop being a Muslim, and his heart told him it was right. He needed Paige's promise of help.

CHAPTER THIRTY-FIVE:
The Chase and Justice

* * *

Khan's men were putting up a good fight as Khan sprinted from the garage to find transportation to facilitate his escape. The rain stopped; the humidity pressed down on him. A sudden terror overtook his mind creating doubt his plan would not work. He knew the gunfire gave his plan a chance to work. As he ran, the shooting stopped, *no gunfire, he thought*. The silence brought back his doubts.

In the distance, he spotted the airport and knew from the maps to keep the airport to his left, making sure he traveled north. His feet stomped a constant plop, plop, plop as he ran on the wet streets. The sound echoed like gunshots off the buildings that formed an urban canyon in the pre-dawn darkness.

* * *

As Jack rolled out of the van going straight to Paige, he observed her wound as one of the PJ paramedics dressed it. The other operator, along with Evans, worked on Tomkins. Jack knelt by Paige and assisted the PJ by applying pressure on her side wound.

"She'll be fine," the PJ explained. "The bullet's out, leaving a hole in her side. We need to get them to a hospital."

Jack dialed the General. "General McDaniel, we need medical help at our location. We have several people wounded as a result of a firefight. Notify the Chicago police and get their bomb tech here. I believe I stopped the detonation but would feel better if an expert examined the device. Khan escaped, and we're going after him."

"Medical personnel have been dispatched. I was monitoring the police band; heavy gunfire was reported coming from your location. Could you give me a complete report when you can? I am heading there now." The phone went dead.

"Lee, how are you doing? Any wounds?"

"No, I'm fine."

Noting the mess inside the garage, and the pools of blood and bodies, Jack's shallow fatigued voice, directed, "Evans, you stay here and take charge. The General is on his way. Lee and I are going after Khan. Abbas, come with us."

"Got it," Abbas replied.

"Paige, you're going to live. What did that woman yell at you?"

"She said something about her son and husband. I think the old guy is her husband, and the young one is the son."

"Hang in there, babe. Medical help is coming. We have to go."

"Go ahead, get Khan, don't stop until you find him."

With a quick kiss on the forehead and a gentle squeeze of her shoulder, Jack rose.

Jack and Lee, Abbas, ran across the street where the SUV sat in the garage. The rain subsided; the thunder and lightning moved off to the East. On the horizon, the sun began to rise as a sliver of light peeking through heavy clouds.

At the wheel of the SUV, Jack reeled out of the garage, racing in the direction Abbas last saw Khan. Abbas strapped into the front passenger seat, Lee in the back, both bouncing against the doors. Jack's mind raced through the training he'd received at the "crash and bang" course in West Virginia. He knew how to use a vehicle as a weapon. Breaking out of ambushes, do "J" turns and pit maneuvers, and drive at high speed backward. He accelerated the SUV to eighty miles an hour as it slid onto the main street, still wet from the rain.

The suburbs of the greater Chicago area were waking to a new day. As each minute passed, more and more vehicles and people bustled along the streets and sidewalks. Jack slowed the truck down to the posted 35 mph speed, searching the streets for Khan, as Lee and Abbas studied the crowds of people on both sides of the roadway. "How far could he have gotten in forty minutes?" Jack asked.

"Assuming he is in shape to run, eight to ten minutes a mile," Lee responded. "I would put him somewhere between four and five miles from the target building."

"I agree," replied Abbas as he calculated like a mathematician. "His legs are strong, and he must be thinking about the blast of the device. He wants distance between the explosion and himself."

Jack's eyes strained against the glare of the rising sun to scrutinize the people on the sidewalks. Scanning as he drove, he divided his concentration on traffic, avoiding running into the back of another vehicle, and watching for Khan.

* * *

Soaked in sweat and laboring to breathe, Khan stopped near an unopened furniture store. To hide and catch his breath, he stepped back off the sidewalk into an alcove. Most early morning travelers never even looked his way; they walked past him without a glance. His disheveled appearance gave the impression of another homeless soul.

Khan struggled to think clearly. *Why has the explosion not taken place? I failed!* He scolded himself. His mind grappled with panic as he tried to plan his escape. He had manipulated multiple attacks on the west coast of the United States, yet, somehow managed not to prepare a well-executed escape route because he assumed it would be comfortable in the mass confusion of a nuclear explosion.

Stepping out of the cubicle, he continued along the sidewalk, panic easing in his brain. Perhaps he had outwitted the infidels after all. He could vanish into the population. His disciplined mind would win out over the flawed thinking of his pursuers. The original plan was to locate a known Islamic neighborhood located twenty-five miles north of Chicago to wait out the explosion results. He began to search for a vehicle.

Khan spotted a delivery truck. The driver appeared to be busy taking items from the back of the truck. An opportunity arose as he heard the gentle thumping, thump of the truck's engine. Each time the driver went into the store, he reappeared within a minute for more items. Too risky. The vehicle had high visibility. Not good. He looked around but saw nothing on the main street. He turned down a side street in hopes of finding a vehicle.

A woman coming out of her brownstone got into a car parked on the street. After starting the car, she abruptly pulled away. Two young girls entered another vehicle parked on the road. An older woman left the house-entering the driver's side. Khan lunged at the driver's door, jerked it open, grabbed the woman, and pulled her out. Khan hit her with his fist, knocking her to the ground, blood oozing out of her mouth as she fell.

The girls in the backseat shrieked as Khan jumped into the vehicle. They opened the rear door fell to the sidewalk in their hast to get out. Khan fumbled with the BMW instruments and, at first, could not get the vehicle into drive. Both girls ran to the unconscious woman and pulled her away from the BMW. Khan stepped on the accelerator as tires smoked and screamed on the asphalt. He headed back to the main street, without regard to traffic, blasting into the intersection, squealing tires, as he made the turn north.

* * *

Jack stopped at a traffic light, staring ahead, yet, seeing nothing that aroused his interest. The light changed, and Jack pulled ahead, searching for Khan. A red BMW passed the SUV at high speed. "I bet that's Khan. No one drives like that unless they are trying to escape something."

Jack accelerated, driving up the center of the road, barely avoiding oncoming traffic. Irate drivers honked at him as he avoided a collision. He quickly gained on the red car; he could see it was a smaller, more agile BMW than the SUV and knew it would be a bitch to stay up with it. Traffic was slowing Khan down. Jack managed to draw near the side of the car.

"That's Khan!" screamed Abbas. "I see his face in the side mirror." The Beamer picked up speed putting several cars in-between them. Jack heard Lee chamber a bullet into his snipers' rifle.

"Get closer, Jack," Lee demanded.

Jack pressed hard on the gas pedal, but traffic prevented him from getting closer. Now was the time to use some of the "crash and bang" maneuvers he learned. "Hang on, guys; it's going to get bumpy."

Jack pulled alongside a green car, moved slightly into the side of the vehicle. Bumping the car caused the surprised driver to pull away from the encounter, making a better path for Jack. Unfortunately, the next driver was not as accommodating. Jack touched the vehicle's bumper, creating a reaction for the driver to slam on his brakes. Trying to stop, the driver only made the second contact a lot harder, causing Jack's SUV to ram into the rear of the vehicle, knocking it onto the sidewalk. Now Jack was directly behind Khan.

Jack looked in the rearview mirror. Lee lowered his window and leaned out with his rifle. Placing his hand over his ear, Jack braced himself for the noise of the shot as the muzzle sat close to his left ear. The only separation between the sound and his ear was a thin piece of glass. Lee's shot blew out the BMW's rear window, shattering the rearview mirror by Khan's head.

Jack immediately accelerated, ramming the red BMW. Khan almost lost control. Recovering from the surprise attack, he increased speed, hitting another vehicle in the side as he tried to get away from the SUV.

With shots fired, traffic quickly cleared a pathway for both vehicles. Jack was having a hard time staying up with the BMW. "Lee, take another shot before there is too much distance between us. Try and slow him down."

This time Lee went to the other side of the vehicle. Abbas pulled away and placed his hands on his ears as Lee fired once again. The Beamer's gas tank ignited. Within moments the back end was burning. Fuel splattered onto the street, leaving a fiery trail.

* * *

Khan drove erratically, trying to evade the infidels, and turned onto another side street. He raced through the intersections, focusing on getting away.

* * *

Jack throttled his vehicle forward, gaining on Khan. It was just a matter of time before the red BMW would burn up all its fuel. Jack was calculating his next move. The BMW slowed down and jerked as it ran out of gas. Khan pulled the car sharply, losing control and slamming into parked cars.

Jack abruptly braked, bringing the SUV to a screeching halt. Before the vehicle entirely stopped, Lee and Abbas were out, followed by Jack seconds later. Jack could see Lee, with his rifle up, scanning the burning car. Abbas was off to the right side of the SUV, looking for Khan.

Jack moved to the left side of Khan's vehicle; his handgun pointed at the driver's open door.

Khan was not inside the BMW.

Jack heard sirens in the distance. Hopefully, help was on the way. Enough people indeed would have called 911 by now. Jack looked around but saw no one. Lee gave him a signal to look in another direction and then quietly stepped off to the right. Jack scanned the line of parked cars expecting to see Khan at any moment. To the right of Jack, a shot rang out, and Jack saw Lee fall. Abbas ran toward Lee and stopped before he reached him.

* * *

Khan faltered and stared in disbelief at Abbas. "You…you're dead."

"No, I'm alive. Your Jihad is over, Khan. It is no use to continue."

"You helped the infidels…you traitor!"

Abbas shook his head. "No, Khan, you are the traitor. You want to murder innocents who do not even care about you or what we believe in, just because they are different from us."

Khan's intellect failed to grasp Abbas's complete betrayal, "You are violating the Qur'an Abbas, I order you to kill the infidels NOW!"

Jack eased up on a distracted Khan. He aimed for Khan's right ear and prepared to squeeze the trigger.

"Khan, I denounce Islam as I denounce you. You're mad. A nuclear bomb to incinerate humanity…for what purpose? For what gain? You cannot rule over the ashes of humanity. I do not know what I believe anymore, but there must be a better way. Your way is not the right choice. Therefore, Islam is not the right way."

"Apostate! I shall kill you myself," shouted Khan rising from behind the car.

* * *

Jack was twenty-five feet away and slightly to the rear of Khan, "Khan, look at me." Jack hissed.

Startled by Jack's voice, Khan turned to face him just as he fired. The bullet traveled straight and true, striking Khan in the throat. It ricocheted off his jaw and severing his spine, paralyzing him, causing him to fall to the ground. Jack rushed to Khan's side, kicking the gun out of his hand. Seeing Khan was unable to move, he ran to Lee.

Lee was unconscious with a chest wound but still breathing. Jack immediately put pressure on the wound and yelled at Abbas, "Get the first aid kit out of the SUV. It's in the back."

Abbas jerked open the rear hatch door and rummaged until he located the kit. He returned to Jack, dropped to his knees, opened the box, pulled out fresh gauze and pressure packs for Jack.

As Jack treated Lee, a Chicago police cruiser arrived, lights and siren blazing. An officer jumped out with his weapon drawn, yelling at Jack and Abbas to stop what they were doing and get down.

"Get an ambulance and medics here now!" Jack shouted as he continued to apply pressure to Lee's wound. Abbas bent over Lee to protect him. Jack noticed his move as another police car arrived. While applying pressure on Lee, he directed the officers to Khan, "The terrorist is over there. We are from the Department of Defense." Jack heard the first officer calling for an ambulance. Jack pleaded with God, *don't let this soldier die. Bradley, please don't die.*

Epilogue-One and a Half Years Later:
The *Silent Storm*

The ship smoothly plowed through the blue waters of the Mediterranean Sea with little effort. Jack looked over his balcony rail and watched dolphins jumping alongside the vessel in the frothy white wake. The ship appeared to be a luxury ocean liner that has sailed these waters for years.

After the attempt to radiate Chicago, the Navy built the *Silent Storm*. Its operation was controlled by the United States Navy, housing a warehouse of special operations and intelligence officers. There were four Navy SEAL Teams, four US Army Special Forces operational alpha detachments, and four US Air Force Special Operations Squadrons.

Additionally, a full complement of intelligence services included CIA and DIA analysts. A Special Operations Forces headquarters element was on board to keep it all glued together. Jack was the senior polygraph examiner for the eight examiners from CIA and DIA and worked directly to support the combined field operations.

The interior of the ship was equipped with a full-size gym and running track. It contained two full surgical theaters to treat any combat casualties. The operations center was state of the art and could communicate with any unit worldwide via direct access to satellite systems.

Above the deck, cleverly disguised as swimming pools, were landing pads for helicopters, two located on the ship's aft and one forward. From a distance, the vessel gave the impression of an ocean liner plying the waves for the wealthy.

Periodically the ship was put into ports throughout the hotspots of the world. Originally the *Silent Storm* sailed from Tampa, Florida, on her maiden voyage. Men and women debarked and embarked like on any other cruise liner. No one ever left the ship without being in civilian attire — the Navy crew dressed like ordinary cruise ship employees.

The difference was everyone had a TS/SCI clearance, was subject to an extensive background check and polygraph examination before deployment for a year on the ship. The ship was a deadly platform for immediate interdiction of terrorist operations in the Middle East, Africa, and Southeast Asia.

The Silent Storm pulled quietly into its next port of call, Athens, Greece. Jack anxiously stood near the embarkation gangplank, waiting on new arrivals. Newly minted Chief Warrant Officer Bradley Lee walks up the gangway carrying a small bag. Wearing a pair of Levi's and a sport shirt, he looked fit and light on his feet. Jack offered his hand, "Welcome aboard, Mr. Lee." Jack was already informed of his new rank, Chief Warrant Officer, and "Mr." or "Chief" was an appropriate greeting.

"Well, I'll be damned. I heard you might be aboard this boat. Good to see you," grasping Jack's firm hand.

"I hope you are ready for some action. I think we have something on the horizon."

"I'm ready; immersed in a rehab is a real bitch. I need something to bring my spirit back," Lee grinned.

"I'll let you get settled and discover the ship. I am in Stateroom 6085, sixth deck. Come up for a drink before dinner around four. We'll tell each other lies." Jack said, wearing a grin.

Laughing, Lee agreed, "I'll do that. See you at four."

Jack watched as his friend walked away and returned to his stateroom. The stateroom was decidedly more extensive than found on any cruise ship with a separate bedroom, bathroom, and living room, more like the penthouse version of a cruise line. The only area missing was a full-size kitchen. The dining room for all passengers was located on the seventh deck and open twenty-four hours a day. The ship never slept.

"Lee will join us for dinner and drinks at four," He told Paige.

"That's great, looking forward to catching up with him," Paige replied, her sparkling blue eyes and gorgeous smile accentuating her red hair folded in layers atop her head.

"What's going on in the analytical world. Anything of interest?" Jack asked.

"There may be a couple of events. We're getting some fragmented information about a major bio-attack in the works. The intel suggests some highly contagious pathogens. Also, the usual cyber-attack issues are popping up. Trying to work out the details now with the CIA. I'll fill you in when I learn more information."

Jack stood on the veranda overlooking the Athens dock. The last year or more had been a rough one — Paige and Lee were both in medical crises and recovered. Abbas was now considered a critical operational source on classified operations since his transformation from terrorist to a controlled asset.

He was embedded at GITMO on a mission with his Jihad buddies, collecting intelligence for six months. They believed him to be a hero in the Islamic cause. At least those were the rumors. Those rumors worked to bolster his status as he collected intelligence against ISIS from recent arrivals at GITMO.

* * *

Jack's idea was daring, and he used Paige's sharp analytical mind to firm up the concept: the escape of Abbas from GITMO. They approached General Webster to discuss their plan. This plan was filtered through the multilevel government system of the Department of Defense and presented to the White House. After hearing the plan's concept, President Turnbull's initial reaction was rejection before knowing the details. Being an action-orientated President, he decided to listen to it directly from the creators and requested Jack McGregor and Paige Anderson to present the plan in a formal briefing.

On the day of the briefing, Jack was sweating bullets. He did not mind doing presentations and had done a few, but the President of the United States' briefing added an entirely new flavor and meaning to the ordeal. On the other hand, Paige was used to presentations; after all, analysts do this for a living, research, and then brief on their findings.

Both were escorted to the situation room, more for controlled privacy than anything else. Entering the room, Jack stared straight into a large screen, multiple speakers, and an ungodly large table. Around the table sat General Webster, his boss, General Donnelly, Vice Chief of Staff, the President, the Vice President, the Secretary of Defense, the Secretary of State, the Commander of CENTCOM, and commanders of the Special Operations Commands in the military. Jack's first thought, *"I would rather be shot at than be here."*

Almost at the same time, Jack and Paige noticed that Captain Joe Miller was sitting in the corner. Miller slightly nodded toward both. Paige gave her best sexy smile in return, and Jack respectfully nodded back. Somehow, Miller's presence made Jack feel more comfortable and less intimidated. As he and Paige took their assigned seats, General Webster started the briefing.

"Mr. President, my team, developed an incredible plan, unorthodox, but that is what I have come to expect from Jack and Paige. If we can pull it off successfully, it is a plan that has far-reaching consequences and rewards. I will now turn the brief over to Jack and Paige."

Both Jack and Paige stood up with Jack, beginning, "Mr. President, what we have in mind is to allow our embedded GITMO asset, Abbas, to escape. Right now, his stature is elevated, and we made sure Abbas is a hero of Jihad. We manufactured a believable story of how he fought against us, was captured, intentionally misled us, escaped, and recaptured. The past six months at "Hotel GITMO" have proven invaluable in the collection of intelligence about ISIS operations from recently captured terrorists."

Paige picked up as Jack finished his sentence, all eyes glued to her. She knew she commands the room, "Mr. President Abbas received two pieces of critical intelligence we believe is a new plan to attack the United States with a weaponized pathogen of unknown toxicity. This pathogen manufacturing is at an unknown location, we believe in Africa, by ISIS or ISIS sympathizers. Abbas believes he can track the information to its source and uncover the operation during the process. Our one problem; he needs to be out of GITMO to accomplish the mission."

Jack continued, "Abbas has been polygraphed, and unbeknownst to him, another asset in GITMO has given him an operational test verifying everything Abbas has reported to us. We have vetted Abbas fifteen ways to Sunday. Our next step is escaping. What we propose is a manufactured escape. The problem is since GITMO is on the island of Cuba, how can we make this look real?"

Paige took over, "Using the various teams of special operations, SEALS primarily, since this will have to be an ocean escape. Our plan has Abbas cutting through the wire of GITMO fences, entering the sea, swimming to a small craft, and heading for one of the many islands in the area of South America with the help of "pseudo jihadists." Next, we would hide Abbas for a month or two before transporting him to Africa, where he would be released on his own to track the location of the pathogen laboratory facility."

Jack picked up the brief, "While he is in hiding, we will provide more training for Abbas, place a tracking chip in the back of his left shoulder and make sure he is physically fit for his journey. As part of his security and training, a cadre of Green Berets will be with him during this whole process and manufactured escape.

"In the meantime, we will make sure we elevate his importance, along with his stature, within the terrorist community so he will be welcome anywhere as a hero of the Jihad. We use controlled information spread out through the entire world, allowing it to filter to ISIS and al-Qaeda and any other terrorist group on Africa's continent.

"We'll have tracker teams, special operations personnel of SEALs, Army Special Forces, and Army Rangers near him based on satellite tracking of his chip. Once the group involved in the pathogen operation is identified, and the pathogen is determined, we can launch a strike team to kill or capture the terrorists."

Jack and Paige sat down. The silence in the room was deafening as each person thought the plan over. Jack eyeballed Miller, who gave a stealthy thumbs up.

The briefing was well received, and a spirited discussion followed, giving birth to Operation Raven.

* * *

The rest of the team involved in the past operation to locate Khan, who survived so long ago, had different stories. Some wounded to a point requiring medical discharge from the military service.

The one terrorist left alive in the firefight landed in the prison system. He survived for several months in a prison ward. Subsequently, someone murdered him over some dispute concerning another inmate touching his Qur'an. An infidel can't pick up or, for that matter, touch in any way a Qur'an, and a fight ensued that did not end well for the terrorist.

Jack made sure the recognition of all the military personnel involved got awards. It took guts to go into that operation, knowing you could turn into dust in the blink of an eye. They did it so others may live.

The trial of Khan, held in a closed court over Khan's defense team's objections and paid for by a mysterious Islamic benefactor, wanted a very public hearing, but the Government refused. Wheelchair-bound he could not move or speak, except with a device that replicated his voice, so it sounded as if he were talking in a tin can through a computer. The court found him guilty on all counts and sentenced him to life imprisonment even though Khan demanded death.

The Bureau of Prisons opened a confinement center in the 1990s in Southern Colorado. A high-level custody prison is often referred to as a "Supermax," a name used in media reports. Prisoners are under scrutiny twenty-four hours a day in single, soundproof cells with facilities made from poured concrete to deter self-harm and one hour for recreation or showers. Direct supervision is a continuous function. There is a high ratio of guards to inmates, and the bar set for security is incredibly high. Some believe the confinement is so rigorous it impacts the mental health of the inmates. Strangely no one, except the prisoner's, cares about that aspect of the imprisonment.

Khan could not move, even to stare at a different spot of the featureless wall in his cell. He also lost control of his bladder and bowels. His care required twice a day intervention by medical staff. The only company he had was his fantasies.

Time is an intangible puff of air. You know it exists, but you cannot feel it, taste it, or see it. Embedded in your perception of movement is time. It advances with each daily task. Everyday life is marked by increments that control and advise you when you need to be somewhere or doing something specific. That is how people live. If it all comes to a stop, common sense implies you're dead.

Khan had no control over movement, no daily task, only his thoughts, only his dreams. He tried to force his mind into his dreams and fantasies, yet it became increasingly more difficult. Khan's ability to separate his reality and dreams is fractured. The tears that often rolled down his cheeks could not even be wiped away as he desperately yearned for his fantasies to be his escape. The prison staff ensured that Khan would survive his sentence by feeding him through a tube rather than trying to end his life by starvation. He would live out his life in a self-made hell. Trapped in a non-functioning body, he thought of Abbas and screamed his name in his mind.

* * *

From the balcony, Jack looked back into the stateroom, watching Paige. He was in love. Jack searched his inner soul, explored the depths of his passion, and knew deep in his heart. Jack loved Paige. There wasn't anything he would not do for her. No personal sacrifice was too big.

She brought stability and order to his life, giving him a feeling of peace, he had not thought possible. She held the ghosts of his past at bay. He thought about settling down in one day with her. Maybe a small ranch in Wyoming. He wondered if it was wishful thinking, but it felt good. That discussion with Paige would happen very soon. He'd already floated the idea with her about having a dog, a golden retriever. Paige was receptive. She knew retrievers were his favorite.

She knew him.

* * *

The DIA asset known to a few, by the code name Butterfly, moved through Mombasa's city to arrive in three hours to a meeting, which would bolster his stature as Islam's hero. On either side of the town, the tracking teams were not far behind.

Abbas thought *it is interesting that all the researchers agree that the human race started in Africa. Now all the most horrible pathogens such as Ebola and HIV potentially could wipe out humanity are also found in Africa. What pathogen has ISIS developed?*

THE END

Acknowledgments

No one writes a book alone. Many authors like to think they do, but reality sets in, and they discover they need outside input. If nothing more than to erase the alarm bells going off in their heads, what they have produced from pure imagination is readable. I am no different.

I would like to acknowledge that my editor, Chris Evans of Reedsy, was a tremendous help. Without his knowledgeable guidance, I would not have reached my goal.

There is a group in Phoenix known to the select few as the Writers Round Table, broken down by color-coded tables, my table being the Green Table. We meet every two weeks or so, at least until COVID-19 reared its ugly head, and we sat around for several hours discussing each other's attempts at writing. No subject was off-limits. My fellow writers and authors gave sage advice, and I thank them for their exacting input and professional comments. They are much better at writing than me and quickly put me on the right path of expression. Rick Adelmann published author *The Greek Coins Affair*, *The Hilltop Ranch Affair*, *Francis March's Visions*, Elliott Munson, Kathleen Parrish, JoAnn Senger, and Marilyn Bostick. Their advice was taken to heart.

I would like to thank Minda and Lenny Chernick for their constant contribution to my efforts to correct the story and make it exciting for the reader. Minda, a retired English schoolteacher from New York and New Jersey, made me feel like I was back in school again. Thank you.

I have two dear friends, both polygraph examiners working in the federal government, who took valuable time away from their jobs and pursuits to guide me on some of the polygraph's excellent points. JW Gee, published author of *King Down, Dodge City* (both Byron Becker Crime Novels) and *Reflections of a Partly Cloudy Mind*, and Esther Harwell, made sure I stayed faithful to the science and art of polygraph examinations. These two polygraph examiners have served in various parts of the world, testing some of the worst types of people. I thank them for their service and sacrifice to our country and the help they rendered to a struggling author.

Another special friend helped me, and his thoughtful advice was instrumental in completing my book. Retired Special Agent Ernie Dorling, published author of *With Consciousness of Guilt, Murder: A Family Affair* featured on two national TV shows of Discovery Channel and *Criminal Investigations for Practitioners,* graciously reviewed my efforts and provided guidance and encouragement to finish the project.

Finally, my beautiful wife, Patricia, somehow managed to put up with my constant questions and discussions on my book. Her gentle reminders to push ahead and get it done were instrumental in arriving at the end of a long effort on days my head refused to cooperate with my writing efforts. I love her for her patience and her thoughtful encouragement.